Leaves
of Hope

**Center Point
Large Print**

**This Large Print Book carries the
Seal of Approval of N.A.V.H.**

**This Large Print Book carries the
Seal of Approval of N.A.V.H.**

Leaves
of Hope

**Center Point
Large Print**

Leaves of Hope

CATHERINE PALMER

CENTER POINT PUBLISHING
THORNDIKE, MAINE

This Center Point Large Print edition
is published in the year 2006 by arrangement with
Harlequin Enterprises Ltd.

Copyright © 2006 by Catherine Palmer.

The text of this Large Print edition is unabridged. In other
aspects, this book may vary from the original edition. Printed in
Thailand. Set in 16-point Times New Roman type.

ISBN 1-58547-818-0

Library of Congress Cataloging-in-Publication Data

Palmer, Catherine, 1956-
   Leaves of hope / Catherine Palmer.--Center Point large print ed.
      p. cm.
   ISBN 1-58547-818-0 (lib. bdg. : alk. paper)
   1. Large type books. I. Title.

PS3566.A495L43 2006
813'.54--dc22

2006009898

For Tim Palmer, whose humble service to "the least of these" bears daily witness that any man who is in Christ is a new creation.

Acknowledgments

A book's roots run deep. This story's legacy goes all the way back to the tea and coffee fields of my childhood in Kenya. To Carol Lloyd, whose friendship saved my mother and brought intense joy to my young life. To her husband, Thomas Lloyd, manager of Tinderet tea estate, a man whose life demonstrates that hard, honest work can break down every barrier. To Richard Wilson, who brought me more happiness than he will ever know. And to his family, whose life in Kenya helped spark the very essence of my imagination.

While the oldest and deepest roots hold a plant in place, the newer ones provide the nourishment that gives it life. For this book's existence, I thank my husband, Tim, who patiently lived the story of Jan and Beth with me and who edited every word of the manuscript before it left my hands. I am so grateful to my Steeple Hill editor, Joan Marlow Golan, who listened to my heart and gave me freedom to stretch my wings in writing the story of two generations bound by a message in a teapot. My gratitude also to Karen Solem, my agent, a woman who always keeps me pressing forward in the Christian race. May God richly bless all of you!

Chapter One

Being home again felt better than she had expected. With her mother living in a new house by the lake and her father gone, Beth Lowell had feared things might seem strange. But there in the pink armchair sat her mom reading a magazine. By the door stood the familiar brass coatrack. On the table sat a bouquet of fresh roses, as always. As much as she wished her mother would wake up and do something exciting with her life, Beth couldn't deny the pleasure in the familiar aroma of Jan Lowell's warm cherry cobbler. The taste of her famous chicken salad. The tang of fresh, home-made lemonade.

"Do you realize how many times your phone has tweedled, sweetie?" Jan lifted her head from the magazine. "I bet you've had fifteen calls since you got here this afternoon."

"Is that bothering you?" Beth asked as she set the phone beside her on the old beige sofa.

"It does make conversation difficult. I haven't seen you in almost a year, but we can hardly finish a sentence. Before this last call, you were telling me about your boss."

"I don't want to talk about Joe anymore." Beth crossed her legs and rubbed her toes, determined to avoid the subject of the man she had been dating for two months. "He's a good guy, but he doesn't understand my job. They bought us out because they knew they needed us, but Joe hasn't found time to learn what we do."

Her mom's eyebrows lifted. "I have no idea what you're talking about, Beth. Who's *they,* and who's *us?* And what do you really do?"

"My division of the company used to be an independent consulting firm. We assisted various corporations with international transitions. Last year, Global Relocation Services acquired the firm and moved us to New York. Now we help their clients."

As Jan shook her head in confusion, Beth wondered why her mother suddenly looked so old. Why did she wear a faded pink chenille bathrobe and that ancient flannel nightgown? And why did she still have those awful fake-fur slippers she'd gotten for Christmas a jillion years ago?

"What is an international transition, honey?" Jan asked. "I'm sorry, but I can't picture what that means."

She adjusted herself in the chair, Beth noticed, as though her back were hurting. Could she have osteoporosis at age forty-five?

"You're the English teacher, Mom," Beth reminded her. "International refers to the world. Transition means moving and changing. I help people move around the world. Industry executives. Diplomats. Oil field managers."

"You pack boxes for them?" Jan glanced at the stacks

of cartons still lining the edge of her living room. Though she had been living at the lake for more than a month now, she had yet to sort through all her possessions. The guest room where Beth would sleep was a maze of lamps, side tables, artificial flower arrangements and boxes.

"The moving company takes care of people's furniture and possessions—the packing and unpacking," Beth explained. "My division handles the rest."

"What else is there?"

"Everything. Families are uprooting their lives and settling into a new community. That's where I come in."

Jan flipped a page in her magazine without looking down at it. "Like helping them find a good school?"

"That and a hundred other things. For example, I just spent three months working with the family of a plastics company executive moving from Chicago to Colombia."

"Colombia? South America? Where they have the drugs and cartels and kidnappings? You didn't go down there, did you?"

"Sure, I went. This family—Dad, Mom and three children—were moving to the city of Cali. I interviewed each person to learn what they needed in order to be happy. Then I went to work. I helped them find a great house—five bedrooms, swimming pool, wonderful yard. There's a wall with Spanish lace on top— that's broken glass and barbed wire. And I set them up with a reputable security company, so they've got armed guards and watchdogs 24/7."

"How horrible!"

"No, it's great. It's safe, too—that's the main thing. Their car has an armed chauffeur, and the house features a state-of-the-art alarm system. I found the kids an international school where classes are taught in English. Fully accredited—kindergarten through twelfth grade. Ninety-five percent of the students go on to university, most of them in the United States."

"Well, that's impressive. But what a scary place to live. Armed guards?"

Beth shrugged. "Families like that are prey for kidnappers. They're wealthy, they're American and they work for Fortune 500 companies. Unfortunately, Colombia has a number of guerrilla organizations. Ransom money helps pay for their activities. So does drug money."

"Beth, what kind of parents would move their children to such a place? It's so risky, so irresponsible! And how could you go there without telling me? If I'd known, I would have been frantic!"

"That's why I didn't tell you. I loved every minute of it, and I was perfectly safe. Cali is an enchanting city—flowers, a perfect climate, wonderful people."

"Except for the drug lords and guerrillas," Jan said drily.

"What country doesn't have a criminal element?" Beth countered, trying to squelch her resentment that her mother was putting her on the defensive about her work . . . her life. "The family was thrilled with my

12

work. Before the move, our transition team briefed them on what to expect—not just the change in lifestyle but the emotional impact of the move. I heard from the mother the other day. They're enjoying their new life, the kids are excited about school and everyone is taking Spanish classes."

Jan leaned back and set her magazine on the table. "I don't know how you became this person, Beth," she said softly. "You grew up in Tyler."

"Everyone grows up somewhere. I've always wanted to travel, Mom. You make it sound like a bad thing."

"It's dangerous."

"Not really. And the adventure is more than worth the risk. I'm going to Botswana in a couple of weeks!"

"Africa? Oh, my."

"Are you really worried, Mom? Or is it that you don't like change, so you can't believe someone else would?"

"Probably a little of both. Frankly, even hearing about it wears me out. I wouldn't know where to begin doing what you do. And those poor wives. If my husband had moved me around like that . . ."

She paused, her eyes drifting to the corner of the living room as if she were looking at something far away. Then she shook herself and focused on her daughter again. "I'd be scared to death, and I would probably hate it. I'm glad you're happy, though, honey. That's all I want for you."

Beth rearranged herself on the couch. "I wish you'd come to New York for a visit, Mom. I'd show you my apartment, my job . . . my life. We could go to some of my favorite restaurants. And see a play. When was the last time you saw a Broadway production?"

"I've never been to New York," Jan admitted.

"Mom, that's *awful!* You've never been to a Broadway show? You were an English major. You directed plays at John Tyler High School for the past twenty years. Didn't you have a chance to go when you were young—on a band trip or during college?"

"New York City is a long way from Tyler. Besides, I've never wanted to leave Texas. I'm sorry to disappoint you, honey, but I like my quiet life out here by the lake."

Beth gazed out the window at the mown green lawn, the strip of gray road, the yard across the street and the lake beyond. The sunset reflecting on the water flashed periwinkle and pink sparkles as snatches of foamy white scattered across the surface. Birds wheeled and screeched overhead—seagulls and pelicans—dipping to pluck fish from the water.

Jan followed her daughter's gaze. "I don't know how those seagulls dare to wander so far from the ocean."

"Maybe they're the adventurous ones."

"Or lost." Her mother returned her focus to Beth. "You can come to the lake any time you want. I'll always be happy for a visit."

"Is that the only way I can have you in my life? You and Dad helped me become who I am. I want you to know me now, Mom . . . as an adult."

"I do know you, sweetie," Jan said. "Better than you

think. I'm just not one to go places—I never have been. Now I'm forty-five and a widow and an empty-nester, and my life isn't going to change drastically. It's like the quote I love so much, remember? 'That that is, is. That that is not, is not. Is that not it? It is.' I painted it on the wall of my screened porch. I used brown to contrast with the white clapboard. It's the theme for my new life here at the lake."

Beth reflected a moment. "Mom, that's the theme you've always had. *Que sera sera*. What will be, will be. Or Shakespeare's 'I scorn to change my state with kings.'"

"Sonnet Twenty-Nine," her mother clarified. "'For thy sweet love remembered such wealth brings That then I scorn to change my state with kings.' It's better when you say the whole thing. You know I taught English for twenty years, Beth. These quotes crop up in conversation now and then."

"But they're always the same, Mom, like memos to yourself—reminding you to shrug off any possibility of change." Beth's eyes widened and she sat up. "I just thought of another one. 'God, grant me the serenity to accept the things I cannot change, the courage to change the things I can—'"

"'And the wisdom to know the difference,'" they finished together.

"What's wrong with that?" Jan asked. "Your daddy grew up in a houseful of reformed alcoholics, and they lived by that saying."

"They weren't *reformed* alcoholics when Dad was

growing up." Beth tucked a strand of brown hair behind her ear. "Dad was the only stable one of the whole bunch. I'm surprised they didn't all fall to pieces after he died."

"I'm surprised none of *us* did." Jan swallowed, and looked down.

Beth felt again the huge hole her father's death had left in his family's world. Two years had gone by, but it seemed like yesterday. And forever.

"The point I'm making, Mom," she continued gently, "is that you took a big step—retiring from your teaching job, selling the house you and Dad lived in your whole married life, leaving good ol' Tyler, Texas, and moving to a new house fifteen miles away. But then you painted the same old motto on your porch."

Jan's blue eyes narrowed. "Young lady, 'what is, is.' I will accept it and try to be happy."

"So, you're just going to roll up like a little pill bug and bury your head?"

"Of course not! I have plans. Things I'm doing. But I won't spend my life longing for what was. Or wishing for what might have been. It's called acceptance."

"It's called boring."

"Well, that's your opinion."

Beth's heart grew softer as she heard the pain in her mother's voice. "When I heard you were moving, I was thrilled. I thought, *now.* Now, she'll do something with herself. You taught school to earn a living, but inside, you had art, poetry, imagination bubbling up and seeping out. I thought I might come to the lake and find a bohemian mom with candles burning and red velvet couches and books of poetry lying around. But you have another tidy little house with the same curtains, beige furniture and throw rugs, just like in Tyler. You're still making chicken salad sandwiches and lemonade. And you've painted a saying that means 'Accept life and do nothing different.' "

"First of all, I loved teaching," Jan told her daughter. "It was never just a job. Second . . . well, I am doing things differently. My art, for example."

"Watercolors?"

"Pastel chalks, as a matter of fact." Jan lifted her chin as though she had just reported recently climbing Mount Everest. "So you see? It's not the same. I took a class years ago. A woman taught us how to create portraits of Native Americans."

"You're painting Native Americans?"

"Of course not. What would I know about Native Americans? But one day I got out the old pastels, and I've been experimenting. I'm trying new things."

"It doesn't count if you're still doing roses, Mom."

"I'm painting people."

"People!" Beth sat up straight. "Let me see!"

"Absolutely not. I'm still learning. Besides, all my people still look like Native Americans. Pastels aren't as easy as watercolors, where you can blend until you get the exact tone before you put brush to paper. With chalk, it's all about how you use your hands. Look at my fingertips. The prints are worn off from rubbing the

17

paper. I could commit a crime, and they'd never catch me."

Beth laughed. "You've never done anything wrong, Mom."

Jan gave a demure smile. "So, now you know what's new with me . . . tell me more about you. Are you seeing anyone?"

Beth groaned. "You are *way* too predictable."

"Well?"

"Are *you?*"

"Me?"

"You're allowed to date, you know. Bob, Bill and I talked over the idea, and we're agreed. We think you should start going out. Maybe even marry again."

"So my children are discussing me behind my back," Jan said. "Well, save yourselves the trouble. I'm not interested in dating—or remarrying—ever. It hasn't been long since your father died, and that was very traumatic. Besides, look at me. I've spread out in all the wrong places. I'm sagging and drooping and wrinkled up like one of those Chinese dogs. But let's talk about *you.* Have you met any nice men in New York?"

"Look, Mom, I know losing Dad was devastating, but he died two years ago, and was sick for three years before that, so it's not as if you haven't had time to work through your feelings. And why do you make yourself sound like a bag lady? You're pretty, Mom."

"I know what's under this bathrobe. Believe me, there's no chance I'm ever going to marry again, so you can put that notion right out of your head."

"If marrying is such a bad idea, why are you always pushing *me* to connect with some altar-bound guy?"

"Well, for pity's sake, Beth, you're beautiful and smart, and you have your whole life in front of you. Don't you want to build a family? Buy a home instead of living in that cramped apartment? And what about children? What about love?"

"You tell me."

"There's nothing more wonderful than a happy marriage. It's what I want for all my children."

"Then why won't you marry again?"

"Beth, stop! I've been there, done that, okay? Look at who's available for me to choose from, anyway? The single men my age will have failed marriages or be old, lonely widowers with too many needs or have resentful children. Even if I did find some never-before-married man my age, what sort of person could he be?"

Beth rolled her eyes. "Everyone has baggage, Mom. None of the men I meet are pristine young innocents."

"Have you been going to church?"

"Of course. I've met some decent men—but everyone has baggage."

"You don't have any baggage. You grew up in a two-parent home in Tyler, Texas, with a nice church and an active social life. You got a good education, and now you have an interesting job."

"I'm practically perfect in every way, like Mary Poppins?" Beth grinned. "Yeah, you and Dad did a fine job raising me, Mom. I'm just not in a hurry to marry. I have other things to do before I settle down. And I want you to come to New York and visit me."

Jan reached over and fiddled with the magazine. "I might," she said finally. "I have time now, and your dad left me in good financial shape. So I suppose I could."

"How about this summer?"

"Oh, no, I'm still settling in here in Lake Palestine. I have a lot to do."

"I'll help you unpack. I'm here for three days. I bet we can take care of it all before I leave."

"No." Her voice growing serious, Jan rose from her chair. "Don't touch anything, Beth. Leave those boxes in the guest room exactly as they are. I'm the only one who knows where things should go. Seriously. Hands off."

Beth studied her mom, who looked shorter and tinier now than ever. Despite her auburn hair and pert blue eyes, Jan showed her years. Did she want to shrivel up and fade away as her husband had done? Disease had robbed him of all movement, and then his breath and finally his life.

Before the tears could start, Beth stood. "Good night, Mom," she whispered as she folded her mother in her arms. "I love you."

In the guest room, Beth rooted through her suitcase. She had grown so accustomed to living out of it that she hardly had to search for things. Underwear on the left. Toiletries on the right. Casual clothes at the bottom. Business attire near the top. She bought knits that needed no ironing, and lingerie she could wash at night and wear by morning. Her mother had no idea of any of this.

As she tugged her T-shirt over her head, Beth focused on a plaque Jan had painted long ago. It had always hung in the spare room at their house in Tyler. "Welcome, Friend," she had painted in delicate, curling script—black ink on a pale purple background. And then beneath it she printed words from a William Cowper poem:

Now stir the fire, and close the shutters fast,
Let fall the curtains, wheel the sofa round,
And, while the bubbling and loud-hissing urn
Throws up a steamy column, and the cups,
That cheer but not inebriate, wait on each,
So let us welcome peaceful evening in.

Beth wondered if this was truly what her mother desired most. Shutters fastened, curtains drawn, cups of hot tea and a quiet life in which nothing ever changed.

She mused on their evening together. While talking of New York and her job, Beth had felt her mother's scrutiny. It was as if Jan were trying to read her offspring, define her, decipher this odd creature in her living room. If only she could label her daughter in the same way she tagged other things, the child would make sense at last.

In fact, now that Beth thought of it, her mother *had*

21

branded her. Near the window in her cotton-candy pink bedroom, Jan had hung this verse:

What are little girls made of?
Sugar and spice, and everything nice,
That's what little girls are made of.

Sugar and spice? Hardly. Now, as she opened the closet door to toss in her travel bag, Beth wondered where the framed sayings and poems had ended up. Were they in one of the boxes stacked around the guest room? Or had her mother thrown them into the trash on moving day?

Of course, the inscription painted in bright pink letters over the bed in Beth's room would have been left behind. She recalled gazing at it for hours, wondering if it were true. "Queen rose of the rosebud garden of girls," read the words by Alfred, Lord Tennyson.

Queen rose. Beth had pondered the elaborate calligraphy as she lay in her pink bedroom with its reproduction white French Provincial furniture, its flowered spread and curtains and its pale pink carpet. She had imagined the Tyler Municipal Rose Garden, a fourteen-acre park with five hundred varieties of roses among its forty thousand bushes. She had pictured a girl's face inside each rose . . . her friends, models in the Sears catalog, actresses on television. In the center of the park grew one large bush with a single deep red blossom . . . the queen rose of the rosebud garden of girls. And whose face did Beth see when she peered among the petals of that marvelous flower?

Her mother's.

Janice Amelia Calhoun Lowell.

In her heart, Beth knew she herself was no rose. She inhabited the pink room, but it had never belonged to her. She didn't match the soft hues, fragile blossoms and sweet poetry. An olive-skinned tomboy, she ran around the neighborhood with scuffed sneakers, scabby knees, tattered shorts and skinny arms. Twigs of hair stuck out in every direction from her long brown braids. She climbed trees and built forts. She was a pirate king, a mermaid ruling an undersea city, a soldier slogging through the jungle, a spy on a secret mission. She hated pink.

"I don't know how you became this person," her mother had mused aloud. But had Beth changed so much?

As she set out her toiletries and Bible, she tucked a length of hair behind her ear. Scripture taught that change was not only possible but essential. In his second letter to the Corinthians, Saint Paul had written that a Christian must become a new person in Christ. A different creature.

This was troublesome for a girl who had given her life to Jesus at a church revival when she was eight years old. How much sin could a child that age have committed? How much change could one expect? Yet, Beth sensed that because of Christ, she was changing all the time—renewing, working out her salvation, striving toward righteousness.

The more she dug into Scripture, the odder and less normal she became. These days, she felt transparent and single-minded and deep and narrow and open and loving and intolerant and all kinds of contradictory things. In the same way that she had failed to blend into her pink bedroom as a child, she now failed to identify with most of her coworkers and friends. She was metamorphosing into an alien, someone not even her own mother recognized.

With a sigh, Beth pressed a dab of toothpaste onto her toothbrush, picked up her cleanser and comb, and cast a last look at the Bible on the bed. Tired and a little cranky from trying to communicate with her mom, she considered skipping her daily Scripture reading. But she knew she wouldn't. The ritual had come to mean too much.

As she brushed her teeth in the guest bathroom, Beth could hear her mother in the kitchen—putting away dishes, opening and closing the refrigerator, tucking place mats back in their drawer. Touching everything and setting little bits of herself here and there, shaping and molding her small, well-ordered world.

Did her mother feel she had failed? Skinny, dark-haired Beth, Jan's only daughter, hadn't grown up to become the queen rose. She certainly wasn't sugar and spice and everything nice. Beth had traveled away from her family and had kept on going, until she was someone else entirely.

As she headed back into the bedroom, Beth recalled her mother's insistence that she was doing different things now—using pastels to create portraits. As though that were a radical change from her watercolor bouquets.

Perhaps such an alteration was more fundamental than Beth supposed. Curious about her mother's art, she peeked behind the coats and sweaters in the closet. What sort of people could Jan Lowell be sketching? Rose-cheeked children? Ladies in pink flowered gowns? The high school students she had taught so many years? All of them looking vaguely like Native Americans . . .

Smiling at the thought, Beth knelt and pushed aside a cardboard box in search of an artist's pad or a hidden portfolio. The new sketches were probably in her mom's bedroom, stashed away until she deemed them ready for presentation. In the past, Jan always held a little ceremony, complete with chocolate cake and punch at which she debuted her latest rose paintings. Her children chose their favorite, and their mother framed it—hanging the selected piece in a special place beside the front door.

As Beth began to uncurl from the floor, she spotted a black-marker notation on the cardboard box she had pushed aside in the closet. "For Beth," it read. The carton wasn't large, and she wondered what could be inside it. Old school papers or childhood treasures? Perhaps a collection of mementos from Beth's grandparents or sweet old Nanny, the children's favorite babysitter?

Beth ran her hand over the tape that sealed the

carton. Odd that this box had been so well packed while the others in the room were simply folded in on themselves. She shouldn't open it. Her mother had told her not to touch anything in the room. Hands off. But this carton was clearly meant to be Beth's. "For Beth," it announced in bold black ink.

Glancing at the door, she noted that the house had fallen silent. Her mom might be upset with her for opening a box so carefully sealed, but maybe their talking about the items would draw them closer together. It would be interesting to see what bits and pieces had been saved from the big house, the old life in Tyler, where school and friends and family had been all Beth knew of the world.

As she popped the tape and the carton's flaps sprang up, Beth saw she had guessed correctly. Relics of the past. Her baby blanket—a soft knit in shades of white and pink—lay on top. A tag fluttering from one corner read, "Crocheted for Beth Lowell by her mother, Jan." Next she lifted her red velvet Christmas dress with its row of tiny holly leaves across the hem. Her mother had printed on the tag, "Beth's church dress when she was three years old." Farther down, she unearthed small white shoes, worn and battered, her first pair. A sealed envelope under the shoes had been printed in her mother's handwriting, "A curl from Beth's first haircut."

Continuing to sift through the box, Beth found more carefully packed mementos. Jan Lowell's handwritten tags provided each item's history. How sweet that her mother had saved these things . . . cherished and gently tended, like the daughter who once had worn them. Misty-eyed, Beth ran her fingers over a lumpy mass of bubble wrap taped around some bulky object. As she lifted the keepsake from the bottom of the box, she saw it had no label.

Sniffling, Beth began to peel away the plastic wrap. She had the best mother in the world. Chocolate-chip cookies and cold milk after school, freshly ironed dresses for church, a new lunch box every year and paintings of roses beside the front door. Unlike many of her friends, Beth had been held in her daddy's arms and fed with her mother's warm love and nourished by all the security, peace and hope her parents had been able to provide. How truly blessed she was.

As the bubble wrap crackled and fell open, Beth smiled at the sight of still more roses. A small sugar bowl, pale ivory with tiny pink, blue and yellow blossoms scattered across it, lay nestled in the plastic. How beautiful and delicate it was. She set aside the sugar bowl and discovered the plastic wrap held two more items. She lifted a creamer rimmed in gold, and then a teapot, plump with a curved spout that surely would never spill a drop.

Who had these belonged to? Beth couldn't recall ever seeing them. Brushing her damp cheek, she turned over the sugar bowl and read the name of the manufacturer. Grimwade, Royal Winton. How fragile and perfect it was. At last, she cradled the teapot in her lap and peeked under its lid. A thrill ran up her spine as she spied a folded piece of paper lying at the bottom. She opened the note and read her mother's inscription.

"Beth, this tea set was given to me by your birth father, Thomas Wood. He was a good man."

The words sat on the page, unmoving, clearly legible, yet indecipherable. "Your birth father." What did that mean? Beth read the note again. "Your birth father, Thomas Wood." That wasn't right. Her father was John Lowell, history professor at Tyler Junior College, barbecue king, TV football addict, Halloween treat dispenser, Easter egg hider and picture of health until he was stricken at fifty by Lou Gehrig's disease and died at fifty-three.

Beth picked up the teapot and studied it. Whose was this thing? Not hers. She didn't have a birth father. She had a father. This "Beth" on the label must be another girl. A different person entirely.

Confusion filled her as she glanced at the items scattered on the floor. These had been hers. The Christmas dress. The lock of hair. But not this tea set. Not this birth father. Not this Thomas Wood.

But the china had been packed and put away in Beth's box. The note inside began with her name. "Beth . . . this tea set . . . your birth father . . . Thomas Wood . . . a good man . . ."

Impossible. No way.

Shaking, Beth got to her feet and gathered up the teapot along with the bubble wrap and the note. This would make sense in a minute. Things would fall into place. The world would come back together.

As Beth stepped out into the living room, the lid clinked against the teapot. "Mom?" she called out. "Mother, where are you?"

Chapter Two

Jan pushed her toes down to the very end of the bed and wiggled them inside her socks. No matter what time of year, her feet were always cold. Her husband had gotten used to it after a while. Sometimes in the night John would roll over, gather her in his arms and let her tuck her feet between his. Even now, two years after his death, she could recall the warmth of his feet seeping through her socks and between her toes. Human warmth. Male warmth. A heating pad or an electric blanket could never replicate that. How she missed him.

Moving to the lake had been a good idea, Jan confirmed to herself once again. She pulled the quilt up to her neck and listened to the utter silence outside her bedroom window. A small neighborhood surrounded her own little cottage, but at this time of night no one stirred. The couple next to her had retired years before. Another widow—in her nineties—lived catty-corner across the street. Few of the homes belonged to permanent residents. Most people came and went on weekends. RVs pulled into driveways. Boats and Jet Skis zipped across the water. Outdoor grills scented the air with barbecue and charcoal. Firecrackers popped, and dogs howled. But by Sunday night, the week-enders had gone away, and the lake resumed its peaceful repose.

Though she hated to admit it, Jan knew she would feel relief when her daughter loaded the rental car and sped away, too. After a sudden change of plans gave her a free weekend, Beth had arrived at the lake house unannounced. Her shoulder-length dark hair slightly mussed from leaning back against an airplane seat, she wore a tight black top, a black skirt that clung to her nonexistent hips and a black jacket. To Jan, none of the fabrics matched, but Beth never noticed details like that. Leather, denim and silk—well, they're all black, Beth would argue. Despite her annoyance at her mother's predictability, Beth hadn't changed much, either. She had always been difficult . . . so odd and indecipherable.

Her younger brothers were teddy bears—freckled and floppy replicas of their pudgy, amiable father. They laughed, wrestled, accidentally knocked things over, told jokes and rolled along with good-natured ease. Bobby had clowned his way through school and almost succeeded in goofing off his entire college career. Now he held a job with a computer company in Houston, but Jan had little doubt that he was still making everyone around him laugh. Billy had been so easygoing, happy to just hang around his big brother and play with his friends and do his chores. He had just graduated from Texas A&M and was back in Tyler working for one of the rose nurseries.

But as a child, Beth had been a dark-eyed, wiry loner—climbing rock piles or hiding in treetops, building forts out of cardboard boxes, staring at bugs and reading until dawn. She rarely giggled, hated cuddling and deplored the girly aura her mother had tried so hard to create around her. A pink bedroom. A pretty velvet Christmas dress. Dolls. Ribbons. Beth preferred blue jeans, sneakers and a compass or a pair of binoculars.

Off to see the world! That was Beth's motto—then and now. Jan sighed and rolled over. It wasn't that she didn't love her daughter. Nor was she disappointed in the way Beth had turned out. Just the opposite. But why wouldn't Beth let her come closer? Why was she always pushing away from the slightest touch or snapping out some witty retort? If only they could be friends now that Beth was grown.

"Come to New York," her daughter had begged. The very thought of it made Jan queasy. A huge city, sidewalks jammed with people, taxi drivers yelling and honking. And terrorists. You could never forget about that possibility.

No, Jan would much prefer to stay here by the lake and work on the portraits she had started. She liked puttering. She enjoyed strolling. Solitude pleased her.

Let Beth and the boys come here. They could watch their mother slide gently into old age, getting creakier and maybe even crankier with time. She would bake her famous cobbler for the neighbors. Paint roses on her walls. Plant petunias, marigolds and roses in her front yard. Maybe she would even stop coloring her hair that familiar auburn shade. What an unexpected thought. Gray at last.

Beth had described her mother as a pill bug. But that wasn't right. Jan didn't intend to roll up and hide her head from the world. She simply didn't need people as much now. She didn't have to mingle with professors' spouses or attend PTA meetings or be in the Lady Lions or even go to church. None of that was required.

In fact, Jan hadn't been to church once in the weeks since she'd moved to the lake. And so what? Who would notice if she never showed up at a worship service? She didn't need sermons to know what she believed, and she certainly had no desire to walk into a Sunday school room full of strangers. If some church wanted her to be a member, well, let them come find her. God knew where she was, and that was all she cared about.

Turning over again, Jan debated what to do with her daughter for two more days. It wasn't like Lake Palestine was a dream destination for a single, twenty-five-year-old female. Formed by damming the Neches River, the lake covered 25,000 acres and dropped to fifty-eight feet deep in places. It was a fisherman's paradise. Largemouth bass, white and striped bass, channel and blue catfish, crappie and sunfish drew people all year long. The white bass had just completed their spring run up the Neches River and Kickapoo Creek. But Jan didn't own a boat, and she wasn't fond of fishing. She and John had often taken their children to the smaller lakes around Tyler. Jan had preferred to sit on the dock and read a book or prepare the picnic lunch while her family fished and swam.

That was what Beth just didn't understand about her. Jan *liked* being sedentary. She didn't want to see the world. Or even New York. The thought of flying to Botswana made her shudder. And as for that poor wife whose husband had dragged her and their children to Colombia to live inside a fortress with armed guards outside—

"Mom?" Beth's voice down the hall sounded troubled. Instantly Jan threw back the quilt. What was it? A bad dream? A spider?

"Mother, where are you?"

"I'm coming!" Jan stepped into her slippers and started across the room. "Beth, what is it, honey?"

The door swung open, and there stood her daughter holding Thomas Wood's teapot.

"What is this?" Beth demanded. She could hardly hold back tears. If her mom said the wrong thing . . . if this was what it seemed . . . if the note had been true . . .

"Where did you find that?"

"What is it, Mother?"

"Well, it's a teapot, of course." Her mother reached for it. "Give me that, Beth. Where did you get it?"

"You'd better tell me what it is right now, Mother. And don't even think about taking it away!"

"Don't use that tone of voice with me, young lady."

"Mother, where did this teapot come from?" Beth let

out a breath, tried to calm herself. "Tell me whose it is."

Jan crossed her arms over her chest and turned away. "I'm going to put on my robe," she announced. "And you had better adjust your attitude by the time I'm done."

"Adjust my attitude? What is this, Mom? Do you think I'm fifteen?" Beth followed her mother toward the rocking chair where the robe lay. "I found this teapot and the note inside it. And I want to know what it means."

Jan pursed her lips as she pushed her arms into the pink chenille robe, folded the edges over each other and tied the belt into a half-bow at her waist. She walked to the closet, opened the door a hair and shut it again. Then she switched on the lamp beside her bed and adjusted the shade.

"Mother!" Beth stepped to her side and took hold of her arm. "You can't fidget your way out of this. You can't deny it. Now sit down and tell me what is going on here. Why was this teapot in my box? What does this note mean? And who is Thomas Wood?"

"Nothing and nobody," Jan said, dropping onto the edge of her bed. "That's all you need to know. Nothing and nobody."

"That's not true! You wrote this. What does it mean—'your birth father'?"

"Where did you find that teapot? I told you not to touch any of the boxes in the guest room!"

"You wrote my name on it—'For Beth.'"

"So what if I did? You were not to open anything in the room! Where did you find that box?"

"It was in the closet."

"In the closet! Were you digging around in my private possessions? Snooping? Is that it?"

"Mom, that is beside the point."

"It certainly is not. The things in this house are mine, and I told you not to touch any of them. I warned you! I said, 'Hands off.' But you didn't listen. You poked and pried, just like you always do. Getting into things that aren't any of your business. That box was for later. After I'm gone."

"You mean dead? You wanted me to wait until you were dead to find this teapot?"

"I put items from your childhood in the box. You don't need any of them now. They're just mementos. I should have thrown them all out when I moved."

"And then I wouldn't have known. You would have preferred it that way."

Beth stared at her mother. Jan looked across the room toward the curtained window, her lower lip quivering. "Obviously I did not want you to know anything about it at this time," she said in a measured tone, as if trying to corral something that was determined to escape. "I put the teapot in the box. I sealed the box. I told you not to get into my things. And you disobeyed me!"

She whirled on her daughter. "You never do what you're supposed to do, Beth! You think it's fine to just go wherever you want to go, do whatever you want, act however you please! You don't care about privacy and silence and decent, normal behavior! I'm sorry I let you come here this weekend. I wasn't ready for you yet. And now you've gone and done this—this thing."

Beth clutched the china teapot to her belly, wounded by her mother's accusations, in spite of her determination not to care. She was the one who should be angry—not her mother! Beth had found the note. The secret. She deserved to be furious. But her mother had turned her own guilt into fury, as she always did. And soon the anger would transform into cold, bitter silence.

"Mother, I'm sorry I failed to honor your request not to touch the boxes in the guest room." Beth sat down in the rocking chair next to the bed. "But you have to tell me what this note means. Is it true?"

Jan reached for a tissue and blew her nose. "I don't even remember what it says—and don't read it to me! Just put it back in the teapot. And give that to me. I'll take care of it."

"Get rid of it, you mean? No way. It's mine. You put it in my box. I'm not turning it over to you to throw in the trash." She spread her fingers over the teapot's smooth, porcelain shape. "You wrote that Thomas Wood gave you the tea set. Who is he?"

"Someone I knew a long time ago. He's gone, all right? Dead."

"Dead? Was he my father?"

Her mother's blue eyes crackled. "John Lowell was your father, Beth, and don't you ever forget that. He

36

was the best father a girl could ever have. He loved you so much! He did everything for you! He treated you like . . . like—"

"Like I was his own?"

"Like a princess!"

"Like the queen rose in the rose garden of girls? But that's not who I was! It's not who I am! Who am I, Mom?"

"You are Bethany Ann Lowell, and you know it. Now stop all this nonsense. I'm exhausted, and I'm sure you must be, too. Go back to your room and . . ." She paused. "Better yet, I'll make you some hot chocolate. You can drink it while I clean up the mess you made in the guest room."

"Then what? We'll go to bed and pretend this never happened?" Beth's jaw clenched. Her mother would try to sweep this under the family rug—Beth just knew it. But not this time. She lifted her chin. "How did my father die?"

"He had ALS. Lou Gehrig's Disease."

"I'm not talking about Dad. I mean *him*. Thomas Wood. When did he die? What happened to him?"

"He wasn't your father. He was just a man I knew. A college acquaintance. A friend."

"A boyfriend."

"Okay, maybe. We dated in college, and then he moved away, and that was that."

"Except that you were pregnant with me."

Jan heaved an enormous sigh. "All right, so what if I was? Does that part matter—really? The point is . . .

37

John and I married, and he raised you as his own precious daughter. He gave you everything you could need, and he loved you dearly. Certainly as much as Billy and Bobby."

"But they were his natural children."

"By birth. Yes, they were. Yet, you were as much John's natural child as your brothers, Beth. He loved you every bit as deeply. He never showed any preferences. You were his little pumpkin, remember? His ragamuffin. His Bethy-boo."

"Mother, you know I loved Dad. Nothing will change that. Certainly not this teapot. But why didn't you tell me about Thomas Wood? Why wasn't I allowed to know?"

"What for? It made no difference to your daddy and me. Why should you care?"

"Because!" Beth stood and shook her head. "Because I'm different! I'm not the same as the rest of you."

"That's ridiculous. Every child is unique. Look at your brothers."

"Peas in a pod. That's what Dad used to say. Billy and Bobby, peas in a pod. He never included me."

"You were a girl."

"I wasn't his child."

Jan exploded up from the bed. "Yes, you were, Beth, and don't ever let me hear you say such a thing again! You are John's daughter every bit as much as your brothers are his sons. If you deny that, you deny everything he was!"

"How can you say that?"

"Because he was the man who married me! He did what he didn't have to do. That's who John Lowell was—decent, faithful, steady. I could count on him. He never gave me a moment's doubt about his love for me—or for you, either. The very essence of your father was his willingness to set aside the past and face the future. Did you watch him die?" As she asked the question, Jan's face hardened. "Oh, I forgot. You were away at college. And then traveling. Colombia and Botswana and places like that. You weren't here to watch your daddy's battle."

"I came home."

"How often? In his last year, you were home maybe twice."

"Mother, it was hard to deal with. It was hard to see what was happening to him."

"Hard to deal with? He didn't find it hard to deal with the fact that you were another man's birth child. He didn't find it hard to deal with his pregnant bride. He accepted all that—just the way he accepted that his disease was going to rob him of every ounce of strength . . . the ability to talk . . . even his eyes, at the end. He couldn't move his eyes, Beth. Did you know that? Because of it, he couldn't even communicate with me. That brilliant man—silenced by a disease! But he kept on. John pushed forward, never feeling sorry for himself, never looking back. That was your father. That's who raised you and loved you and gave you everything he had."

39

Beth sniffled as she looked down at the teapot in her arms. Why did she feel guilty about even holding the thing? She had been a terrible daughter. And she was even more despicable now that she had opened the box, seen the tea set and read the note.

But she couldn't help how she felt. She needed to know. Who was the man her mother had named in that cryptic message? What sort of person had given her an ivory, rose-strewn tea set . . . along with an unexpected baby . . . ?

"Just tell me one thing," Beth said. "Did he know about me? Thomas Wood?"

"It wouldn't have made any difference to him. He had his own plans."

"So you never told him."

"I hinted. He probably knew. He left anyway."

"Where did he go?"

"That's enough, Beth. You don't need all these details. Let's go into the kitchen and get some cocoa. Here, give me the teapot."

Beth clutched it tighter. "It's mine. You put it in my box."

"Thomas gave it to *me*."

"And you gave it to his daughter. A childhood memento, you said. *My* childhood. And I'm keeping it."

"Fine, then." She flicked her hand in a gesture of disregard as she walked past her daughter. "I don't care if you keep it. Take the whole box when you leave. Put it into that tiny little roomette you call an apartment."

"It's a studio."

"Whatever."

Jan could hardly blink back the tears that kept filling her eyes. As she filled the kettle with tap water, she wanted to shout at her daughter. Go away! Just leave me alone! What do you know about anything? You had life handed to you on a silver platter, and it was all thanks to John Lowell.

Oh, John! If only he were here right now. But that would be awful. Thankfully he had died before Beth found the teapot. He would have been crushed to see her reaction—so demanding and curious and stubborn. Hugging that teapot as though it were her own unborn baby. Clinging to it!

Jan sniffled and dug in her robe pocket for a tissue. Why had she even kept that stupid tea set? She should have thrown it out the moment Thomas turned his back on her and walked away. Thomas had professed to love her, but he had no idea what that really meant.

John, with his blond hair and gentle smile . . . he was the king of true love. He had heard about her predicament in a Sunday school class at church. Jan's older brother had brought up his pregnant, unwed sister as a "prayer request." Right. Perfect fodder for the holy gossip mill. But then John had come knocking on her parents' door, asking if Jan would enjoy going out for ice cream, wondering how she liked her college history class, volunteering to lend her his books for a research paper.

At the time, he had a job as a college teaching assistant while working toward his master's degree in history at Tyler's branch of the University of Texas. It wasn't exactly proper etiquette for John Lowell and Jan Calhoun to date, seeing as he was a teacher and she was a student at the same school. But she hadn't been in his history class, after all, and he was a friend of her brother's. In the end, no one from the college seemed to mind, and their awkward first dates quickly turned to love. At least John had fallen in love with Jan. She was still a wreck over Thomas when she agreed to marry.

But time took care of that. Did it ever! John became everything to Jan. Her lover, her supporter, her encourager, her best friend. Father to her daughter, and then to their sons. Those were happy days, for the most part. Jan could look back on her marriage with satisfaction. She had done the right thing. The smart, sensible, level-headed thing. All except for that tea set.

She set a mug on the counter and dumped in an envelope of instant cocoa powder and tiny, dried-up marshmallows. Well, she wasn't about to give in to her daughter's curiosity. Beth now had all the information she needed about Thomas Wood. He had given her his DNA but nothing more. He had vanished. And he was dead.

At least, Jan was pretty sure Thomas had died. So that was that. *Que sera sera.*

"I thought we might drive to Tyler and visit the rose garden in the morning." Jan forced a lightness to her

42

voice as she poured steaming water into the mug and began to stir. "It's a little early in the season for the best display of flowers, of course, but there will still be a lot to see. I'm thinking of putting in a bed of roses here at the new house, and I'd like to get some ideas for which variety would work best. Maybe you could help me choose. I may plant some climbers up the south side, too."

Her daughter regarded her coolly. "How did Thomas Wood die?"

"Stop this, Beth." Jan slid the mug across the counter, sloshing hot chocolate over the rim and down the side. She stomped to the sink for a rag. "That subject is closed. Now, do you want to go to Tyler tomorrow or not? We could stop at the cemetery and visit your father's grave."

"Do you think I actually want to look at some stone stuck in the ground where my father's body was buried? Dad isn't there. He's in heaven, Mom, and that's how I want to think of him."

"Well, you ought to at least see the marker. It's very nice. Mine is right beside it."

"Oh, Mother!"

"What?" Jan wiped up the spilled chocolate. "I'm planning ahead. I have a plot right next to your father's. It's not far from Nanny's grave—near an oak tree."

"So you and Dad can listen to the acorns fall while you're lying side by side in your caskets?"

"That's it." Jan flung the rag into the sink. "I'm

going to bed. If you want to stand there and say one ugly thing after another, you can just say them to yourself. I have better things to do."

"Mom, don't walk away. You cannot leave in the middle of this discussion."

As Jan started toward her room, she could hear Beth following. "We're not having a discussion," she informed her daughter. "I was trying to make plans for tomorrow. Trying to say something nice. Hoping you might want to visit your father's grave and remember what a wonderful, perfect man he was."

"Dad was not perfect. He was funny and smart and kind and lots of good things. But he wasn't perfect." Two paces behind her mother, Beth stepped back into the bedroom. "I'm not living in some fairy-tale world, Mom. I remember Dad's flaws, just like I see my own. And I'm not mortified that you're imperfect, either. So, you got pregnant by your boyfriend before you were married. We're humans. We do some stupid, wrong things. I forgive you."

"I don't need your forgiveness. I need you to stop making such a big deal out of the whole thing." Jan pulled off her robe and sat on the bed. "It's so far in the past. Let it go. Do what your daddy did and move ahead."

"It's in *your* past, but not in mine. I just found out about it, remember? Thomas Wood is news to me."

"He wouldn't have been if you had kept your nose out of my things. Now go to bed, Beth. I'm exhausted."

44

Her daughter stood near the door, staring at her. Hating her. Reviling her. Jan had always known this was how it would be. If Beth ever found out the truth, she would despise her mother for making the decision to keep Thomas Wood a secret.

But that had been the best way. The right way. John was able to raise Beth without any interference from a shadowy, mythical father figure his daughter might throw at him in her anger. The family had been able to be normal. To behave as a family ought—no skeletons in the closet stepping out to bother them.

Of course, there *was* a skeleton in the closet. John and Jan knew it. But Beth and the boys . . . they hadn't needed to be made aware of that potentially harmful information. Jan and John had made a choice, and they never once second-guessed it.

The only problem had been that tea set. Jan had considered getting rid of it, but the fact was . . . she couldn't. Somewhere in her heart, she needed her daughter to know the truth. And she needed to preserve that tiny spark of memory that had been Thomas Wood.

So she had wrapped the set of china in layers of bubbly plastic and hidden it at the bottom of a box. No one was to open it until after her death. Then, if the box happened to get lost somewhere or was put into the trash or given to charity, fine. Or, if Beth actually opened it, she could deal with the truth then. When she was older. Wiser. Less prone to outbursts.

Her daughter's dark brown eyes accused Jan from

45

across the room. "I'm not done with this, Mom," Beth vowed. Her lips tightening, she turned and left the room, shutting the door a little too hard behind her.

Jan let out a breath and dropped back onto her pillows. She knew Beth too well to think her daughter would drop the subject now . . . or ever. Beth would bring it up again and again. She would want to look at it the way she used to examine rocks she dug out of the dirt and washed in the kitchen sink. She would turn it one way, then another, asking questions and making speculations, the way she'd done as an inquisitive child. *Do you think there's a diamond inside this rock? If I cut it in half, would it be the same color inside as it is on the outside? What are rocks made of? Are rocks alive? Why do they keep coming up out of the ground?*

Rolling over, Jan covered her head with the spare pillow. But nothing would block the image of her daughter's accusing brown eyes, so like the eyes of Thomas Wood. The floodgates of memory burst open, and suddenly Jan was immersed in the past she had thought was buried forever.

Chapter Three

*H*is *eyes like deep pools of chocolate, Thomas sat on the doorstep at the back of the Calhoun house and gazed at Jan. "Why not?" he asked her. "You could at least come and see it."*

Why not? *Seated beside him, so close their hips*

touched, Jan hugged her middle. Thomas had graduated from college a week ago, and two days later, she had learned the awful, wonderful truth. Snuggled down inside her, in the soft folds of a perfect nest, their baby was growing.

So, why didn't she want to spend next semester's savings, risk the life of her unborn child, freak out her parents and board an airplane bound for a war-torn island off the coast of India? Why didn't she want to just go off with Thomas Wood, unmarried and pregnant, like a couple of hippie backpackers with no ties and no morals, living on nothing but love? Who did he think she was, anyway?

"I can't go with you, that's all," she said. Her hair, a waterfall of thick auburn curls, tumbled over her knees as she crouched barefoot on the step. "I'm only nineteen, and we're not married and besides . . . I don't want to go to India."

"It's not India, Jan. It's Sri Lanka." He picked up a strand of her hair and twirled it around his finger. Thomas had wonderful hands—big, brown, manly fingers with thick nails and calluses that proved he knew hard work. Of all the things about him that made her stomach do flip-flops, his hands were the best. She recalled the first time she had met Thomas—he'd been lifting a rosebush from a flower cart into the trunk of her mom's car at the nursery his parents owned. She had noticed his hands first, loved them instantly, then looked at his face and realized she had seen him in school.

47

"Hi," he had said to her, and hooked his thumbs on the pockets of his jeans. He gave her a crooked smile. "I think we were in biology together last semester."

She had nearly melted into a puddle in the parking lot. How could any man have fingers like that? And those eyes! And that mouth! And why hadn't she paid better attention in biology?

Now, almost two years later, she still felt the same. But it was no longer just a physical spark between them. Thomas had walked into her heart, broken down all her restraints, taken her body, given his in return, become her whole world. And now he wanted her to abandon family, friends, stability, security—every-thing—to follow him halfway around the globe.

How could she say yes?

How could she say no?

"We'll be in India for less than a day," he told her, as though that were the most natural thing in the world. "The plane lands in Madras, and then we switch airlines and fly to Colombo. Someone from the tea company will meet us in the city and drive us up to Nuwara Eliya."

"I can't go, Thomas."

"I'll help pay your way. It's not as expensive as you think. Besides, you got a scholarship last year, and you'll get one when you transfer over to UT-Tyler. I know you will. C'mon, It'll be fun, the two of us together."

"My parents would have a cow."

"You're not a kid anymore, Jan. They like me. So what if we travel together?"

"So what? We're Christians! They would die of embarrassment if I went off on a vacation with my boyfriend. The whole church would know."

She swallowed as she thought of the months to come. Everyone would soon know about the baby she was carrying. An abortion was out of the question. Jan was studying to become a teacher, and she loved children. All her life, she had dreamed of having a big family of her own. This was an unplanned beginning, but she wasn't about to cut short her child's life just because things had started badly. No, she would simply tell her parents what had happened, and then she would have the baby . . . and move into an apartment of her own . . . and try to finish school . . . and . . .

Fighting tears, she dipped her head. "Just go, Thomas. Go home. Do whatever you want. This isn't going to work out."

"What's that supposed to mean?" He turned and caught her by the shoulders, forcing her to face him. "Listen, Jan, I wrote you the whole time I was gone, didn't I? It's not like we were apart that long anyway. Three months. We both stayed faithful, and nothing changed between us. Why are you acting this way all of a sudden?"

"Nothing changed? You changed."

"I did not. I just evolved into who I was already becoming. We've been together two years, Jan. You knew what I wanted out of life, and now it's within my *grasp. I got a great internship, I finished up my courses, I graduated, and now Wilson Teas wants me to come back and work there full-time. Management level. This is a great opportunity for me. And Sri Lanka is an amazing place. You'll love it."*

"I'm not going, okay?" She pushed away from him and stood. Walking across the yard, she tugged her shorts down on her thighs and wondered how long she would even be able to wear them. By the end of summer, she'd be in maternity clothes. Unbelievable.

She could hear Thomas behind her. "What's the big deal, Jan? Why are you pushing me away? I came all the way back to Texas to see you."

"You came home to graduate."

"And to be with you again. I care about you. I love you—you know that. Now come with me to Sri Lanka. Just for the summer. If you hate it, fine. But you won't."

She turned and set her hands on her hips. "You got cholera over there!"

"Yeah, and then I got well. I'm fine, now."

"They're having a civil war!"

"Not up in the mountains where we'll be. The country's an independent republic. It's mainly just a problem between these two groups, the Tamils and the Sinhalese. The Tamils want an independent homeland, because they're Hindus. The Sinhalese are Buddhists, and they're the huge majority, and they've got the power."

"I don't care!" she sang out. "Tamils, Sinhalese—"

"But the government isn't going to let the Tamils do

50

anything too bad. Americans aren't even a target. And the people I worked with on the tea estate are all really nice. I never felt afraid." He raked his fingers through his long, shaggy brown hair. "You'll be there with me for the Kandy Esala Perahera in July. It's this amazing pageant with ten days of torch-bearers, whip-crackers, dancers and drummers. They've got elephants all decorated and lit up. Everyone told me it's spectacular. We'll see so much other stuff, too. This ancient ruined city called Anuradhapura has a temple that supposedly contains the right collarbone of Buddha."

"What? Buddha's collarbone? Come on, Thomas! That's ridiculous!" Frowning at the very idea of herself in a place where people worshipped things like that, Jan stepped away from Thomas again. She spoke over her shoulder as she walked toward her mother's flower garden. "That's stupid! I mean, it's just not for me, you know? I'm from Texas, Thomas, and I don't need Buddha's dumb collarbone to make my life complete. I don't want to see a temple, and I don't want to visit a place with malaria and cholera and bullets flying around. Okay? Okay? Can you just drop it?"

He stood by the picket fence, thumbs in his pockets the way she loved, staring at the ground. This conflict had been building between them for weeks. The moment Thomas got back, he'd begun putting subtle pressure on her—dropping hints, talking nonstop about the wonderful island and the amazing tea estate and the fascinating people. She kept her mouth shut, hoping the whole thing would go away.

Finally he mentioned that he might be offered a full-time job in Sri Lanka. Then he actually got a letter from the company offering him a contract. He wavered, talking about it one way and then another every time they were together. She'd tried to change the subject or ignore him. But today, after Jan had spent the morning hanging over the toilet vomiting, he'd told her he wanted her to go with him.

Not married. Nothing permanent. Just a trip. A summer vacation. See the place. Have a look around. Do some touring. Then she could return to Tyler and start her junior year at UT. A wonderful plan.

Right.

"Are you telling me you don't ever want to go to Sri Lanka?" Thomas asked. "You wouldn't even be willing to visit me there?"

"That's what I'm saying."

"But I want to work with tea!"

"You majored in agriculture, Thomas. Your parents own a rose company. Why on earth can't you just stay here in Tyler and grow roses like everybody else? Why does it have to be tea?"

"I told you. I don't want to be like everybody else. I want to see the world. I want to live in different places. Tea can take me wherever I want to go. They grow it in Kenya, Tanzania, South Africa, India, China, all over the globe. It will be an adventure. Don't you see? A great life."

"Well, have fun on your big adventure, then." She

turned away, blinking back tears. "Go, Thomas. Just go home. I don't even want to see you again. You've changed so much."

"I have not, Jan! Why do you keep accusing me of that?" He caught up to her again, setting his hands on her shoulders. "Please, babe, don't be this way. It's me you're talking to, okay? The same guy as ever. Only, I found out the world is a big place, and I want to experience it. I want you with me. I want it to be us . . . together."

"What are you saying?" She looked into his brown eyes. Was this a marriage proposal? If so, he wasn't doing a very good job of it. "You said you wanted me to go to Sri Lanka with you for the summer and then come back here."

"Right. That makes sense, doesn't it? I mean, you'd have to leave so you can finish college." He scratched the back of his neck. "You couldn't stay there. You wouldn't have a work visa. Besides, you're not even twenty yet."

"But I'm old enough to travel halfway around the world with you? Old enough to flout my parents' belief system and throw it in their faces? And then what? Come sashaying back to Tyler like nothing happened? Is that what you're asking me to do, Thomas?"

"Is this about us having sex? Because if you're going to go into your major guilt trip again—"

"This is about you telling me to act like an adult by going to Sri Lanka with you, and then turning right around and telling me I'm too young to marry you."

53

"Marry me? I'm not ready to get married! I'm only twenty-two."

"Fine, then. I don't want to marry you, either."

"Who said anything about getting married?"

"Nobody, because it's not happening. Ever! Go to your stupid island and see Buddha's collarbone and grow tea and have a wonderful life. I'm staying here in Tyler where I belong."

"Come on, Jan. Don't make such a big deal out of everything. I'm just talking about summer vacation. The two of us together. And maybe in the future . . . maybe if you like Sri Lanka . . . and after you get your degree . . . and I'm more settled . . . and older—"

"No, Thomas." She brushed the tears from her cheeks. "No, no, no. If you want us to be together, you'd better stay here in Tyler. Because this is where I live. This is my home, and that's my family in that house, and I'm going to get a degree and teach school, and have a baby and—" She hiccupped. "I'm going to marry someone who wants the same things I do, and we'll have babies. Children, lots of them. And I won't have to worry about my kids being blown up with land mines, or mosquitoes giving them all malaria, or any of that stupid stuff!"

"I love you, Jan! How can you tell me just to walk away from you like this?"

"I have my priorities." She folded her hands over her stomach. "I know what's most important in my life. And it's not Sri Lanka."

"It's not me, you mean."

"I didn't say that." She was crying so hard now that her nose had begun to run, and she felt like she might throw up again. *"I love you, too, Thomas. I do. But I want the guy I met at Wood's Nursery and Greenhouse. Not this foreigner you've turned into."*

"Jan, please. Try to understand. Try harder."

"I can't. No matter how hard I try, I don't understand where you're coming from. I want security. Stability. I need it. Nothing's going to change that about me. You can't change who I am into someone you want me to be."

"And you can't change me, either."

They stared at each other. He was crying now, too, his eyes red and tears hanging on the fringes of his lower lashes. He swallowed and jammed his hands into his back pockets.

"Okay, then," he said. *"I guess this is it. It's over between us."*

She nodded as bitter bile began to back up into her throat. "Bye."

Before he could see her completely lose it, she ran across the yard, flung open the back door, made it to a bathroom and retched in the toilet.

Jan pressed her pillow against her face, blotting her tears. Dumb, dumb, dumb to be crying about Thomas Wood after all these years! She had done the right thing. To protect herself and her baby, she had cut him out of her life. Everything about him. She had thrown away the letters he had written her from Sri Lanka. She had packed the little gifts he had given her over their two years together—a pretty candle, a picture of the Rocky Mountains, a couple of science fiction novels she had forced herself to read, photos of the two of them together. Before he was scheduled to leave town, she had taken the box over to his house and dumped it on the front porch.

Three days later, she had discovered a box on her own front porch. Even now, the memory of Thomas's handwriting on that brown cardboard made her heart hammer so hard, her pulse rang in her ears. She had knelt on the painted boards and pulled apart the flaps of the box. Expecting to find things she had given him, she was shocked to see a tea set sitting inside a nest of white foam peanuts.

It was beautiful. Covered with pink roses, her favorite flower, the teapot was rimmed in shining gold. Jan had lifted the pot in both hands, holding it to the afternoon sunlight, marveling at the glow of the glaze on the ivory china. Delicate bluebells, green leaves and yellow daisies mingled with the rose blossoms. The pot itself was a strange shape, squared into four corners with four small feet, yet somehow still soft and undulant. She had lifted the lid and peered inside to find a tiny white envelope wedged at the bottom of the pot.

Even now, lying in bed, a forty-five-year-old widow with three grown kids and a whole other life, she could see the words Thomas had written to her in blue ball-point ink. "I bought this tea set for you at an antiques shop in London on my way back to Texas. I knew you would like it. The pattern is Summertime, and I had hoped that would be our time. I will always love you. Thomas."

Setting the lid on the porch floor, Jan had turned over the teapot. Grimwade, it read. Royal Winton. Summertime.

She had taken out the creamer, a funny little squared-off thing with four feet that matched the teapot. And then she had studied the rectangular sugar bowl and the matched pair of gold lines that rimmed it on the inside. The set looked so pretty . . . too pretty . . . on the old, creaky porch.

Crying all over again—it seemed she was either crying or vomiting in those warm days of early summer—Jan had settled the china pieces back into their foam nest and carried the box upstairs to her bedroom. Briefly she had considered putting the tea set on her bedside table. But the thought of Thomas holding that delicate china in his big, wonderful hands . . . walking into an antiques store just for her . . . writing her the note . . . loving her . . .

"Oh, rats!" she breathed out. Jan threw back her covers and swung her feet out of bed. Plodding to the bathroom, she thought of how slender and long-legged she once had been. And how pudgy and ancient she felt these days. Thanks to her daughter's snooping, she wasn't going to get a wink of sleep. Tomorrow she would have swollen eyelids and a fat nose from crying all night. She would be irritable, and Beth would start bugging her about the tea set and Thomas and all the things Jan had worked so very hard to put away.

Well, Beth was *not* going to get the whole story. And that was that. Thomas was a good man, just as she had written. But he had not hesitated to walk out of the Calhoun backyard that afternoon. He hadn't called or dropped in to say goodbye before flying off to Sri Lanka again. Only four short letters with strange stamps had appeared in the mailbox in Tyler.

Gone, just like that. Pfft. Out of Jan's life, as though a match had been snuffed by the wind. Nothing had remained of those two years of passion, two years of insane, crazy, mad love. Nothing but Beth. Little brown-eyed, brown-haired Beth, who looked so much like her father, sometimes it was all Jan could do to keep from showing how deeply the child affected her.

Beth would stare long and intensely at her mother, just the way Thomas had, and Jan wanted to grab the little girl and hold on so tightly that maybe she could feel Thomas's breath against her cheek again. And other times Beth would give a toss of her hair and go wandering off from the house for hours, never bothering to tell her mother where she was. That was when Jan fought to keep from snatching her by the shoulders and shouting out the speech she had often rehearsed for Thomas.

Stop leaving me! she wanted to yell. Stay with me, where you belong, and stop running away all the time! Don't leave me alone! Need me . . . want me . . . be lost without me, the way I am without you.

But Beth had too much of Thomas Wood in her to read beyond her mother's placid face and calm words. She didn't see or understand or even care how much she meant to Jan. Like her father, she would happily jaunt off to Sri Lanka or Botswana or some other foreign place where you could die of cholera or require armed guards and Spanish lace to keep your house secure.

Genetics. All the nurture in the world couldn't overcome a wanderer's nature.

After blowing her nose and splashing water on her face, Jan walked back into the room and checked the clock on the bedside table. Nearly three. Great. And there was John, sitting in his oak picture frame, looking at her like he always did. "Get a grip, Jan," he would say when her nerves unraveled and she began to fall apart. Nothing's that bad. It's not a big deal. Relax, honeybunch. Let it go.

She ought to paint some of John's platitudes on her bedroom wall. They would comfort her the way her husband had with his calm, quiet smile and a pat of his hand. He would lean over and press his lips to her cheek and make that little smack.

"There you go, sweetie pie," he would say. "Better now?"

And she was. Truly, John always made things better. From the day he had offered to marry her and become the father of her baby, to the day he exhaled his last, labored breath, John had brought peace and security into Jan's life. He had given her everything she wanted

59

and needed. Always. He hadn't asked her to change. Or leave. Or go to strange places. He had just patted her hand and planted a kiss on her cheek and called her honeybunch. And that had been more than enough.

"Oh, John." Taking up the photograph she had framed not long after his death, Jan gave the glass a wipe with the sleeve of her pink robe. "What am I supposed to do without you? You weren't supposed to leave me. Thomas did that already. *You* were supposed to stay."

Battling a new wave of tears, Jan took off her robe, lay back on her bed once more and shut her eyes, hugging the frame against her chest. Maybe she ought to pray. Beth always chided her mother for not being more religious. What would she say if she knew Jan wasn't even going to church these days?

Well, what was the point? You prayed, and your husband died anyway. You went to church, and then what? Your kids grew up and left home. Your Sunday school class just got older and older until you couldn't believe you belonged in the same room with those wrinkled, gray-haired fogies. Your preacher kept yammering on the same Bible verses again and again until you could practically preach his sermon for him. Potlucks and Bible studies and revivals and prayer meetings and on and on.

The thought of it all made Jan tired. Still holding John's picture, she turned onto her side and pulled the sheet up over her ears. Just as she was sure she would never get to sleep, she realized she had been imagining herself in a shoe store buying a pair of hiking boots, which had nothing to do with anything. And then the hiking boots turned into furry yellow puppies. And that was the end of that.

Jan woke with a gasp. A slanted sunbeam warmed her cheek. It must be after nine! Good grief!

She sat up in bed, rubbed her face with her hands and blinked, trying to see through the residue of last night's tears. Oh, great. This was not good. She needed to be up fixing breakfast for Beth. She ought to have taken a shower by now. Dried her hair. Put on makeup. Dressed in a pair of slacks and a nice top. She was still determined to take her daughter to the Rose Garden. Or the Azalea Walk. Either would be beautiful this time of year.

As she fumbled her way out of bed, Jan saw that she had slept with John's framed photograph all night. Poor John . . . How hard he had battled that awful ALS—three years of fighting, until he had looked nothing like the man in the picture. She set it up on her bedside table again. This was how she would remember him—pudgy and freckled and grinning from ear to ear.

"There," she said, taking a last look at the picture. She grabbed her robe and slipped it on as she hurried out into the kitchen. Thank goodness there were no signs of life. Beth must be sleeping in, as she always had on school holidays when she was younger.

Jan padded in her thick socks to the coffeemaker. She

would get the pot started, and then she could run to the bathroom for a quick shower. This was going to be a better day, she thought as she stood at the sink to fill the glass carafe with water. She and Beth would start off on the right foot, and that way Jan could head off any . . .

She stared at her empty driveway. The rental car was gone.

Chapter Four

"I'm looking for yearbooks." Beth leaned against the reference counter. "From John Tyler High School."

The librarian was a nice-looking young man with dimples. "The *Alcalde!* Are you an alum?"

No one in New York would have asked such a personal question. In large cities the world over, Beth had discovered, people got down to business. Chitchat took too long, didn't really matter, and you'd never see the person again, so why bother?

With a fair amount of chagrin, she recalled her first week in the Big Apple. She had walked into a perfume boutique, said hello to a saleswoman and—like a good Southern girl—she began with a comment about the weather and then moved on to discuss her own favorite fragrances, how she enjoyed floral scents because she was from a town in Texas where roses were grown for export, how she had just arrived in New York and was excited to have found a studio apartment she could afford and on and on. Finally, Beth had realized the woman was staring at her as though she had just landed from Jupiter. Not only had Beth breached the "no small talk" rule, but her Texas twang had no doubt branded her as someone who just fell off the turnip truck.

This wasn't New York or London or Toronto, though, so Beth smiled back at the young librarian. "Yep, I graduated from JT a few years back. Go, Lions!"

He laughed. "I went to Robert E. Lee High. I'm working on my library science degree at UT-Tyler now. It's a good school, but I'll be glad when I've got my degree and can move away. *Tyler.*" He rolled his eyes. "My ancestors were some of the town's first settlers, and we've been here ever since."

Beth nodded. "Time to set forth into the world. I live in New York."

"Really? Wow. I bet that's different."

"You can say that again." Beth reflected for a moment on the number of old families still living in the area. "Did you ever hear of anyone named Wood around here?"

"Wood? Like Wood's Nursery and Greenhouse? Wood's Landscaping? Wood Tractor and Lawn Service? There are several businesses by that name."

For some reason this shocked Beth. Of course she knew about the Wood family. The name was on any number of small enterprises around the city. She could have been living among her relatives all her life and not realized it.

Had they known about Beth? Was her heritage a Tyler secret? Did people elbow each other as she went by . . . ? *There's Thomas Wood's daughter, but don't let on that you know.* . . .

"I'm looking for someone," she told the young man. "His name is Thomas Wood. Or was. I think he might have passed away a while back. I'm pretty sure he would have graduated from John Tyler High in the early eighties."

"All our copies of the *Alcalde* are down that row of reference books across from the soda machine. You can't check the yearbooks out, but you can use our copier if you need certain pages. Dime a page."

Beth thanked him and headed across the library. As she crossed the reading area, she glanced at an elderly man browsing the *Dallas Morning News*. Did *he* know? If she walked up to him and said, "I'm Thomas Wood's daughter," would he reply, "Oh, I know that. He left town, but your mother stayed here and married John Lowell."

Why not? In a city of around ninety thousand, people ran into each other now and then. They joined things together—churches, PTAs, Lions and Rotary Clubs. They congregated at the Tyler Municipal Rose Garden or the Caldwell Zoo. They celebrated annually at the Azalea and Spring Flower Trail, the Festival on the Square and the Texas Rose Festival.

And they talked. They talked at grocery stores, on the sidewalks, in church, at the coin laundries, even in the library. How many had known about Beth's lineage and said nothing to her—but plenty to each other?

The thought of people gossiping behind her back made her feel sick. And angry. She stepped between the tall bookcases and spotted the rows of yearbooks. But as she started to reach for one, she hesitated. Maybe she didn't want to know what Thomas Wood had looked like. Maybe she ought to be like her mother and pretend he really hadn't existed.

Thomas Wood had been a mistake, Jan seemed to be saying.

The pregnancy had been a mistake.

Did that make Beth a mistake?

A brief time in Jan Calhoun's distant past had been nothing more than a blip in the comfortable straight line of her life. Just a small error that she and John Lowell had rectified with their careful, structured and secure marriage. Running her fingertips across the spines of the royal-blue-and-white yearbooks, Beth reflected on the man who had raised her from birth. Her daddy.

As much conflict as she now felt about the whole situation, she would never deny that John Lowell had been her true father. The family photo albums proved that. As an infant, she had spat processed carrots right in his face. He had held her tiny fingers when she was taking her first baby steps. He had pushed her on the swing in the backyard and taught her how to bait a fishhook, and he kissed her cheek when she graduated from high school. She had loved her daddy.

So why bother to look for a picture of a stranger

65

whose DNA she happened to share? A guy who had impregnated his girlfriend and then walked away . . . a loser who had sowed his wild oats, never imagining a baby girl would grow from a night of furtive wrestling in the back seat of some car . . . a dead man whose brief life had meant nothing to his daughter . . .

Clenching her fists in the anguish of uncertainty, Beth read the dates stamped in gold letters on the volumes of the *Alcalde*. What was the point of looking for him? But then again . . . why shouldn't she? How could it hurt?

She was reaching for a yearbook when her cell phone went off. Jumping at the unexpected sound in the cavernous library, she jerked the device from her purse and frowned at the caller ID. It was her mother. Beth silenced the phone and let her voice mail answer. No way was Jan Lowell going to butt into this decision.

Beth had been unable to sleep the night before, alternately furious with her mother, sad at the memory of her father's recent suffering and death, curious about Thomas Wood. She had tried to piece things together, mentally walking back through the years and wondering if one thing or another had held more significance than she thought. It was a nightmare—only she had been awake through it all.

As the sun was coming up over the lake, she had packed her bags, thrown them into the rental car and driven back to Tyler. She cruised around town, looking at the Lowell family's old house, remembering friends

66

and events. She passed her brother's home and considered knocking on his door to ask him if he knew she was just his half sister.

But Bill hadn't been aware of anything, Beth realized. If he had, he would have blabbed years ago. So would Bob. Crazy little brothers. Neither one could resist telling on each other or on Beth. If they had known their sister had a different birth father, they would have told her.

Waiting for the public library to open that morning, Beth had eaten a doughnut at her family's favorite restaurant just off the town square. Every Sunday after church, the whole Lowell crew had traipsed in, settled at their regular table and ordered the same meals they always did. Fried chicken for Dad, roast beef and gravy for Mom, pork steak for Bob, ribs for Bill. Good old Southern dishes.

Beth always ate spaghetti. Italian. She had been ready to taste the world even back then. Like Thomas Wood, who had left Tyler and never come back. Had her parents sensed a difference in her? Had it affected the way they treated her?

Unwilling to hesitate a moment longer, Beth grabbed an armload of yearbooks and carried them to a table. She sat down and flipped through the index at the back for the most likely year. In moments, she had found him. Thomas Wood.

And he was a dork! In his senior photo, he wore a wide tie and a too-small, pin-striped jacket, and his hair hung in strange, choppy lengths almost to his shoulders. He wasn't smiling.

Beth stared at him, trying to see through the black-and-white photograph into the truth of who Thomas Wood had been. Dark eyes . . . like hers. Dark hair . . . like hers. Straight nose . . . like hers.

But there was a lot of him that looked nothing like his daughter—a pronounced Adam's apple, a square jaw and those hands! Beth studied the one hand that the photographer had evidently posed so it showed Thomas's class ring. Huge fingers stretched across the sleeve of his jacket. Big, rough hands roped with veins. Callused knuckles. Round white nails.

She lifted her own hand and studied her slender fingers and manicured nails, turning them one way and then another. No, she hadn't gotten them from him, that was certain. But so many other things . . .

Bob and Bill had inherited a mix of their father's sandy hair and their mother's auburn curls. They both had freckles and a tendency to go soft in the middle. Their noses tilted up at the ends, like Jan's. And their ears stuck out a little, like John's. But big sister Beth had brown eyes and board-straight brown hair and olive skin.

"Did you find what you were looking for?" The reference desk clerk startled Beth as he pulled back a chair and sat down at the table. "Thomas Wood—well, there he is. Guess you struck oil after all. Get a load of that tie!"

Beth tried to smile. "Yeah, I found him. Thanks."

"It's possible we would have pictures of him going

all the way back to kindergarten. You want me to look?"

Actually, she wanted the librarian to go away. But Beth pushed the yearbooks in his direction. "Sure. See what you can find."

"Thomas Edward Wood." The young man flipped to the index in the back of a volume of the *Alcalde*. "Did you come all the way from New York to look him up? Because, in case you didn't know, we can do research for you and communicate online. We're glad to do that. Not all libraries have those kinds of reference services, but we do. And it's free!"

"Great. I'll remember that." While the clerk went to do some more digging, Beth read the inscriptions under her birth father's senior year photograph. Thomas Wood had not held a class office or worked on the yearbook staff or acted in a play. He hadn't done much in sports, either. His freshman year, he had played junior varsity football. He had been on the basketball team—first JV and then varsity—all four years. And that was it. His future? The caption said he planned to attend Tyler Junior College and major in agriculture.

An ag major! He was a hick! Her father was a dork and a hick. A goofball with a tight sport coat and big hands and no more aspirations than to be a farmer.

Of course, being a farmer wasn't exactly an easy life. Beth knew many of them couldn't make a go of it. To take college classes showed Thomas Wood had some gumption. And he had chosen that beautiful antique tea

69

set. Maybe there was something ambitious and romantic in him after all.

Beth read the quote he had chosen to have placed beneath his photograph. It was from Richard Bach's *Jonathan Livingston Seagull,* a book she had never read but had heard was one of the most saccharine pieces of schmaltz of all time.

"There's a reason to life! We can lift ourselves out of ignorance, we can find ourselves as creatures of excellence and intelligence and skill. We can be free! We can learn to fly!"

Yeah, right. *We can be free!* Good motto, Thomas Wood. Get your girlfriend pregnant and then abandon her. If you had been a creature of excellence, intelligence and skill, you would have stuck around and done your duty. At least you could have paid child support.

The fact was . . . she hated him. There, she had acknowledged the truth. Beth stared at the picture of the teenager in the tight coat and wide tie. He was a dweeb, a dork, and she hated him. Good riddance, loser.

Shutting the book, she pushed back from the table. The desk clerk glanced up. "I found him for you in these," he said. He pointed to a stack of yearbooks opened and placed one on top of the other. "Here, I'll show you."

Beth could hardly refuse to look after he'd done all that work. She leaned on her elbows as the young man pointed out his discoveries. "Eleventh grade," he began, his stubby finger jabbing at the photograph of a skinny-faced, even longer-haired version of Thomas Wood. "Tenth grade, ninth. And then we go to grade school. He went to Douglas Elementary."

"You're very good."

"Thanks. It's my job." Dimples deepening, he beamed as he handed her the Douglas Wildcats yearbooks one by one. "Right on down the line. He sure is a beanpole, isn't he? Look at this one—he's got a Band-Aid on his chin. Short hair in these younger versions. I guess that was the style back then. And here's the last one—first grade. There you go. I don't guess there was a yearbook for kindergarten in those days."

Beth stared down at a toothless little boy who was looking back at her with big brown eyes. "He was my father," she murmured. "This . . . person."

"Your father? Thomas Wood?"

"My birth father. I was raised by a different man . . . my real father. He died two years ago."

"They're both dead? I'm sure sorry to hear that."

Beth nodded as she slid the open yearbooks across one another, looking at the pictures once again. "I just found out. My mother . . ." She bit her lower lip. "I'm just blabbing. Forgive me."

"No, it's okay. Do you want me to make photocopies for you? I'll do it for no charge."

"That's all right. I'm just—" She rubbed her eyes. "Okay, yes. Make copies, if you don't mind. I'd appreciate that."

"Sure." He scooped up the yearbooks and headed for a back room.

Beth dropped her head onto the crook of her arm and fought tears. Why should she be sad? Thomas Wood had never been a part of her life. And now he was dead, so why cry? Maybe she was weeping for her daddy. For John Lowell who had carried the secret to his grave. She couldn't be angry with him. He had given his whole adult life to her. His love, his time, his attention, his money.

What had possessed him to do that? Had he loved her mother so much that Beth became part of that passion? Or had he actually loved his adopted daughter, too? Had her father ever felt Beth really belonged to him? Or did her dark eyes and hair always remind him that another man had preceded him in Jan's life?

Beth lifted her head as the eager reference desk clerk returned with a sheaf of photocopied pictures of Thomas Wood from first grade through high school graduation. He handed them to her and waved away her offer of payment. "It was fun," he said. "Like a quest. If you need any more help, my name's Brian. Kids used to call me Brain. That bugged me in the old days, but now I don't mind. It fits."

Beth stood and slid the sheets of paper into her purse. "Thanks, Brain."

He laughed. "You're welcome. Enjoy your visit to good ol' Tyler."

Giving him a thumbs-up, Beth left the library carrying information she had needed, and didn't want, and could no longer live without. Why hadn't her parents told her years ago? What was the point in keeping

72

such a secret from their only daughter?

As she slid into the seat of her rental car, Beth knew she had to make one more stop before she could leave town.

An oak tree. Beth drove the wide turn around the cemetery as she looked at the trees and wondered which one of the many oaks now dropped its acorns on her father's grave. She should have come more often. In the two years since John Lowell's death, his daughter had visited his final resting place only twice. The first time had been at his burial service. And the second time, when Beth was back in Tyler for one of her quick visits, her mother had impulsively driven them to the cemetery after church.

Unable to express how very much she did *not* want to see her father's grave, Beth had wordlessly endured the endless minutes. She and her mother had left the car and stood in silence near the headstone that listed the dates of John Lowell's birth and death but told nothing of who he had been and what he had meant to those whose lives he had touched. Beth had tried not to think of her father's body lying deep in the earth, decaying and transforming into something fit for a horror movie. Instead, she had studied the sky through the oak leaves and thought about the family she was preparing to move to a nice house in Panama.

John Lowell was not inside that casket, Beth had reminded herself at the time. She still believed that. Parking the rental car near the cemetery's old iron gate, she walked toward the one grave she did know how to find. Beth's beloved babysitter had brought her to the memorial park on regular occasions. While Nanny knelt and rearranged the silk flowers at her husband's grave, Beth and her brothers had chased each other up and down the rows, hiding behind headstones and trees, throwing acorns or sweet gum balls at each other and generally behaving like little pests.

There it was. Beth crossed a path and approached the small plot that she remembered Nanny tending so faithfully. Nanny now would be buried beside her husband, though the child she had babysat for so many years had never once visited her final resting place. Stopping at the spot, Beth gazed down at the bright green grass, neatly mown without a dandelion in sight. Then she looked up at the pair of matching headstones. *Theodore Wood. Nancy Wood.*

As if a sudden wash of ice water had slid down her spine, Beth stiffened. Again she read the two names. Theodore Wood. Nancy Wood. But this was where Teddy had been buried . . . Nanny and Teddy. Two people without last names. Without pasts or futures. Without children, grandchildren, nieces or nephews. Nanny had just existed to babysit Beth and her brothers, hadn't she? She had been an icon, never changing, never growing older, never acting any different than she always did.

While Jan Lowell had taught English at John Tyler High School for twenty years, Nanny had looked after the three little Lowells. Every weekday morning when they were preschoolers, Beth, Bob and Bill had gotten out of the car at Nanny's house and spent the day there. Their mom picked them up about four every afternoon. When they were old enough to start school themselves, they went to Nanny's house in the afternoons for visits or on weekends to splash in Nanny's big plastic pool and eat Popsicles from her freezer.

Nancy Wood. Nanny.

Could it be? Beth walked around the two stones, looking for some kind of clue. Might Nancy and Theodore Wood have been Thomas's parents? But that would make Nanny Beth's grand—

"Hey, there."

Giving a start at the interruption, Beth swung around and saw her mother approaching down the path. Jan had left her car next to Beth's near the cemetery gate. Wearing jeans, a knit shell top and bleached white sneakers she looked younger than she had said she felt. Younger even than Beth had thought the day before.

"She was Thomas's mother," Jan said, answering the question before Beth could ask it. "After you were born, Nanny put two and two together. She wanted to be a part of your life, and I thought that was a good idea. She loved you so much."

"Why didn't you tell me?" Beth demanded. "Why didn't she say something? It's not fair that I never knew. I treated her like . . . like nothing! She was my babysitter, not my grandmother."

Beth turned away again, consumed by sorrow and regret. As the truth dawned, she fought tears. "I came and went from her house nearly every day when I was little, and I never asked her any questions. I never looked at her photo albums or paid attention to the pictures on her walls. I didn't even ask if she had children."

"She had one. After Thomas left Tyler, Nanny sold the nursery and greenhouse that had been in her husband's family for three generations. That gave her more than enough money to live on, and all she really wanted to do was dote on you."

"But why didn't someone tell me? That's such a . . . It's wrong! It's just wrong!" Beth clenched her fists. "How did you find me here, Mother? I don't want to talk to you right now. I need to be by myself."

"I saw your car parked by the gate." She pushed her hands into her jeans' pockets. "You didn't think I was going to let my daughter just run off like that, did you?"

"You let my father run off."

"John Lowell was your father!" Jan exploded. "Listen, Beth, you had better show respect for the man who raised you. You owe him that."

"Fine, then. You let my *birth* father leave. You didn't even try to make him stay."

"You don't know that."

"I don't know anything. And why is that? Because you won't tell me. It was your big secret. You and Dad. You even got Nanny to join in the deception."

"We never deceived you, Beth. None of us. We just chose not to tell you something we felt you didn't need

76

to know. If it was wrong, it was a sin of omission and nothing more. We didn't want to hurt you. Nanny agreed with your father and me. Her desire was to spend time with you. It never mattered to her if you knew she was your grandmother. She didn't care that you weren't so interested in *her*. That wasn't important at all. What she wanted was to be with you, to dote on you and give you her time and her love. She had lost her husband, and her son was far away, and you were all she had left."

Beth tried to absorb the significance of this new reality. The whole time she had been skipping in and out of Nanny's house—selfishly focused on her own life—Nanny had been gazing at her with the loving, mournful eyes of a bereft grandmother.

"Maybe it wasn't important to Nanny to tell the truth," Beth said finally, "but it would have been helpful for me to know who she really was. I might have treated her better. Been nicer. Kinder. Less self-centered. Did that ever occur to any of you coconspirators?"

Jan clenched her jaw for a minute. "Beth, I don't want to continue with all this hostility. Let's get back to being mother and daughter, the way we were before."

"We can't ever be the way we were before, Mom. Don't you see that?" Beth opened her purse and took out the stack of photocopies. "Your life may not have changed, but mine sure has. See this person? He wasn't there, and now he is. I can't erase him."

"What are those?" Jan reached for the papers as she had the teapot, but Beth pulled them back. "Where did you get those pictures?"

"I got them from the library. Because I wondered what Thomas Wood looked like."

"Why? What use is that? You shouldn't have—"

"Seeing his picture helps me. Now I understand why I don't have freckles and a pug nose."

"Oh, for pity's sake! That is just ridiculous. Your appearance is absolutely unessential to this issue!"

"Wrong, Mother. Now I know why I look the way I do. And I want to understand how he fits into who I am. Mom, I'm not going to stop searching until I've found out everything I can about him. Thomas Wood is part of me."

Jan shook her head. "No, he isn't. Genetically you're connected, but that's it. That's all there is."

"That's a lot."

"It is not! Freckles and pug noses are nothing. Come over here, and let me remind you who was *really* a part of you."

Taking Beth's arm, the older woman tried to pull her away from the graves of Nancy and Theodore Wood. "Don't take me to Dad's plot," Beth warned, brushing off Jan's hand. "I know who he was. I loved him, and I called his parents my grandma and grandpa. Now, I want you to tell me who these people were. Nanny and Teddy."

"You knew Nanny better than I ever did, Beth. Why don't you tell me who she was?"

Beth brushed some dirt from the top of Nanny's marble headstone, then she sank to the ground and crossed her legs. She spread the photographs of Thomas Wood on the grass before her. For a moment, she could hardly remember anything about the old woman who had looked after her when she was a young child. And then it came.

"Nanny was funny," Beth began. "She had little songs for everything. She made buttered popcorn every afternoon. Our favorite lunch was fish sticks. She gave us lollipops when we won games. Billy used to cheat at Candy Land, and I would catch him and cry. Nanny rocked me in her lap until I fell asleep. She called me Bethy. Bethy-Wethy."

Closing her eyes, Beth fought tears as she sang the funny little song Nanny had adapted just for her. "My Bethy lies over the ocean, my Bethy lies over the sea. My Bethy lies over the ocean . . . oh bring back my Bethy to me."

Jan joined in softly. "Bring back . . . bring back . . . oh, bring back my Bethy to me."

But Beth wasn't ready to be brought back to her mother—her sense of betrayal was still too strong.

Chapter Five

Just like that, Beth had gone away. As Jan dug a deep hole for the first of the climbing roses she had bought to plant beside the deck of her lake house, she recalled how stunned she had felt that morning at the cemetery. Tears streaming, her daughter had walked away from Nancy Wood's grave, climbed into the rental car and driven off. Jan had phoned her repeatedly, but Beth refused to answer, letting her voice-mail system pick up the calls and never returning them. Two days later, an e-mail message appeared on Jan's computer.

I'm back in New York. On my way to Botswana for three weeks starting Monday. Love, Beth.

That was the extent of her daughter's communication. Jan had phoned the studio apartment in New York, but Beth didn't return her call. E-mail messages received no reply.

It wasn't as though she had purposely hurt her daughter, Jan reasoned as she pushed her fingers through the ball of roots beneath the rose's graft. Loosening the dirt would give the roots room to breathe in their new home. Now that the whole situation with Thomas had unfortunately come to light, she was even making an effort to explain it to Beth. She had sent a pretty "I love you" card with a lovely poem inside, and she had written a lengthy message on the computer in an attempt to make things better and heal the breach between them.

Your birth father and I did care about each other, Jan had typed in finally—after deleting three previous efforts and revising the current one countless times. *Thomas was a good man. He was intelligent and kind. But he and I had different goals. He longed to travel, while I planned to stay in Tyler. I never wanted to be far from my family, but Thomas had no desire to work in the Wood nursery business or live close to his mother. He cared about Nanny, and I know he wrote to her, but he did not come back to Tyler often. Even though Thomas and I were friends, we both knew we did not belong together as husband and wife. I hope you can find a way to be grateful that I married John Lowell, Beth. Your father and I were happy in a way that Thomas and I never could have been. In the long run, sweetheart, your childhood was better for this difficult decision, even though you may not believe it.*

After much soul-searching, Jan had pressed the send button and released the letter to her daughter. Later, consumed with worry when Beth made no response, Jan had printed it out and read it at least fifty times, checking to make sure she had said exactly what she meant. She didn't want to hurt Beth further, but she couldn't condone this futile quest that seemed to have consumed her daughter. The memory of Thomas's school photographs spread across his mother's grave still filled Jan with a mixture of shock, grief and anger. Maybe the reminder that Beth's happy home was a gift from her parents and her grandmother would help ease the hurt she felt over the secret they all had kept.

"Is that a Climbing Peace you've got there?"

As she patted dirt around the rosebush she had just planted, Jan recognized the voice of a neighbor who lived four houses down. Pasting on a smile she didn't feel, she turned and waved to the widower. "It sure is,

Jim. You can't do better than a Peace if you want the perfect rose."

"I couldn't agree more." Jim Blevins was walking his dog, a mixed-breed poodle-like creature that had a tendency to roll in nasty things. Jan noticed they were both overweight as they sauntered off the road and started up her drive.

"I've got two Peace Roses in my yard," he said. "A climber and a regular bush rose. But you know what really has me intrigued? Zepherine Drouhin."

"Gesundheit!" Jan exclaimed, throwing up her hands in mock surprise.

Jim laughed, his blue eyes disappearing into folds of soft skin. "It's not a sneeze, it's a rose. I hadn't heard of the Zepherine Drouhin till last year. Found it at one of the nurseries and planted it next to my front door."

"Did you like it?"

"Did I *like* it? The thing turned out to be a stunner. Climbed up nearly ten feet in the first year, if you can believe that. It puts out a dark pink rose, and the canes are almost thornless. Great if you've got grandkids around, you know. Of course, mine are nearly grown, but still, it's a comfort not to have to worry about anyone snagging a sleeve as they go inside the house. Best part is, the Zepherine Drouhin tolerates a little shade, and I've got a pin oak near the drive that keeps the sun off the front of my house about half the day."

"That does sound wonderful. I never heard of a rose that could stand much shade at all."

"This one can, and the fragrance is out of this world.

It's a Bourbon, so it's got that heavy perfume, you know what I mean." His dog was nosing around the Peace Rose Jan had just planted, and she hoped the scrawny little fuzz ball wouldn't get any ideas about digging it back up before it had a chance to settle in properly. Jim gave the leash a tug. "Come here, Trixie. Leave Mrs. Lowell's rose alone."

"Oh, it's all right. Trixie's no trouble," Jan said, meaning the exact opposite. Why did her Southern upbringing make her say polite things that often stretched the truth? She shrugged. "And you might as well call me Jan. After all, I'm a full-timer now. Part of the neighborhood."

Jim gave her a big grin. "We're all just tickled to death to have you here. You know, Jan. I was thinking about heading over to Tyler this afternoon to the nurseries. I want a Zepherine Drouhin to put at the other side of my front door. Kind of like an archway. They repeat bloom like crazy, so you really can't beat them. Would you like to drive in with me and pick one up for yourself? I noticed you've got a patch of shade over by your side porch there, and a thornless rose might be just the thing."

"Oh, well . . . my goodness . . ." Jan tugged at the fingers of her gardening gloves as she tried to think how to get out of this. The last thing she wanted to do was be seen driving off to Tyler in Jim Blevins's car. Tongues would wag. She certainly had no interest in the man beyond a neighborly chat. He was at least twenty years her senior, for one thing.

Did Jim see her as a potential date? What a thought! Jan reached up and patted her hair, deciding immediately that she would *never* let it go gray, not even when she was ninety-two.

But maybe she was overreacting. Maybe all he really wanted to do was shop for roses.

"Thank you, Jim," she finally fumbled out. "Actually, I went rose shopping last Saturday, and I've still got all these bushes to plant. Not to mention the annuals on my porch. But that's a kind thought. I'll remember the Zepherine Drouhin next time I'm in town."

"Sure thing! Not a problem." He leaned over and patted Trixie's round white head. "I'd be happy to help you put in your plants this afternoon. Wouldn't we, Trix? We'll help Miss Jan dig those rose holes, won't we, girl?" Straightening, he jabbed a thumb over his shoulder at his own neat white house. "Tell you what. I'll be back with my shovel right after lunch. Unless you'd care to come up to my house and have a bite to eat on the deck? The Zepherine Drouhin is just budding out, and you can decide if you like it. I've got tuna salad from yesterday."

"Well, that is so nice of you, but if you don't mind, I'll just stay here and keep on working. I do enjoy getting my hands in the dirt in springtime, don't you?"

"I certainly do. All righty, then—Trixie and I'll be right back after lunch. C'mon, girl. Let's go make us a sandwich, and then we can come back and help Miss Jan out with her planting." He called back to her. "I always put some of the best bread-and-butter pickles you ever tasted in my tuna salad, Jan. I'll bring you a jar. My wife canned them last summer just before she died. Here, Trix. Stay out of that ditch, now!"

As he walked away, Jan blew out a breath that sent the damp hair on her forehead dancing. Great. Just what she did *not* want. If anything, she had moved to Lake Palestine in the sincere hope of being left alone. Her past few years in Tyler had been utter chaos and so stressful. First she had been torn between taking care of John and continuing to teach in order to keep their health insurance. Then she had been compelled to take off a month of school and devote her entire summer to tending to her increasingly helpless husband. His death had come as a sad relief, for she knew John had been ready to go. Such a terrible, aching, futile struggle . . .

Two more years of teaching had brought her to early retirement, but they hadn't been easy. Jan had mourned her husband so acutely that at times she was sure she couldn't go on. Their finances had been a confusing mess, their friends either tried to adopt her or discarded her like yesterday's dust rag and their home suddenly felt like a mausoleum. The pressure had been nearly unbearable.

Jan had been looking forward to this first summer in her new home with great eagerness. She would paint her favorite sayings on the walls, plant roses in the yard, read all the bestsellers she had missed out on in the past five years, take long baths and generally tend to herself. What she had not envisioned was a nosy neighbor. A messy dog. And an angry, unforgiving daughter.

And memories.

Now that she had seen those photographs of his face, Jan could not stop thinking about Thomas. Had she been wrong to keep her pregnancy from him? She would never forget the slope of his shoulders as he had walked away from her that day in the backyard. Had he truly loved her? Or had she been simply another adventure on the pathway of his life?

Even now, Jan could hardly believe Thomas had expected her to follow him to Sri Lanka. Wherever *that* was. But his feelings for her must have been stronger than she imagined. His letters from those months of his internship revealed a depth of thought and emotion she hadn't seen during their casual dating and then their growing physical passion. Maybe there had been more to Thomas Wood than a handsome, physically striking rogue who wanted to wander the world.

Had Jan been right in telling Beth that they would have been unhappy together? Yes. There could be no question about that. A tea plantation in some far-off country would never have felt like home. Jan would have been miserable and Thomas resentful. Their marriage could not have lasted. And besides, Thomas was dead now—Jan had looked into that herself several years ago. Whether Jan had married John or Thomas, Beth would have lost her father.

Her heart heavy, Jan pulled her gloves back on. She had to stop her daughter from continuing to pursue this mythical image of her birth father. Thomas Wood wasn't meant to be in Beth's life—everyone, even his own mother, had agreed about that. Somehow Jan needed to find a way to put an end to her daughter's feelings of anger and betrayal over the secret they all had kept. She had to help Beth see that it was over now . . . over and best forgotten. Resolved, Jan knelt to pat down the dirt that Trixie had scattered from around the Peace Rose.

That's all she really wanted. Peace. She was beginning to think it an impossible dream.

If she could live anywhere in the world, Beth had concluded, she would choose Botswana. As the taxi sped down the streets of Gaborone toward Sir Seretse Khama International Airport, she tried to take in every detail of the capital city she had come to know so well in the past three weeks.

What a wonderful country! About the size of France, Botswana was landlocked in the heart of southern Africa. In compiling research for her clients, the Furman family, Beth had learned that although the Kalahari desert stretched across Botswana, abundant wildlife filled the northern Okavango Delta. She had yet to fly there, but the stories she had heard filled her with determination to see it on her next visit.

With a population of only 1.5 million people, Botswana had been one of the poorest countries in Africa before its independence in 1966. But the discovery of vast diamond reserves had brought a prosperity that enabled the new nation to build one of the soundest infrastructures on the continent. Beth found that the roads—though few—were well maintained. The electricity rarely failed except in times of extreme drought. The postal and telephone systems were kept in decent working order. Most important, the government functioned as a politically stable democracy, largely free of corruption. The people proved intelligent, kind, generous and welcoming.

In fact, the only blight Beth had been able to uncover in Botswana was the tragedy of HIV and AIDS that ran rampant in sub-Saharan Africa. Botswana and neighboring Zimbabwe had been among the hardest hit, and the government now used billboards, secondary school classes and pamphlets in its campaign to prevent spread of the deadly virus. Treatment for the disease was scarce and expensive, but it was available. Officials at Princess Marina Hospital in Gaborone had admitted to Beth that sixty to eighty percent of their inpatients had HIV, and several orphanages in the area cared for children of AIDS victims.

Despite the epidemic, Beth felt sure her clients were going to fall in love with their new home, just as she had.

"Excuse me, please, Mma." The taxi driver spoke up, addressing Beth with the polite Setswana title of respect. Like most citizens, he spoke the capable British-accented English he had learned in school. "Did you come to Botswana as a tourist?"

"Actually, I came on business, *Rra,*" Beth replied.

She had managed to learn a few words and greetings during her three weeks, but she regretted her inability to converse in the native language. "I'm employed by a company that moves people and their possessions around the world. My job is to help make our clients' transition as smooth as possible. In Gaborone, I've been looking at housing and schools for a family from America."

"Gaborone is a good city for new people," the driver observed. "Did you find a house?"

"I toured several and sent the information to my clients. They selected a home in Mokolodi."

"A fine area! I am certain this house will have many large rooms and a big yard."

Beth smiled at his obvious pride in the city. "In fact, there are five bedrooms, three bathrooms, a wonderful kitchen and a swimming pool."

"Ow!" he exclaimed in the Setswana expression of amazement. "How can your clients be unhappy with such a fine house? And they will place their children in the Westwood International School, of course. The school owns forty hectares of land, and all the class-rooms are air-conditioned. It has a twenty-five-meter swimming pool and cricket nets. The fees there are very high, but not for Americans."

Beth nodded, recalling the well-equipped school that provided the children of diplomatic personnel, busi-nessmen and missionaries with a solid education. For a man like the taxi driver, the school's laboratories, library, computer center, auditorium and gymnasium must seem like an extravagant luxury. Yet his voice held no tone of resentment. Rather, he exemplified the pleasure all Batswana seemed to take in their country's progress and success.

"We have the Princess Marina Hospital here in Gaborone," he was saying. "It is a good hospital. You have already seen our international airport, named for our first president, the late Sir Seretse Khama. Also, in Gaborone and even in Francistown, we have excellent hotels, and markets for buying food and clothing."

Beth leaned forward, arms on the seat in front of her. "I've been very impressed with your city, *Rra*. I believe the Furman family will be happy here."

"Are they indeed Americans?"

"Yes. The husband is a scientist, a geologist. Your government has hired him to help determine where to build dams and lakes that would help supply water during droughts."

The driver fell silent as he maneuvered in traffic. Finally he spoke again. "The droughts are brought to us by God, *Modimo,* who lives in the sky. His rules should not be broken, or He will send retribution. God is very kind and understanding. But He does not approve of those who disregard Him."

Beth considered his words. Most of the people she had met in Gaborone considered themselves Christians. But their theology allowed for spirits and manifestations of past pagan belief systems. She certainly didn't want to offend the friendly driver, but Beth had never been good at keeping her thoughts to herself.

"Do you believe God would punish people for trying to ensure they had water during the droughts?" she asked.

"God has established rules, *Mma*. In Botswana, we have drought and rain. These two seasons were given to us by God. Who are we to believe we can change them?"

"Perhaps God Himself has decided to send Dr. Furman to help the Batswana. If God truly cares for His people, how could He want them to suffer during the droughts?"

"All people must die, *Mma*. If they have been good, God will welcome them after death. If they have been bad, they must be sent to a terrible place. This is God's rule. It cannot be broken."

"*Rra,* I believe something different about God. I believe He loves change. In fact, I believe God sent His Son Jesus to earth to break all the old rules. He came to set people free from rules."

In the rearview mirror Beth saw the taxi driver's eyes widen. Clearly, he considered this idea revolutionary, and therefore suspect. Oddly, his expression reminded Beth of her mother's face when they discussed her taking the job with the moving company. Jan Lowell didn't like change any better than this taxi driver. As different as they were, both believed God had set up a system of rules that shouldn't be broken. If a person broke a rule, he or she must suffer the consequences.

"I do not wish to show disrespect, *Mma,*" the driver

said. "But my church teaches that Jesus, though He is the Son of God, is the same as God. Why do you say that Jesus came to earth to break God's rules?"

"Do you believe God is great?"

"God is greater even than Sir Seretse Khama, and he was the greatest man who ever lived."

Beth smiled, noting again the reverence with which the Batswana regarded their first president. "Yes, God is so great and so holy and so perfect," she told the driver, "that He could not allow people even to look at Him. He spoke to Moses from a burning bush in the desert. He killed men who touched the box where His laws were kept. And God did set up rules that people had to follow to earn His forgiveness—by sacrificing animals on an altar to pay for their sins. But God was not satisfied with the sacrifices of the people, and He didn't like the distance that separated Him from those who loved and honored Him."

She paused as the driver steered his taxi through the airport's main gates. Then, praying that God would give her the words, she went on. "So, that's why God sent His only Son, Jesus. God did away with the old rules. He said we didn't need to sacrifice animals any-more, because Jesus took their place on the altar."

"You are speaking of the cross on which Jesus died."

"Yes, *Rra.* And when Jesus died, His sacrifice gave us new life, you see. We're free from death. We can change and grow and become new people by following Jesus. Do you believe this?"

The driver pulled his taxi to the curb and switched

off the ignition. "I do believe Jesus died on the cross and came alive again. But how can any man become a new person? This is not possible."

"I believe it is not only possible, *Rra,* but it is required."

His dark eyes assessed her. "I cannot change the color of my skin or the tribe into which I was born. How can I be a new person?"

"By releasing your own spirit and allowing yourself to be filled with the Holy Spirit of God. He will change you on the inside, *Rra,* and that's how you'll be a different person."

The driver's mouth widened, and his white teeth shone in the sunlight as he smiled at her. "I know what you are telling me! It is like the snake that sheds its skin. The snake may look the same as before, but after shedding the skin it is different."

Beth nodded and gave a little shrug. "Yes. The Bible promises that if any man is Christ, he is a new creation."

The driver adjusted his meter and took out a receipt book. "You are a wise woman, *Mma,*" he said as he handed her the slip of paper, and she gave him a stack of *pula* in return. "I hope you will return to Botswana very soon. If you come back, perhaps you will ride in my taxi, and we can talk about God again. Until that day, I will consider this situation which you have presented to me—a God of rule-breaking who wishes for His people to change."

As Beth slipped out of the taxi, she wondered if she

had made a mess of the man's whole theology. Obviously, he had been to church, and he understood about Jesus. Maybe she should have kept her mouth shut and let someone better qualified explain things to the driver.

He was lifting her suitcases out of the trunk of his car and setting them on the sidewalk. Beth pulled out the handle on her rolling bag and settled her smaller case atop it. As she started for the terminal, the driver touched her arm.

"These are fierce things which you have spoken," he said, holding up a single finger. "Very strong and powerful ideas. If you are correct, perhaps God will be happy to permit your American client to help Botswana in the times of droughts. And . . . perhaps I, who carry the Slim disease in my body, can become a new man."

Beth caught her breath. "Oh, but you must understand, *Rra*—"

"I understand that I will die from this illness. But you have taught me that if I replace the inside of myself with the Spirit of God, at the time of my death, only the old skin will be shed. The new man will live with God forever."

Her eyes filling with tears, Beth clasped the man's hands in her own. "Speak to your minister about this, *Rra*. He will help you understand it better."

"Thank you, *Mma*. Good day to you."

As he climbed back into his taxi and shut the door, Beth grasped the handle of her bag and headed for the terminal. Nothing had to stay the same, she thought. Not an African taxi driver with AIDS, and not Bethany Ann Lowell.

Chapter Six

Jan held her hand on the telephone receiver, closed her eyes and lifted up a quick prayer. She hadn't been in the mood to pray much these days, but this situation called for divine help. *Please let Beth answer her phone.*

For days now, Jan's calm demeanor and hard-won sense of peace had been crumbling like a stale cookie. She couldn't put her finger on the cause. Certainly Jim Blevins played a part in her discomfort. The man always found some excuse to drop by. Trixie evidently required five or six walks a day, so the pair were always sauntering past Jan's house, interrupting her reading, her gardening, even her painting. One day she barely resisted the urge to soak them both with her hose.

But Jim and Trixie could be tolerated. So could the air conditioner, which suddenly gave out on the hottest day of June. Then a blocked kitchen sink drain necessitated a call to a plumber. Next came the unexpected visit from the pastor of a nearby church.

One Thursday afternoon, Pastor Mark Jackson and his wife had dropped by with a box of Stella d'Oro daylilies thinned from their garden. Apparently someone from the lakeside neighborhood had mentioned Jan's landscaping efforts. Pastor Mark thought of his overgrown lily bed and decided to take her an offering for her new garden. Although she had made up her mind that she no longer needed church fellowship or sermonizing, Jan had visited Pastor Mark's congregation in the small town of Palestine the following Sunday and found it to be a warm and welcoming group. Unfortunately, the neighbor who had told the minister about her turned out to be Jim Blevins—which meant Jan had to sit next to him during the worship service.

Overneighborly neighbors, a broken air conditioner, a plugged drain, a persistent pastor . . . Jan's life was getting more complicated than she liked. She had borne everything in stride until yesterday afternoon. She had been doing some leisurely shopping. When she and her cart arrived at the hair care aisle, Jan glanced at the central shelf, expecting to find her usual shade of permanent coloring lotion, Desert Sunset.

The brand and hue could always be found in every grocery store in the area, right between Amazon Lily and Auburn Glow. But not this time. Desert Sunset was gone. Vanished. Jan had stared at the other two boxes for a moment in disbelief. They had been renumbered, completely omitting Desert Sunset. She dug through the two rows of dye boxes for the shade she had been using at least ten years. Nothing. Feeling as though a trusted friend had just disappeared into the witness protection program, she stood gulping and trying not to cry as she gave up the search.

What could this possibly mean? Had Jan Lowell been the only woman in the world to use Desert Sunset? Had studies shown it to be unpopular? Or too brash? A silly or unnecessary color? Should she write to the company and beg for its reinstatement?

Trembling at yet another shift in the axis of her world, Jan had reluctantly dropped a box of Auburn Glow into her cart, waited through a checkout line and then driven back to the cottage on Lake Palestine. By the time she got home, her dismay had turned to indignation. She plopped down on her sofa and punched the toll-free number of the company into her phone.

"Where is Desert Sunset?" she demanded of the woman who picked up the line at the customer relations department. "I'll have you know I've been using Desert Sunset since my first gray hair, and now it's not in the store. You've renumbered all the boxes! You haven't left room for my color!"

"I'm sorry, ma'am, but Desert Sunset has been discontinued. Auburn Glow is the shade most women have preferred since we reconfigured our line. They're very similar."

"But Auburn Glow isn't my color. It's not the real me, don't you see?" Even as she said the words, Jan realized she was ranting about a dye . . . a mask actually intended to disguise the real her, who was graying and forty-five years old and somehow attractive to a man with a portly dog and several grown grandchildren.

"I'm sorry you feel uncomfortable with the company's decision," the customer relations person said, "but I would encourage you to give Auburn Glow a try. I think you'll be pleased with it."

"I will *not!* How can you expect me to alter myself just like that? I was Desert Sunset one day, and I'm supposed to step out my door the next day as Auburn Glow? That's ridiculous. Don't you think people will notice that I've changed? Don't you think they'll see the difference?"

"The changes in dye lots are subtle, ma'am, and I assure you that—"

"This is not fair, and it's not right. You don't eliminate something like a color. Colors ought to stay the same. A woman's hair is important to her, and your company should know that. My hair color is *me*. It's who I am, and you cannot . . . you simply can't expect me to change. I've changed enough . . . I've been through too much . . . and you can't think that I'll be able to . . . to simply . . ."

By that time, she was sobbing in great, loud gulping hiccups, so she hung up the phone and buried her face in her hands. That was it, then. Desert Sunset's demise was her undoing. But the issue was not hair color, really. It was the loss. The terrible, irredeemable loss of herself.

As she hunched over on the sofa and wept, all Jan could think about was how Beth had turned and walked away. Just like Desert Sunset and John and even Thomas Wood. Gone. Vanished from Jan's life.

Why? The unanswerable question sat atop everything that had tried to destroy Jan. Why had her daughter fled? What had caused this seemingly unbreachable rift between them? Nothing. Nothing except Thomas, who had really been nobody.

Oh, why had Jan ever let that boy into her life? It had been his fault for holding her and kissing her so passionately that her every reserve had melted away. He had not given a single thought to anything but satisfying his own desire. For that matter, neither had she. The two of them, crazed with nothing more than plain old-fashioned lust, had thrown every ounce of caution right out the window of his car.

And not just once. That would have been bad enough. But no, they had acted like a couple of squirrels chasing each other around a tree, through the branches, back and forth. Jan went after Thomas. He went after her. They were insatiable, never giving more than a passing consideration to the consequences of their behavior.

Then look what had happened. *Beth.*

Those days with Thomas had been the final rash and heedless period in Jan's life. From the moment she discovered she was pregnant, her world had changed irrevocably. Each day, each month, each year revolved around the single task of keeping everything under control. Marrying John Lowell. Earning her teaching certificate and graduating from college. Tidying her home and cooking nutritious meals. School and church and the garden club. Order. Security. Stability.

Change was not a good thing. As Jan had sobbed her way through the loss of Desert Sunset, she knew she had to put the most out-of-control part of her world back in order. She had to fix things with Beth.

Today, with her hair Auburn Glow—a much darker shade—Jan searched through her purse for her daughter's cell phone number. "I don't know where you are, Beth," Jan whispered as she opened the address book on her knee, "but you had better answer this time. Dear God, please let Beth talk to me. *Make* her talk to me."

Probably, it was not a good idea to order the Lord around, Jan realized as she punched in the number. On the other hand, did He really even listen? There were only a few times in Jan's life when she had prayed earnestly, from the very bottom of her heart—and God hadn't answered any of those prayers. She had prayed not to be pregnant, but Beth was already on the way. She had prayed for John to live, but he had died. So what was the point in asking God nicely?

"Hello? Mom?" The voice on the other end sounded groggy. "What on earth? Why are you calling me at this hour? It's three in the morning in Nairobi."

Beth was to have been in Botswana for three weeks, wasn't she? "I'm sorry, honey, but I never know where you are or what time it is there. Did I wake you up?"

"Actually, no. I'm sitting in the Nairobi airport. I've been here all night. My flight to London was canceled, and none of the passengers was allowed to leave the terminal." The sound of Beth sipping something came through the receiver. "It's so dry here. I'm just exhausted."

Her heart aching with the instant urge to protect and comfort her daughter, Jan's face softened. "I'm sure you are, sweetheart. Isn't Botswana near a desert?"

A sigh of impatience. "The Kalahari desert crosses Botswana, but I'm not there anymore. Nairobi is the capital of Kenya."

"My goodness, Kenya? What are you doing there? I don't think you mentioned anything about Kenya in your last e-mail."

"I'm passing through. My flight out of Gaborone took me to Nairobi. I should have been able to get right on the plane to London but . . . wait, hang on a sec . . ."

After a pause, Jan heard Beth's voice say, "Excuse me. Excuse me, sir, but that's my bag you just put your feet on."

Jan could hear a deep male voice in the background. And then Beth spoke again. "I realize I'm not using it at the moment, but it isn't a footrest. My clothes are in there. Now move them."

The man's voice sounded again, but Jan could not make sense of his words. When her daughter spoke again, she sounded annoyed. "This is so irritating. The airline won't announce the next flight to London. All the passengers have been sitting here since seven last night, just endlessly waiting. There's nothing to eat in the terminal, and we can only buy warm soft drinks. I could scream."

"Is someone bothering you?" Jan pictured her pretty

daughter sitting there in the airport. Beth had turned out to be so beautiful. Tall, thin, sculpted. Her thick, straight brown hair fell in drapes and sheets that slid like maple syrup across her shoulders when she bent over. It would be no surprise if some man was trying to draw her attention.

"It's all right," Beth said. "Mom, why did you call? Is everything okay? Are Bob and Bill okay?"

"Everyone here is fine. Really, we're all doing very well. I just . . . well, I wanted to talk to you. It's about the problems we were having before. You know . . . when you were visiting at my house."

"Okay, Mom. But I'm not going to apologize for opening the box, if that's what you want. It had my name on it."

This was Beth, her mother realized. Of course she was intense. She had to be—living in New York and working at such a strange job and becoming so successful at an early age. But she had always been that way. Confrontational. Blunt. Ever determined to stick to her guns. She took everything so seriously—unable to move on if she couldn't have her way. As a toddler, Beth had once chewed up a cardboard puzzle piece that refused to fit into a puzzle depicting Winnie the Pooh with a honey jar on his head. Jan had discovered the wad of damp gray paper, dried it under the pressure of a stack of books and then put it back in the box.

That was a long time ago, Jan thought. Another time, another place. Yet the essence of her daughter was the same. Never mind that Jan had specifically said to leave the boxes in the bedroom alone. Never mind that no guest should ever go snooping around in someone else's closet. Beth wouldn't apologize, and Jan was just going to have to accept that if she wanted to reconcile with her daughter.

"What I wanted to tell you about was *him*," Jan said. "Thomas Wood."

"What about him?" Beth's voice was softer.

"I know you can't understand why your father and I made the decisions we did. And you don't seem to want to accept that even Nanny agreed with us. We all felt it was best to let you believe John was your birth father."

"Mom, you were going to tell me something about Thomas Wood."

Brash. Cutting right to the quick. Oh, how had such a blunt creature emerged from that pink bedroom with the ruffled lace curtains?

Jan swallowed, trying to remain calm. "I wanted to talk to you about . . . to tell you how . . . or why . . ." She shook her head, trying to remember the way she had planned the conversation. "The thing is, you see, Thomas Wood is dead. I thought I ought to explain about that, so you would understand. Then you'll know."

"I'll know how he died?"

"Well, you'll understand that he's not worth searching for. Not that Thomas was worthless. That's not what I'm saying. He was a good man. But, Beth, he's gone now, and you need to accept it."

103

"Are you really saying I should just leave it at that? Why should I?"

"Because you need to go back to being the way you were before. You need to forgive your dad and me, and even Nanny, and get on with your life. I want you to let it all go. Let *him* go."

"Tell me how he died."

Jan steeled herself against her daughter's harsh tone. Taking out her reading glasses, she slipped them on and scanned the sheet of paper she had saved . . . hidden with Thomas's old letters at the bottom of her jewelry box beneath ropes of pearls her mother and grandmother had worn.

"When he left Tyler, Thomas had a job in Sri Lanka," Jan said. "It's an island near India. Ceylon is what it used to be called. They grow tea there. Thomas was in the tea business, you see. That's why he bought me the antique tea set. He thought it was wonderful . . . tea."

"Okay," Beth said, a long question mark buried in the word. "So he went to Sri Lanka."

"Well, doesn't that ring any bells for you? Something in the news a while back?"

"No."

"That tidal wave!" Jan exclaimed, wondering why her world-traveling daughter hadn't automatically made the connection. "That tsunami caused by an underwater earthquake. Don't you remember? It was the world's worst natural disaster, or one of them. Beth, it hit Sri Lanka."

"Thomas Wood died in a tsunami?"

"Hundreds of thousands of people died. You must remember it. It was right around Christmas in 2004. Every channel carried the news—day after day for at least a week. And then CNN and the talk shows had guests with all those heartbreaking testimonies. People telling how their loved ones were washed away. Babies ripped out of their mothers' arms. Children sucked into the riptide. It was a terrible event."

"Of course I remember, Mom. I can't believe he was there when it happened. Did he drown?"

"I'm not sure. I don't know exactly how Thomas died. To tell you the truth, I hate to even think about it. It must have been awful."

"How did you find out he had died in the disaster?"

Jan moistened her lips, wishing like crazy that she didn't have to confess this part. If only she could get Beth to accept the truth and let it go. But not Beth. Not that little tiger. She would hang on to the last shred, chewing and tugging and ripping away, until she knew everything.

"I looked him up," Jan said quickly. Perhaps if she spoke fast enough, her daughter might not fathom the implications. "I went online, and I searched for lists of the tsunami victims in Sri Lanka, and there was his name. Wood."

"Just 'Wood'? But that could have been anyone, Mom. Maybe it wasn't him. Wood is a common name."

"It was him, Beth. Because I . . . well, I also found the name of the company he worked for. Wilson Teas.

They had a toll-free number. I called it. I shouldn't have done that, considering the situation with your father. But anyway, I did. I thought, well, Thomas was a part of my life long ago, and I ought to find out if he's all right. And so I called."

"Wilson Teas? What did they tell you?"

"They said he had been working for them in Sri Lanka for many years."

"Mother, that doesn't mean he died in the tsunami."

"Yes, but then the woman told me she couldn't release personal information about an employee unless I was immediate family. So, that's how I knew. She said those very words—*immediate family*—and you never say that unless someone has died. I'm sorry, Beth, but that's the way it is."

"That that is, is."

Jan smiled sadly. "Yes, honey. Some things are unchangeable. He was swept away. Or buried under debris. We really don't want to know. The main thing is that Thomas Wood was doing what he loved in a place he found beautiful and fascinating. He must have been happy. In fact, I'm sure he was. Nanny once told me that she got letters from him now and then, and he was enjoying his work and didn't miss Texas a bit. So, you see? That's the whole story right there in a nutshell."

Jan held the receiver tightly, waiting for her daughter's response. She tried to picture Beth sitting in some Third World airport, a stranger's feet resting on her suitcase, her mouth parched, her body exhausted.

106

Oh, why did the child do this to herself? Couldn't she understand that life was hard enough? You didn't need to go to Africa to find beauty or heartache, joy or sorrow. Those things were everywhere, all around. Jan hadn't escaped her problems by marrying John Lowell. Though their marriage was a good one, it had brought plenty of difficulties. And now, after his death, she had tried to flee to Lake Palestine and live in a cottage by herself. But already she had dogs digging up her roses and leaking plumbing . . . and a daughter who was so angry she had run away from home. . . .

"Thank you for telling me, Mom." Beth's voice was flat. "I realize you don't want to talk about him."

"It's hard to have it come up after all these years. But, Beth, I love you. I don't want you to hate me for keeping a secret I believed was for your own good. Please come home again, sweetie. We'll talk about your work, and you can tell me about Botswana."

"I'll be in London for a few days. Then I have a lot of work to catch up on in New York. After that, it looks like I'm going to France, but maybe there'll be time. I could try to shake loose another weekend."

"That would be wonderful."

"Will you tell me more about him?"

Jan stiffened. "About Thomas?"

"Of course."

"But Beth, he's dead. That's why I called you. It's over. There's no more to tell."

"Mother, it's not over. *I'm* not dead. I'm his legacy, and I want to know who he was."

"Oh, Beth!"

"Did you think you could just say my father died in a tsunami and expect me to forget all about him?"

"Thomas Wood was not your father! John Lowell was the best and most loving—"

"Okay, Mom, listen, I'm too tired to argue with you. I appreciate your phone call, and I'll let you know when I'm back in New York. I'm hanging up now."

"Beth, don't do that. Let me try to explain."

"I understand. I really do. It's just that we're so different. I don't sweep things under rugs or hide them on back shelves. I don't have little sayings that wrap everything up in pretty packages with bows on top. Life is my journey. My quest. I want to run the race with eyes wide open—meeting obstacles head on. I'm not going to hide. I won't pretend. If you want us to be close, you'll have to understand who I am."

"The race? What do you mean by that?"

"Mother, I'm quoting from Paul. The Apostle Paul. Hang on just a sec."

Jan tried to blink back the tears that filled her eyes. She had given birth to Beth. She had raised the little girl with her own values and according to her own ideals. Why didn't they connect anymore? Jan could hardly make sense of what her daughter was saying these days. And she certainly didn't understand the motivation for the strange, disjointed life Beth had chosen.

In the background, Jan could hear her daughter's voice. "Sir! Hey, sir. Move your feet please. That's my bag. I need to get something out."

Jan thought about this man who was so recklessly using Beth's suitcase as a footrest. The mother instinct made her want to give the brute a shove! But he was someplace in Africa. So far away it was difficult to imagine. There was no way Jan could protect her daughter. Nothing she could do to save Beth from pain or discomfort or turmoil.

"Here it is." The young, confident voice filled the receiver again. "First Corinthians nine, starting with verse twenty-four. 'Remember that in a race everyone runs, but only one person gets the prize. You also must run in such a way that you will win.' Then Saint Paul goes on to say that we're running for an eternal prize. 'So I run straight to the goal with purpose in every step.' Does that sound like someone who carries secrets around, Mom? If you're running a race, you can't have a bunch of baggage weighing you down and tangling your feet."

"The image of the race is a metaphor, Beth. You can't take the Bible so literally."

"Yes, I can. Listen to this passage in Hebrews twelve. Talking about the race again. 'Therefore, since we are surrounded by such a huge crowd of witnesses to the life of faith, let us strip off every weight that slows us down, especially the sin that so easily hinders our progress. And let us run with endurance the race that God has set before us. We do this by keeping our eyes on Jesus, on whom our faith depends from start to finish.' "

Jan leaned back on the sofa and let out a breath. Her daughter was actually carrying a Bible through Africa. Her daughter could find and quote Scripture faster than Jan ever did. Maybe things weren't so bad. If Beth had her focus in the right place, nothing could go too terribly wrong, could it?

"Honey, if you're saying that keeping the knowledge of your birth father a secret was sinful . . . I'll have to disagree with you. It wasn't wrong. And it won't tangle your feet or slow you down in the race unless you allow it to. Do you understand what I'm saying?"

"Yes, Mom. I hear you."

"Good. Then let's hang up on a happy note." Jan brushed a tear from her cheek. "I love you, sweetie."

"I love you too, Mom."

As the phone clicked off, Jan rested her head on the sofa cushion and closed her eyes.

Beth worked on filling out her customs declaration form as the jet began its descent toward the airport. She would land at Heathrow in London, take a train into Victoria Station, then ride the tube to Bayswater. Finally, she would settle into her usual room at the Sedgwick Hotel. After a long nap, a cup of tea and a stroll around the nearby square, she ought to be in fine form again.

The British division of the moving company had scheduled a meeting the following morning, which would give Beth enough time to wash and dry one of her knit travel suits, shampoo and shower, get a good night's sleep and make herself presentable. The London agents understood her position and responsibilities within the organization fairly well, but this meeting would include franchise owners from Denmark, Germany, France, and Holland. Her presentation needed to be clear, concise and persuasive if she were to garner their business for her group.

The hours between her and the hotel bed felt like an exhausting journey on top of her flight from Gaborone and the long delay in the Nairobi airport. But Beth bent over her declaration form with determination to tackle one thing at a time. When a broad-shouldered granite block of male humanity suddenly filled the seat next to hers, she glanced up in surprise. At the start of the flight, she had managed to trade places enough times to end up with an empty seat beside her. It was at the far back of the crowded plane beside the toilets, but Beth coveted any spare space on a transcontinental or transoceanic jaunt. She had guarded that seat with her life. Now, with her nerves jangling, she found herself looking into the face of the jerk who had used her suitcase for a footrest back in Nairobi.

Blue eyes—reddened and bleary from lack of sleep or too much in-flight alcohol—gazed back at her. A hank of thick brown hair hung over the man's forehead like a haystack that had blown loose in the wind. He was sunburned, in desperate need of a shave, the top button on his khaki shirt had come open and he smelled like the outdoors. Like her brothers and father when they returned from a camping trip taken without her. She disliked him more than ever.

"Nairobi Airport," he said. English accent—she suspected Eton and Cambridge. Upper-class. Another jaded Brit. Probably some expatriate heading back to the homeland to check on his relatives. He cleared his throat and rubbed the back of his neck.

"Overheard the bit about Sri Lanka," he told Beth. "Sorry."

She moistened her lips, trying to summon politeness on less than four hours' sleep. "It's okay," she said. "Cell phones. No privacy."

He smiled. Straight white teeth despite everything else. Then his face became somber. "Your father? The tsunami of 2004?"

"It's a long story. I'm not sure what happened, to tell you the truth."

"You're American?"

Beth looked pointedly at the declaration form on her tray table. The last thing she wanted to do was engage in pointless conversation. She hoped this guy didn't have any ideas of trying to hook up with her while she was in London. Not a chance, buster. First of all, she was semi-dating Joe. And second, the man was a jerk.

"Texan," Beth muttered. "Look, I've got a few things to declare, so I should . . . you know . . ."

He nodded. "Miles."

"Right. Not many left. I think I heard the landing gear come down."

"No, Miles—my name." He set a business card on her tray table. "Better get back to my seat."

She mustered another smile as he stood and worked his way up the narrow aisle toward first class. Beth bent over the declaration form again, but the white card caught her eye.

"'Miles Wilson,'" she read aloud. "'President, International Sales. Wilson Teas, Ltd.'"

Chapter Seven

In the past four days, he had cleaned up well. Beth shook the outstretched hand and marveled at the changes in the man. His morning shave revealed a jaw that formed sharp angles beneath each ear. A shower and shampoo had turned his brown hair a dark sandy gold. A comb had swept the hank of hair off his forehead to set off those blue eyes—now a piercing shade of lapis without a hint of sleep deprivation. A tailored gray suit, white shirt and blue tie took the place of the wrinkled khaki shirt and baggy shorts. In fact, only the straight white teeth gave any indication that this gentleman had been the jerk in the Nairobi airport.

"Miss Lowell." He indicated a leather chair near his massive desk as he set her business card on his blotter. "Bethany Lowell."

"Beth." She took a seat, placed her purse and attaché case on the floor, leaned back and crossed her legs. She felt slightly off-kilter. For some reason, she had envisioned a musty Victorian building with crates of tea stacked about and Dickensian clerks dipping their pens into inkwells as they jotted ciphers in oversize ledgers.

Instead, the headquarters of Wilson Teas, Ltd. occupied two floors of a modern high-rise. This private office looked out on central London, the houses of Parliament and the large clock face of Big Ben. Just beyond the door, a phalanx of employees typed into computers as they spoke to invisible clients via headset phones. The man who now stood behind the glossy mahogany desk had been the biggest surprise.

Beth touched her hair, wishing she had put it up. She could look professional if she made the effort. But this visit had nothing to do with her work persona, and everything to do with who she really was. A missing father. A family secret. A lost legacy. An unknown heritage. Things that confused and upset her.

Though she had prayed long and hard about her mother, Beth felt little peace. She simply didn't understand how a woman could have done such a thing to her child. What was the point? The only reason to keep such information hidden had been to protect Jan Lowell's pride and reputation. How selfish!

Now there was this whole issue of Thomas Wood having been killed in a natural disaster. True? Or another lie? Jan had said she was telling her daughter about the death in order to close the book again. Get over it. Get on with it. Get back to who you were before.

Who was she? Beth hardly knew anymore. She had spent the past four days taking Miles Wilson's business card in and out of her purse so many times, it was going soft and fuzzy around the edges. Had God sent the man to help her? Or was this some kind of test? Should Beth honor her mother and obediently tuck away all thoughts of her two dead fathers? Or should she stick her neck out, go to the address on the card and find out what the Englishman knew?

At last she had made the decision to seek him out. To rebel against her mother's wishes. To satisfy herself instead of sacrificing her own will on behalf of her mother's peace of mind. Now what? The fusty tea office had turned out to be a sleek, modern enterprise. And the galoot on the airplane had managed to transform himself into a *Gentleman's Quarterly* poster boy. The entire situation made Beth feel insecure. Which, in turn, made her testy.

"So," she said, trying to think how to begin a conversation she wasn't even sure she should have. "On the plane from Nairobi the other day, I might have been a little . . . abrupt. You . . . well, you looked nothing like an executive in a tea company."

"And you looked nothing like a . . ." He glanced at her card as he sat down in the high-backed upholstered chair at his desk. "Transition specialist?"

"I assist people who are relocating internationally. I find homes, schools, house help, clubs, churches, that kind of thing. Settle them in."

"Ah. Must be something new. We didn't have anything like that when I was young."

"Are you old?"

His focus sharpened suddenly, the blue eyes intense. "Thirty. You?"

"I'm twenty-five. But it's rude to ask a lady her age."

"Afraid I've never been the courteous sort. Known as a bit boorish, in fact. Uncouth. Brought up in the African bush, mostly. A tea estate in the highlands of Kenya. Been there?"

She shrugged. "Just the Nairobi airport. Not a pleasant experience. Some oaf kept putting his feet on my suitcase."

A grin tilted one corner of his mouth. "People are thoughtless, aren't they? The woman beside me kept ringing people on her cell phone. I could hardly sleep for the constant nattering."

Beth tried to keep a straight face. She wondered if he had been as unimpressed with her appearance as she'd been with his. "What did I look like on the airplane?"

"The material point, dear lady, is that you look lovely today." He picked up a pen and began tapping it on the blotter. "As for me, I'd been on safari."

"That explains it."

"Explains what?"

"The smell." She smiled. "So, Mr. Wilson, despite my appearance, my yapping away in the airport and my unfriendly demeanor as we were landing, you were kind enough to give me your card. Why?"

"Miles. I'd heard you mention Wilson Teas in the conversation with your mother. You were . . . upset. The situation with your father . . . I thought the company might be of service." He pressed a button on his

116

desk. "Jillian, may we have tea, please? For two."

"At once, sir." The response was far too submissive for Beth's taste.

"Miss Lowell," Miles said, facing her again. "I should have spoken frankly to you in Nairobi or on the airplane. Wilson Teas did not lose any employees in the tsunami of 2004."

Beth stiffened. "Are you sure?"

"Absolutely. Our property in Sri Lanka is near the town of Nuwara Eliya. Both tidal waves crashed into the coast around Trincomalee in the country's northeast, sending water about a kilometer inland. Far enough to kill thousands."

"But not as far as the estate?"

"Not even close. Tea grows best in cool, hilly country. At our estate, we produce what is known as 'high grown' tea, which must be harvested 1,200 meters above sea level or more. High grown Ceylon is flavorful and aromatic—extremely desirable on the world market. Nuwara Eliya is a hill station not far from Mount Pidurutalagala, which is 2,524 meters high."

"You've been to the town, then. You've seen the terrain."

"Many times. Lived there twice, actually. I was . . ." His eyes focused on the corner of his office, as though the dates might be written there. "I was five years old the first time. Eight on the second go-round." He returned his attention to Beth. "The town hasn't changed since it was part of the Empire. Odd mix of

Tudor and Georgian architecture, gabled roofs, perfect rose gardens. Old gravestones. Even a club. I assure you, it's well inland. The earthquake didn't even rattle the buildings."

"But an employee might have been visiting the coast. Maybe he was on a vacation."

"The surname was Wood?" He reached toward a notebook computer. "I ran a search after I returned to the office the other day. Didn't find anyone by that name at our Sri Lanka estate in 2004. Let me look again."

Unable to help herself, Beth rose and circled the desk to stand beside him. "Thomas Wood," she clarified. "He interned with your company . . . well, I guess it must have been twenty-five years ago. After that, Wilson Teas hired him full-time, and he moved to the island."

"There's no Thomas Wood listed on our roster of employees in Sri Lanka. Not now. Not in December of 2004." He turned the slim machine in her direction. "You certain he was with us? Wilson Teas?"

"That's what my mother told me." A stab of doubt shot through Beth's chest as she scanned the list of names. There was nothing Jan Lowell would like better than to pretend that Thomas Wood had never existed. Maybe she had invented everything in their conversation at the Nairobi airport. The name of the tea company. The site of the estate. Even the report of his death.

"Thomas Wood," Miles repeated, his voice low.

118

"Perhaps he moved on. Fair number of tea estates around the world, you know. Any number of large companies who might have taken him on. But his name is familiar, though not with our Ceylon division. I can't think where . . . Hang on." He pressed a button on his intercom. "Malcolm, you there?"

"Busy!"

"Ever heard of a Thomas Wood? American employee at Nuwara Eliya?"

"I'm in a phone meeting, Miles."

"I'm thinking India."

"Miles, cheese off, will you?"

"Darjeeling, do you suppose?"

The silence went on so long that Beth was sure the other man had switched off. It was obvious how Miles Wilson had earned his reputation as boorish and uncouth. He was eyeing the intercom as if determined to force this Malcolm fellow to come up with an answer. And he did.

"Darjeeling, yes." The office door burst open and a slightly older, paunchier version of Miles Wilson stormed into the room. "What's this all about? I was on the phone with New York, and now I've gone and lost them." He spotted Beth behind the desk. "Pardon me. Malcolm Wilson."

"My older brother," Miles said, eyes twinkling. "We share presidency of the company. Malcolm, this is Bethany Lowell of New York."

"I may be older, but it's all I can do to keep my eye on my grotty little brother." He gave a slight bow as he

119

shook Beth's hand. "Are you with Lipton?"

"No, actually, I'm—"

"Looking for someone," Miles cut in. "Thomas Wood. Employed with us twenty-five years ago. Sri Lanka."

"Darjeeling, dear brother. He's our production manager there."

"Wrong. You're thinking of Lawford."

"Lawford does the office and the books. He's the one we work with. Wood is in charge of production—the bloke who actually runs the place. You remember him."

"Tall chap?"

"Correct. Been with us forever. Father hired him, I believe."

"Married to an Indian woman, right? Built a house a good distance from the other buildings. He's a thin fellow, isn't he? I believe I met him once or twice. Speaks the language fluently, though he doesn't say much."

"That's him. Look him up."

Malcolm edged Beth against Miles as he crowded closer to peer at the computer screen. She could hardly concentrate on the spreadsheets flipping in and out on the monitor. Thomas Wood was married to an Indian woman? That couldn't be right. She had pictured him much like the youth in the John Tyler High School yearbook. He wasn't some grizzled farmer married to an Indian woman. Impossible.

"Here he is." Miles tapped the screen. " 'India Division. Wilson Teas, Ltd., Darjeeling estate. Production manager.'"

"How long has he been with us?"

"Twenty-five years exactly." He looked up at Beth, a triumphant smile on his face. "There you are, then. Got him!"

She stepped back, nodding. Thinking she might be sick. "Okay. Thank you."

"Who is Thomas Wood to you, Ms. Lowell?" Malcolm Wilson asked. "Friend of the family?"

"He was . . . or is . . . he's my . . . my father. I think."

"Good heavens."

"He's alive, then?" she asked Miles. "Are you sure?"

"He's very much alive." He stood. "Thomas Wood wasn't in Sri Lanka in 2004. Our father had transferred him to India nearly twenty years earlier. Ms. Lowell, are you well?"

"Tea, sir?" Bearing a silver tray with a porcelain teapot and cups, a young woman appeared just inside the office door. "For two? Or shall I fetch another cup?"

"Thank you, Jillian, but I'm sorry to tell you that I've decided to take Ms. Lowell to lunch instead." Miles dismissed the tea girl with a wave. "Back to work, please, Malcolm. You've done your bit. We'll manage from here."

"Honestly, Miles." Malcolm shook his head. "Ms. Lowell, if I may offer some advice—"

"You may not, thank you very much." Miles took

121

Beth's arm above the elbow as he gave Malcolm a not-so-gentle nudge toward the door.

"Do *not* listen to two words my brother tells you, Ms. Lowell," Malcolm went on. "He's a cheeky swain, he is. Rude. Selfish. Stubborn."

"Out, Malcolm." Miles shoved him through the open door and shut it behind him. "He's jealous. I was always the better shot when we were after green mambas in the bush country. I'd kill ten to his two. Pay him no mind."

"You've been warned!" The door popped open again, and Malcolm's head appeared. He focused on Beth. "Forewarned is forearmed, Ms. Lowell."

"Push off, Malcolm!" Miles held up a fist.

"Cheers, then!"

As Malcolm vanished a second time, Beth realized she felt as though she were in the presence of her own two brothers. The easy banter between the men comforted her and eased the knots in her stomach. At the same time, she was disconcerted by the strangely familiar sense that she was home . . . yet so far in both physical and emotional distance from those she had always loved the most.

She detached her arm from Miles Wilson's grasp. "I need to go."

"We'll eat at The Running Footman on Charles Street," he said, ignoring what she'd just said. "Wonderful lunch there. Jackets—baked potatoes, I believe you call them. Or fish and chips. Ideal British meal for a visitor. None better." He was picking up her purse and attaché, handing them to her, taking her elbow again.

"Good, strong tea at The Running Footman, as well," he continued, propelling Beth out the office door toward the elevators as he talked. "We supply them, of course. Wilson Teas—Earl Grey, Darjeeling, Assam, Ceylon, only the finest. Did you know footmen used to run ahead of carriages in order to clear the streets of the poor and vulgar? The aristocracy didn't want to look at commoners. Too distressing. That's how the pub got its name."

"I don't want to go to a pub," Beth protested as he steered her into an elevator. "I don't drink alcohol."

"Nor do I. Vile habit. There's no need to drink anything at a British pub. Think of it as a café. Or, in America, a diner. That's the ticket—we're off to a diner."

"Listen, Mr. Wilson, I need to get back to my hotel. I can't eat lunch with you."

"Why not? Another appointment? Or am I being boorish again?"

She crossed her arms as the elevator descended. "I need to be alone, that's all. I have to think."

"Think aloud. Talking, it's called."

"Mr. Wilson—"

"Miles."

"This is not amusing. Not to me."

"I'm well aware of that. I overheard your conversation in the Nairobi airport, remember? Half of it, anyway. Not a terribly pleasant memory, if you must know. Perhaps that's why I didn't speak to you until the plane was landing. Thought I shouldn't interfere. But now that I've gone and muddled myself in your affairs, the least I can do is take you to lunch."

"I'm not hungry."

"Besides, there's something I want to ask you."

Even though she knew it was a mistake, Beth accompanied him down the sidewalk. "Business?"

"Perhaps. Wilson Teas does move people around quite a bit. But I was thinking of something a bit more personal. Information."

"About me? No way."

"Me, actually. My past."

"I have nothing to tell you, Miles. There's no Thomas Wood in your past. I couldn't possibly have any information for you."

He came to a stop at The Running Footman and held out his hand to usher her inside. "You're wrong on that account, Ms. Lowell."

She paused beneath the pub's creaky sign. "What are you talking about?"

"I may not have a Thomas Wood in my past," he said, his blue eyes fastened on hers. "But I've other things you might be able to help me sort out."

"Me?"

"You and Saint Paul."

Four days! Four whole days, and not a word.

Jan ran her index finger across the tip of a pink pastel crayon. It wasn't the right shade. Too light. Almost

124

silly in its saccharine giddiness.

The child in the photograph clipped to Jan's easel had only the faintest stain of rose in her cheeks. Dark brown hair, dark brown eyes, olive skin, long black lashes. In her pink dress with its lace collar, the six-year-old stared solemnly at the camera. If Jan could pencil in a caption above the photograph, it would read: "I hate this dress. How soon can I put on my jeans and climb a tree?"

Oh, Beth. Letting out a deep breath, Jan reached for her glass of lemonade. What was a mother to do? A twenty-five-year-old daughter couldn't be bribed back into the family. Or punished for wandering away. Or scolded for finding her own life far from home.

Jan had spent eighteen years preparing Beth for independence. More than anything else, a mother wanted a daughter to build a successful life of her own. So why didn't it feel better? Why did this terrible absence feel like estrangement, as though an uncrossable rift were slowly but surely widening between them?

Picking through her collection of broken and worn pastel crayons, Jan realized she was never going to find the right shade of pink for Beth's cheeks. Throughout the child's life, her mother had tried to paint, mold and transform her into a vision of sugary cotton candy. Jan had wanted a baby with pudgy arms that reached for a warm hug. She'd longed for a little girl who would skip through the yard, plucking flowers as her curls danced around her shoulders. She'd wished for a shy teenager standing before a mirror as her mother pinned up her hair for the prom. Pink dresses. Pink ribbons. Pink cheeks.

It was all Thomas's fault. He had endowed his daughter with skin that tanned too easily, erasing all traces of the rosebud beauty for which her mother had ached. Beth had her father's deep brown eyes and sober stare. She had his nose, long and straight and perfect. Not a curve in sight. No dimples. Inquisitiveness rather than sparkle. Nothing that said sugar and spice.

Shaking her head at the unfinished portrait on the easel, Jan stood and padded barefoot into the kitchen. Bobby and Billy had been easy to capture on paper. She'd found the perfect photographs of them in her collection of albums. Her sons were little elves with fat cheeks and freckles and shocks of unruly hair. Bright blue eyes stared out from their portraits, now framed and awaiting a Christmas presentation.

John would have loved the pictures of his boys. Jan regretted that she'd spent so many years painting nothing but roses. These days, children seemed to be rolling out of her imagination as though she were the old woman who lived in a shoe. She could hardly keep up with them. They skipped stones on the lake, played in autumn leaves, held hands and giggled, tiptoed through dandelions, marveled at bumblebees. Sketches and fully executed portraits lay scattered everywhere in the room Jan was using as a studio. These unexpected children fluttered and floated and somersaulted right out of her mind and onto the paper nearly as fast as she could draw them. Truly, she had so many children, she didn't know what to do!

All except Beth. The still, quiet, staring child in the pink dress looked accusingly at her mother day after day, as if to say, "You didn't tell me about Thomas Wood, and so I won't let you draw me." Rebellious child. Resentful. Unforgiving. What was the point in being so hateful, Beth?

Jan took a handful of carrots from a bag in the refrigerator. As she munched, she debated making another phone call. London. At least she knew where that was. But what if Beth had left the city by now? What if she were somewhere over the Atlantic, sleeping in an airplane . . . her preferred womb?

Like Thomas, the child had always been restless. Eager to get on with life. In a hurry to move away. Always ready to leave at the first opportunity.

Well, Jan had learned you couldn't have a happy life without a home. She had no doubt of this whatsoever. *Truly* content people resided in cottages or bungalows or low-slung ranch houses with three bedrooms, two baths and a walk-out basement. Snug homes that hugged and coddled their owners. The less satisfied built cold, massive monuments with too much space and not enough warmth—castles and palaces and 6,000-square-foot mansions. The absolutely miserable had nothing surrounding them at all, no place to call home. They slept in alleys, cardboard boxes, bus shelters. Rented one-room studio apartments. Lived on airplanes.

Returning to her easel, Jan took down the photograph of her daughter, slid it back into a portfolio and tied the ribbon around it. She removed the clips from the heavy paper onto which she had attempted—and repeatedly failed—to capture Beth. That was the problem. Beth didn't want to be caught. Neither had her father. They wanted to run away, both of them. They were eager for escape, like butterflies in a jar.

Oh, far too much like butterflies. Beth and her birth father believed people could change themselves from fat, wobbly caterpillars nibbling at leaves into brilliant, fragile, fluttering winged creatures ever in search of the next bright blossom. Caterpillars were meant to change, Jan knew. But people weren't.

She took out a fresh sheet of paper and clipped it to her easel. Children were allowed to grow up. But as adults, they ought to stay more or less the way they had been raised. Studying the blank white page, Jan saw Thomas's face as he gazed at her that very last time. He had expected her to become a butterfly and glide away with him. He had truly believed she would take his hand and fly at his side like Wendy and Peter Pan on their way to adventures in Neverland. But Jan couldn't do that. She was who she was. Small and quiet . . . and yes, even a little cowardly.

In the Nairobi airport, Beth had said she was running a race, like the Apostle Paul in the Bible. The girl intended to throw off every weight that tied her down. Did that mean she would abandon her own mother? That's not what Christianity was all about! You didn't go sprinting away helter-skelter, expecting other Christians to join you in a mad dash for the pearly gates. A good Christian followed the methodical plan set out in the Bible. Be good. Try not to sin. Raise your children with strong moral values. And go to church.

For a moment, Jan considered searching through her Bible for the verses her daughter had mentioned in their last conversation. How had Beth come up with those passages off the top of her head? And right there in the middle of some foreign airport!

Unfortunately, Jan didn't know where she had put her Bible. It was probably still packed away in one of the boxes in the guest room. Since Beth's visit, she couldn't bring herself to go in there. Certainly none of the cartons had been opened. What if Jan accidentally found something else? Another reminder of Thomas . . . or John . . . or Beth . . . people who kept getting lost or running away or dying . . .

Closing her eyes, Jan fought the tears that welled up from down deep in her chest. Life wasn't a race. And people weren't supposed to change. Were they? She certainly didn't want to do anything more extreme than moving from Tyler to Lake Palestine. That had been enough. More than enough. Now she had planted herself here, like the Peace Rose growing up the side of her deck. A lovely yellow and pink rose with roots down deep and velvety blossoms unfolding beneath the blue sky.

As she sniffled back tears, a child's face suddenly peered around the thorny stem of a rose bush in Jan's mind. A pink-cheeked little girl with golden curls and lace ruffles on her sleeves. She fixed her gaze on Jan, the blue eyes twinkling and the plump little lips drawn into a teasing smile. It was as if the child were begging to be captured. Pleading to be transformed from a thought into one of the soft, smudgy, winsome portraits that lay about in the studio.

Roses and pretty little girls . . . Jan picked up the pink pastel crayon that had been so wrong before, and she began to sketch.

Chapter Eight

"Your brother was right. You're awful." Beth sat on a hard oak chair trying to read the menu in the gloomy light of The Running Footman. "I should have trusted my instincts in the Nairobi airport."

"To run?" Miles Wilson asked. "It usually takes a slightly longer acquaintance with me before a woman heeds her desperate urge to flee."

"You had your feet on my suitcase. Muddy boots, no less."

"Dried mud."

"Big difference." She looked up at him. "So, *jackets* are baked potatoes? You sure about that?"

"Would I lead you astray?"

Beth shook her head in disbelief at the man's cockiness as a waitress took their orders for two baked potatoes and two cups of tea. Darjeeling. This was not at all what she should be doing, Beth realized all over again. She needed to be back in her hotel room sorting through her feelings about the very much alive Thomas Wood. Who was married. And lived in India.

"Darjeeling?" she asked. "Where is it exactly?"

"Top of the world. Another hill station retreat, much like Nuwara Eliya, established during the golden years of the British Empire specifically for the pleasure of the Colonial elite. It sits at just above two thousand meters—that's seven thousand feet to you Yanks—the perfect elevation to grow some of the most expensive tea in the world. Lucky for us. In the mid-1800s, the Viceroys of India would move their families to Darjeeling at the first drop of monsoon rain."

"How long do the rains last?"

"June to September. Unfortunately, that's when the Himalayan mountains are obscured by clouds, and the rain is so heavy it can wash away the roads. The best time to visit Darjeeling is early summer."

"Now?"

"Between April and mid-June. And then it's good again between September and November. In winter, it's much colder than one would think for India. But, of course, Darjeeling sits right up against the lower slopes of the mountains. Fantastic view of Mount Kanchenjunga from Tiger Hill, and on a clear day, one can often see Mount Everest. Shall we go together, Ms. Lowell?"

Beth gaped at him as the waitress set steaming baked potatoes and white teacups on the table. A pot of Darjeeling tea, a pitcher of milk and a cup of sugar cubes took up the rest of the space on the small round oak tabletop. Around them, people were milling about—men and women in business suits mostly, standing at the bar or seated at tables, eating their lunches and chatting.

"I'm not going to Darjeeling with *you*," Beth said, stabbing her fork into the potato. "Don't be ridiculous."

"Who better? I'll think of a vital reason for Malcolm to send me packing. Shouldn't be too difficult. There's always something awry at one of our estates. Labor uprisings. Pests or blights. Someone skimming the books. Machinery breakdowns. We'll fly into Calcutta and then make the short hop to Bagdogra airport near Siliguri. A Wilson Teas man will meet us and drive us the three hours uphill to Darjeeling. Simple enough. I'll put you into one of the guesthouses, show you about the estate and when you're ready, I'll introduce you to Mr. Wood."

As Miles outlined this absurd plan, both Beth's brain and her nose were quickly clogging up from the pall of cigarette smoke in the pub. She couldn't think. Could barely breathe. Miles was crazy. Impossible that she would actually consider going to India to meet her father. Thomas Wood. The man had not existed for twenty-five years. Then he came to life in a rose-strewn teapot, died in a tsunami and now lived again on a Darjeeling tea estate with his Indian wife. It was too much. Yet Miles was dangling the idea before her, tempting her, pressing her toward a moment that might be the worst of her whole life. Or the best.

She couldn't do it. How would her mother feel if she found out! And Jan Lowell *would* find out. Beth had never been good at keeping secrets. Her mother had turned out to be an expert at secret-keeping.

Put that way, why should Beth care how her mom felt about her going to Darjeeling to meet Thomas Wood? So what if it hurt Jan? Look what the woman had done to her own daughter!

"You've gone away," Miles said. "Thinking about your father?"

"I always say grace before a meal," Beth announced as she set her napkin in her lap. "Excuse me for a moment."

She bowed her head, trying to find a stillness within herself to approach her Heavenly Father. Mothers and fathers and brothers and arrogant tea executives. A confusing whirlwind. The words finally came. *Dear Lord, please make clear what You are trying to teach me. Please show me why You allowed Miles Wilson into my life, because he is incredibly irritating and pushy, and please guide me as I work my way to some kind of understanding about what to do with Thomas Wood. Thank You for this meal, Father, and help me not to choke on this stupid cigarette smoke. In the name of Your Son Jesus I pray. Amen.*

It hadn't been a very good prayer, but Beth hardly considered that an issue. Long ago, she had taken the Apostle Paul to heart when he told the Thessalonians to always keep on praying, pray without ceasing, never quit praying. Which meant that Beth more or less kept up a constant inner dialog with the Father, whether she was in a meeting, in the shower, thousands of miles above the earth in an airplane or sitting inside a smoky London pub.

Oh, sure, she tried to pause, bow her head, preface each prayer with praise and end by sealing it with the name of Christ. But most often, it didn't work out that way. Her communications with the Lord usually were breathed up in quick, short, almost unworded impulses. And His messages to her came back in all sorts of nearly indefinable ways—the certain sense of His presence surrounding her and inside her, the sudden recollection of a verse of Scripture that fit the situation perfectly, the actions or words of someone nearby, an event that couldn't be coincidence, an unexplained change of mood or an undeniable assurance that God was with her.

"Are we going to get on with it anytime soon?" Miles asked.

Beth realized she'd been staring at her baked potato for who knew how long. She blinked and lifted her head. "Sorry. I'm sort of in a daze. Sure, go ahead and eat."

"I was waiting for the prayer."

"I said it already."

"I didn't hear a word."

"I wasn't praying out loud."

"How's a bloke to know if a prayer's begun or ended if nothing is actually said?"

"I was praying to God, Miles. And since His Spirit lives inside me, I'm not required to bring you in on the conversation."

"I see. Well, then, on with the meal." He cut into his potato, took a bite and regarded Beth as he chewed. Disconcerted, she took a sip of tea. Darjeeling really was a delicious strain. Light and almost flowery, it lifted her spirits immediately.

"Listen, I'm sorry for being short with you," she told the man across the table. "I appreciate your thoughtfulness in wanting to take me to lunch. And even this idea of going with you to India—crazy though it is— is sweet in a weird sort of way. I don't know why you're being kind to me, but I'm grateful. The thing is, I need time alone to think. These past few weeks have been stressful for me."

"You didn't know about Thomas Wood until recently?"

"I found out when I was visiting my mother last month. She raised me to believe that her husband, John Lowell, was my father . . . and he was. He really was the best father. Dad was great. Of course, we had the normal conflicts through the years, but he loved me. I never had any doubt about that. He was everything a girl could want in a father. He took care of me. He listened to me. He loved my mother desperately."

"Good thing, that."

"Absolutely. We were a happy family. Dad was wonderful."

"Was?"

135

"He died a few years ago. He had ALS . . . Amyotrophic Lateral Sclerosis. In America, it's also known as Lou Gehrig's disease, after a famous baseball player who died of it. It's a motor neuron disease that causes degeneration throughout the brain and spinal cord—"

"I know exactly what it is," Miles cut in. "Here in England, we call it Motor Neurone Disease or MND. I sit on the governing board of the British MND association. It's an independent charity with a national office in Northampton."

Beth set her cup down, missing the center of the saucer and nearly upsetting the whole thing. She couldn't believe what Miles had just said. "You know about ALS? MND? But hardly anyone does. Why do you sit on the national board?"

"I'm on lots of boards. In England, we aristocrats lend our esteemed presence to all sorts of charities. You may recall that Diana, Princess of Wales, had her name linked to literally hundreds of them. It's a way of doing our bit. And more to the point, a way of looking good. My father held the seat before me, and now I've got it."

"Wait. You're an aristocrat? What do you mean by that?"

"Oh, Malcolm and I have a title or two that we toss about on occasion. One can't be in trade as many years as the Wilson family has and not come to the attention of some monarch or another. At any rate, MND is dreadful, and I'm sorry to hear your father suffered from it."

"Thank you." Beth gripped her paper napkin, suddenly and unexpectedly fighting tears. The grieving over her father had been protracted over the three long years of his decline. When he died, everyone who knew him felt a mix of terrible sorrow along with immense relief. The battle John Lowell fought had been hard and unbelievably strenuous, and it had sapped away every ounce of the man he once had been. Beth's mother had hopelessly endured the agony of her husband's disease at his side.

Now, sitting in a London pub far away from Jan Lowell, Beth regretted to the bottom of her heart that she hadn't been a better daughter. It had been so hard to watch her father lose his abilities one by one. She had hated knowing that his mind was perfect—as brilliant and lucid as ever—inside that fragile, immobilized shell of a human body. And so, Beth had found reasons not to go home often. Each time she did see him, it hurt so much that she stayed away longer the next time. Until finally he went.

A thousand times she had wished she could bring him back. Not the silent, shriveled man, but the hearty father who had ridden her piggy-back on his shoulders and had taken her to the zoo to see the zebras and had taught her to love history. She missed her daddy so much.

But he, too, had been part of the conspiracy. Why had her parents lied about Thomas Wood? Why had there even been a Thomas Wood? It wasn't right! It wasn't fair! She didn't want another father—a first father who had somehow preceded the one she had loved with all her little-girl heart.

"You don't care for our jackets?" Miles reached across the table and prodded the edge of her uneaten potato. "Too dry?"

"Hey, you touched it with your fork!"

"I'm perfectly disease-free, I'll have you know, though there might be a parasite or two floating about—left over from my childhood in the tropics. Occasionally, I think I might have a touch of malaria. But you won't catch that from anything but a mosquito. Do give your jacket a try."

"I'm not hungry. I'm just . . ." She pressed her lips together in an effort to force back the tide of emotion that swelled through her all over again.

"I realize you want to be going." He studied her for a moment. "Do you want to know the part of your conversation with your mum that interested me the most?"

"You shouldn't have been eavesdropping, Miles."

"Boorish men do that. Nasty habit. It was the way you described your life. You told your mother you were running a race. You painted a picture of yourself that I couldn't get out of my head. I saw you taking off everything, stripping yourself down—"

"Mr. Wilson!"

"Not like that. The baggage. The past problems, the secrets, the things most people lug around with them everywhere they go, not even knowing they have them. But you said you'd thrown all that off, and you were running unhindered toward the finish line. The idea of it fascinated me. I couldn't get the picture out of my head. You, running that race."

Beth looked into his blue eyes and realized that he meant what he was saying. For once, the uncouth, aggressive boor had taken a back seat to this earnest man who was telling the truth. He wanted to understand.

"Paul," she told him. "The Apostle Paul. He used images of running, training and racing toward a finish line in his letters to the early Christians. I'm guessing he might have been an athlete."

"How did you happen to have that Bible in your bag?"

"I carry it everywhere." She reached down into her purse, pulled out the small leather-bound volume, set it on the table between them and flipped the onionskin pages. "Best guidebook you'll ever find."

"Better than Frommer's?"

"This is the guide to *life*."

"And you've got it memorized?"

"Hardly. But I know it. I use it like a radar screen to sift through everything coming at me. It helps me identify and filter out things I shouldn't have in my life."

He smiled. "Such as Brits with muddy boots?"

"You definitely lit up the screen. Major alert. Proceed with extreme caution."

"That bad, am I? How do you know?"

"I don't. I hardly know you. First impressions can be wrong, but in the airport you came across as incredibly self-centered. You needed a place to rest your boots, and my bag was handy. Didn't matter how many times I asked you to move your feet, you always put them back."

"I did indeed. And you're quite right about me. I'm selfish. That's the essence of it."

Beth prayed silently before responding. "A true Christian ought to be the opposite of self-centered. He's Christ-centered. That's how you can tell. There's a nice line drawn between the two groups. On one side are those who live to please themselves, advance themselves, enhance themselves. You can spot them a mile away. On the other side of the line are those who live to please God, advancing Him and His message. They're usually easy to recognize, too."

"And never the twain shall meet across that impermeable line."

"Actually, we meet all the time. It's just that if you're running the race, you can't afford to get weighed down. You care, love, help, teach—all that. But you don't bond. Paul called it yoking. Don't yoke yourself to unbelievers, he said."

"So, Beth . . . you never do anything to please yourself? I seem to recall a rather determined young lady speaking to her mother in a decidedly defiant manner. She refused to apologize for opening a box she'd been told not to touch. She instructed her mum to get to the point. She even—"

"All right!" Beth held up her hand. "I confess. I'm human. I wasn't very nice to my mother that night. In fact, I haven't been kind . . . or loving . . . not since I opened the box. And you're right about the rest of it, too. I shouldn't have looked inside that carton, because Mom had told me not to touch any of the boxes in the room. I felt justified because my name was on it. But the fact is, I disobeyed."

"Are you still a Christian, then? Still running the race? Or have you gotten your feet tangled and fallen over onto the other side of the line?"

Beth stared into Miles's blue eyes and shook her head. "Why are you asking me all this? What difference does it make to you?"

Miles leaned back in his chair and poured a second cup of tea. Without answering, he added milk and sugar and began to stir. Finally he looked up at her.

"I've never met anyone like you," he said. "Met a lot of people in my life. All nationalities. Hundreds of languages. Different customs. Religions. Rituals. There aren't too many places left in the world that I haven't seen. I'm quite comfortable everywhere—and with every sort of person. I blend in well, like a chameleon. If I choose, I can become almost invisible. And nothing disturbs me. Storms, earthquakes, jet lag, mud, heat, wild animals—not a problem. But you . . . you're troubling."

"Why? You don't even know me."

"I realize that. It's the heart of the issue. I can't pin you down. I can't peg you into your place. You don't fit."

Beth searched the man's face and tried to understand what he meant. She felt overloaded. It was hard enough to adjust to the reality of a living birth father without this persistent Englishman bugging her.

Not only that, but Miles was on target in his assessment of her. Beth had been selfish with her mother. From the moment she read the note in the teapot, Beth had been furious. She hadn't given her mom's feelings a single thought. Her own situation, the confusion and loss and anger, had consumed her. But how was Jan Lowell coping with everything? And why hadn't her daughter bothered to wonder until now?

"I don't know why I make you uncomfortable, Miles," Beth said, setting her napkin on the table and reaching for her purse. "I'm sorry, because you've been very nice to me. In fact, you're kind of a mystery, too. You flared up on my biblical radar screen. My first impression of you wasn't great. I thought you were selfish—and you obviously thought the same thing about me. But when you gave me your business card, and then in your office, and now here in the pub . . . well, you're not like I first pictured you."

"Which side of the line do you think I'm on, then? Am I a Christian, like you?"

"You tell me."

"I am indeed a Christian. Malcolm and I were tottled off to church every Sunday with our mum, if we were living in a town that had a church, that is. We're English, you know, which makes us members of the Church of England by birth. So, you see, that puts me onto your side of the line."

She started to reply, but he held up an index finger.

142

"Am I a Christian *like you?* I'm afraid I am not. No idea where a Bible might be located inside my house. There may not be one. Never go to church. Haven't prayed in fifteen years. Don't think about the Apostle Paul or running races or being yoked with unbelievers. And I suspect all of that puts me on the wrong side of the line, in your opinion."

"My opinion doesn't matter. God is the one who sees and knows our hearts. All I can do is look at how you behave, where you place your priorities, the things you say and do. The way a person actually lives out his faith gives evidence to its reality in his life."

She set her purse strap over her shoulder. "Anyway, listen, Miles, it's been nice talking to you, but I have to go. I've got to figure out what to do about my father. And my mother."

As she rose, he stood, as well. "Come to India with me," he said. "I'll smooth the path for you."

"No part of this is going to go smoothly. It can't. Thanks for asking me again, but there's no way I'll go to India with you."

"Wrong side of the line? No yoking with unbelievers?"

"I don't yoke with anyone, Miles." She stepped past him. "Thank you for the lunch."

"See, now that is exactly what I'm talking about." He followed her toward the front door of the pub. "What did you mean—*I don't yoke with anyone?*"

"You know what I meant." She stepped out onto the sidewalk and began to look for a taxi.

"No, I don't. It's these idioms you toss about. Running races. Yoking. I feel like you're talking in code. It unsettles me greatly, because I've always been good at interpreting what people mean, even when they're speaking some obscure dialect."

Beth stopped and swung around. "Let me give it to you in plain old English, then. I won't go with you to India, Miles, because I'm not interested in our having any kind of a relationship. Not casual. Not serious. And certainly not physical. I realize this sounds weird—and even I can hardly believe I'm doing it, because nobody in my generation seems to understand this—but I'm committed to purity until marriage. The Bible teaches it. I believe it. I'm living it. So leave me alone, okay?"

For some reason, Beth again fought a lump in her throat and the sting of tears behind her eyes. Why was Miles pursuing her like this? Couldn't he see that she needed him to back off? He was just some British tea dealer with muddy boots and a slim connection to her birth father. Did that mean she had to explain herself to him? Did she have to reveal every stupid mistake she'd made in dealing with her mother? Was it necessary for her to divulge her entire world view, including her most private beliefs about intimacy?

"I have to see you again," he said.

A taxi pulled up to the curb. Beth faced Miles as he opened the door for her and then straightened. "You can't see me again," she told him.

"You don't understand. I must see you."

"Why?"

"Because I need to know you better."

"No, you don't. Miles, I'm nothing to you. We're acquaintances. We don't even like each other that much, remember?"

"I'm falling in love with you."

She stared at him, her mouth falling slack. "What?"

"I—I can't understand it. It's never happened to me before. I don't do this sort of thing, honestly. But . . . please. Beth. Let me take you to dinner tonight. At least give me that."

"No." She tossed her purse into the back seat of the taxi. "No way. Absolutely not. I'm returning to the States the day after tomorrow. There's nothing here, Miles. Nothing between us. Nothing."

Without allowing herself to look at him again, Beth slid into the taxi and shut the door.

Chapter Nine

Feeling as though she were balancing a basket of eggs on her head, Jan sat down on the edge of the sofa. She hated coloring her own hair. Such a mess! It didn't matter how carefully she wrapped a towel around her neck or how hard she tried to keep the disposable gloves over her wrists or how perfectly she situated the shower cap over the mass of mucky hair. She always managed to splatter dye across the bathroom walls and sink, down her neck and usually into her eyes.

Then she had to wait twenty tedious minutes, hoping no one would knock on her door, while the color set. And she didn't even get to use Desert Sunset anymore. Auburn Glow was a ridiculous shade. Jan could hardly believe the company would put it on the shelf. But what other choice did she have? If she didn't stick with Auburn Glow, she would have to try at least fifteen different hues from three or four other companies. And how could you trust such a diverse group? Oh, they all promised rich color, silky hair, deep conditioning, total gray coverage, the whole nine yards. But you couldn't be sure.

Disgusted all over again, Jan clicked on the television. She couldn't lean back on the couch, and she certainly couldn't open the curtains enough to let in the last of the sunlight. Tonight she would have to watch her game shows in the dim, murky glow of the lamp on the side table near the couch.

Lately, nothing seemed to be going right. Moving to the lake was supposed to be fun and refreshing. She was going to paint and decorate and garden to her heart's delight. But somehow all she could do was think about her family. They had gone missing. All of them.

John had died.

Beth had gotten into a huff and run away, as usual.

Bobby was busy working on computers in Houston. Evidently he was dating some young lady, but he wasn't ready to bring her to Tyler to meet his mother. This meant he never came home, either, because he always wanted to be with Ashley.

Billy lived in Tyler, but summer was the busiest time of year at the nursery. He rarely visited, and then he only stayed an hour or two. He lived in an apartment with a bunch of his buddies from high school, which didn't bode well at all in Jan's opinion. Those boys had spent most of their free time figuring out how to get into trouble. Just because they were college graduates now didn't mean they weren't capable of mischief. They ought to get married and start families. That would settle them down.

Jan sighed audibly. She sounded like some grouchy old lady. And she looked like one, too, perched on her sofa with red dye in her hair. Here it was, Friday night, and she had nothing to do. No one to talk to. With the Fourth of July holiday coming up the following Monday, even more weekenders than usual had been arriving at the lake all afternoon, unloading their cars, lighting barbecue grills, running back and forth to the shore to play in the water or take boat rides or fish off the dock. Dogs raced everywhere, barking and baying and chasing the children. People wearing bathing suits or shorts strolled up and down the narrow streets of the little community, arm in arm, chatting.

Well, Jan could hardly be jealous of them. She'd had a good, full life—not that it was anywhere close to being over. The weekenders were actually quite annoying. So much activity and so many cars, and then the firecrackers and barbecue grills. Every Friday through Sunday afternoon, the whole area took on a different feel, a different sound, even a different smell.

It wasn't as though Jan were being forced to sit in the half darkness, dyeing her hair on a Friday night. She had plenty of options. Rent a movie. Take a walk to the shore and watch the birds. Order a pizza—though she was on a diet these days. Not two hours ago, Jim Blevins had dropped by with Trixie to ask if Jan wanted to ride into Palestine with him to hear the church choir's Independence Day cantata. Evidently the choir performed the musical numbers for church members a couple of times before the big community picnic and fireworks display in the park in Palestine on Monday. Jan had begged off, telling Jim she already had plans.

Dyeing her hair was a plan. Besides, she didn't want to go out with Jim Blevins, and she couldn't figure out how to get that message across. The man was clueless! No doubt he'd been so used to getting his way in his marriage that he'd forgotten how to read a woman's subtle cues. One of these days, Jan was going to have to tell him point-blank, "You're too old for me, Mr. Blevins, and besides that, you need to lose some weight, and I don't much care for your dog, either. So, if you'd please quit—"

The doorbell sounded so loud in the darkened living room that Jan jumped a foot high and nearly fell off the couch. Oh, no! Who could be outside her door at this hour? Probably a weekender needing directions to a restaurant or wanting to borrow a can opener. She would pretend she wasn't home.

Sitting quietly and holding her breath, Jan waited, hoping whoever it was would give up and go away quickly. The second time the doorbell sounded, she turned around, knelt on the sofa and peered through the lace curtains. A determined bunch, these weekenders, as if the full-timers were just living at the lake to serve them. There was no way Jan would open that door in the midst of an Auburn Glow dye job, no matter how desperate the person happened to be.

"Mom? Are you in there? Open up!"

Good gravy, it was Beth! Jan clapped her hand onto the shower cap that covered the glob of red goo in her hair. This couldn't be happening. Pastel chalk pictures of children lay scattered from one end of the house to the other. The refrigerator was all but empty, because she'd been on her new fruit-and-cereal diet. And what if Jim Blevins dropped by after the choir concert to give Jan a report? What would Beth think of that?

"Mother?" The doorbell sounded a third time.

Jan flinched. There was nothing to do but let her daughter inside. Oh, well. Beth would just have to see how her mother had declined. How things had gone to pot over the past month. How Auburn Glow and Jim Blevins and living at the lake had turned Jan into the Old Woman Who Lived in a Shoe.

"Beth? Is that you?" Jan opened the door a tad. "You're by yourself, aren't you, sweetheart?"

"Mom, what's going on? Is someone in there with you?"

"Oh, for pity's sake, of course not! It's just that . . . Well, get in here quick!"

She threw open the door, grabbed Beth's arm and yanked her into the living room. Beth stared for a moment. Then she flipped on the overhead light.

"Mother! What is going on?"

"I am coloring my hair. What does it look like?"

"In the dark?"

"I don't want people to know I'm home. They come over, you know. To borrow things. Why didn't you warn me you were coming?"

"*Warn* you? Am I that much trouble?"

"No, no, honey. It's just that I'm—I'm not prepared for company."

"I'm your daughter, for crying out loud! I came because I wanted to talk to you. I need to ask you something."

Oh, dear. Jan's shoulders fell. This was going to be about Thomas Wood. No doubt Beth had dug up more information she felt her mother just *had* to know. Which had probably brought on more questions in Beth's mind. What if Thomas had gotten married, and he'd fathered some other children? So now Beth wanted to ask her mother if it was all right to meet these half brothers and half sisters—which it certainly was *not!* Beth's two brothers were all anyone could ask for in siblings. You didn't get better brothers than Bobby and Billy. Well, there was nothing to do now but get this over with.

"Come on in and sit down," Jan told her daughter.

150

"Would you like a cup of tea? I've got a box of Darjeeling."

The look on Beth's face as she gazed at her mother said everything.

Tea.

Thomas wasn't dead. He was still working on that tea plantation in Sri Lanka. The tsunami hadn't killed him after all. Oh, this was going to be much worse than she'd feared.

"Never mind about tea," Jan said quickly. "I'll get us some lemonade. I made a fresh batch right before I put this— Oh, no!" She slapped both hands on her head. "I've got to wash this color off before it eats away my hair! Just sit down, Beth. And stay there. Don't do anything. Don't look at the pictures. Don't touch any of my things!"

Her heart racing, Jan turned on the faucet in the kitchen sink to warm the water. Then she ran into the bathroom and grabbed her shampoo and conditioner and a towel. This was awful. Terrible. Beth would see the pictures of the children. She would ask questions and start prying. Jan's hair would probably fall out in huge handfuls of Auburn Glow. And then they would have to talk about Thomas, right at the moment when Jan felt the most vulnerable—with ratty hair and her drawings exposed to public view and the refrigerator empty except for a couple of oranges and a bottle of milk.

Without knowing why, Jan bent her head over the sink, pushed it under the warm water and burst into tears. Why weren't things turning out better? She was supposed to be happy here at the lake. She was supposed to feel busy and fulfilled and healed. The mourning ought to be over, but it wasn't. John would never come back, but somehow Thomas had, even though she didn't want him. And Beth, Bobby and Billy had wandered off to live their own lives. It wasn't good, or fair, or right that she be stuck in this place with Jim Blevins and Trixie and the wrong hair color.

"Mom?" Beth's voice came from behind her. "Are you all right? You seem . . . upset."

"No, no, I'm fine." Jan sniffled, breathing in a stream of water that instantly choked her. She grabbed the towel and blindly wiped at her face. Beth couldn't know she was crying. A daughter should never see a mother's deepest hurts. It was all right for Beth to know the weekenders frustrated her and Jim's dog dug up her roses. But not this terrible loneliness. Beth should never get a sense of that. She should see Jan as strong and optimistic and hopeful. Full of life and spunk, as always.

"Well, it looks like my hair didn't get eaten up by peroxide, after all!" she sang out as she wrapped the towel around her head. "You sure caught me at my worst, honey. But it's wonderful to see you. Come here this minute and give me a hug!"

Beth obliged, and Jan reveled once again in the sweet pressure of warm arms around her shoulders, soft skin against her cheek and the flowery smell of her daughter's fragrance. Beth might have rejected her

152

pink bedroom and frilly dresses, but she still smelled of roses. Always . . . roses and lavender and honeysuckle. Precious little girl . . . precious child . . .

"Did you bring your bag, sweetie?" Jan asked as she took out two glasses and poured the lemonade. "How long can you stay? I hope you'll be here all weekend this time."

"My bag is in the living room. Mom, have you been crying? Your face is red, and your eyes—"

"You know those awful fumes in hair dye. I think I'm allergic to this new color. It never has set well with me. Here you go. Would you like some cereal? You must be famished."

"No, I ate on the way in."

"That's a relief, because I'm on another diet. Fruit and cereal. Have you heard about it?"

"Mom, you're so tiny. I don't know why you always think you have to diet."

"Tiny? You obviously haven't taken a good look at my hips lately. A woman who bore three children can never be too careful about her hips. They're liable to spread all over the place if she doesn't watch out." She took a sip of lemonade. "Well, let's go sit out on the porch and watch the neighbors' bug zappers. It's quality entertainment, as they say."

Beth smiled for the first time since walking in the door. "Those blue lights on everyone's decks? I wondered what those were."

"I don't understand why people can't just put screens on their porches. That awful sound of bugs being fried

. . . It wears on my nerves. But you can't sit outside on a summer evening without hearing it."

The two women moved through the front door and sat in chairs facing the lake. With her towel-wrapped hair, Jan felt like a foreign queen. She ought to be entitled to make royal maternal pronouncements. *You may not visit your half siblings. You must stay here for a full week, behaving as a daughter ought. You may not ever again mention Thomas Wood.*

Beth spoke up. "It's about my father. I have some questions."

Jan immediately felt her stomach tighten. "If you're speaking of John Lowell, I'll be happy to answer anything."

"Yeah, it's about Dad." Beth moistened her lips. "I've been thinking about him so much lately. I really miss him. I wanted to know what you saw in him, Mom. At the beginning, I mean. What made you agree to marry this man you hardly knew?"

"Oh. Well . . ." Jan couldn't have been more surprised at the question. She plucked the towel from her hair and laid it on the table. Maybe Thomas Wood was old news now. Perhaps the long trip to Botswana and England had given Beth some perspective and had negated the importance of digging around in the past. That would be a definite relief.

"Your father always had a great reputation," Jan said softly. "Even way back then. He was such a wonderful man. So stable and secure. Everyone who knew him loved him as much as I did. He had lots of friends. And he was very nice to my parents. The epitome of politeness. The moment my brother introduced us, I knew John was just the sort of person for me."

"How? How could you tell so fast?"

"Oh, let me think . . ." Reflecting, Jan rubbed her fingers across her scalp, shaking droplets everywhere and enjoying the feel of the cool night air flowing through her damp hair. She actually couldn't remember much about meeting John that first time. He had appeared at the door, and before she knew it, he was a part of her life. The life of the whole family.

"He fit," she said at last. "He and I fit together. We both wanted the same things in life. You, for starters. John knew I was pregnant, and he never once held it against me. I was having another man's baby, and that was that. No big deal."

"Why didn't it bother him?"

"John was quite a bit older, you know, and I think he had almost given up finding the right person to marry. He had wanted a family so much. His own home life was . . . difficult." She lowered her head, remembering the few times she had been over to visit her in-laws. Such disarray and confusion. Such shouting.

"We didn't talk about it much, but it was the alcoholism," Jan said softly. "John had been raised with it, but he was smart enough to see it and avoid it. He knew exactly what he wanted, but he couldn't figure out how to get it. That's how it can be for people who grow up in families with so many problems. They don't know what normal is, you know? And then John heard about me in the Sunday School prayer group. There I was, already halfway to being a little family of my own. So he wanted to become part of it immediately. He said to me . . . and I'll never forget this . . . he said, 'Let's turn one plus one-and-a-half into three.' Isn't that sweet? Marriage would create an instant family for both of us, and we decided very quickly that we liked the idea a lot."

Beth ran her finger down the side of her glass, gathering droplets that fell through the top of the wrought-iron table onto the deck. Jan could see that her daughter was struggling. Had something happened on the overseas trip? Was she still upset about the conflict that had arisen during their last visit? Had Beth discovered information that had brought these questions about her father into her mind?

"We didn't have a fairy-tale beginning," Jan admitted, "but that doesn't change how good our marriage was. Your daddy loved you—"

"Yes, I know," Beth cut in. "I know that, Mom. You keep reminding me, but you don't need to. I have no doubt he loved me. I felt it. He took care of me, and he never treated me any different from Bill and Bob except that I was a girl."

"That part was my fault. He would have taken you fishing and camping more, but I was afraid you'd turn into a bigger tomboy than you already were. All the same, you spent most of your time up in that oak tree in the backyard."

Jan could feel her daughter's eyes regarding her in

the darkness. Around them, cicadas buzzed, crickets chirped and bug zappers sent sparks into the night sky. Someone had lit a citronella candle nearby. The scent drifted through the screen, and Jan considered getting up to light a candle of her own. Vanilla maybe, or magnolia. But she didn't want to break the spell of tentative peace that she and her daughter had managed to achieve.

"I'm sorry about not being all sugar and spice and pink ruffles," Beth mumbled, her head down. "Am I a huge disappointment to you?"

"Honey, of course not! How could you even think such a thing? I'm so proud of all you've accomplished. Look at you—a college graduate living in New York and working at a job that takes you all over the world."

"But you don't like those things. You've never understood me."

"Well, we're different, but that doesn't mean I don't love you and enjoy being with you. I think you've turned out so well."

"I'm not like you or Dad, am I? You married each other because you both wanted security. You wanted stability."

"That's not the only reason. I thought he was as cute as a bug's ear. That round little tummy and all that blond hair. John was just as jolly as he could be, and so much fun! But you know the main thing? He believed in me. He knew I wanted to get my college degree, and he made sure I had the chance, even with you, and then the boys coming along so quickly. He supported my desire to teach English, he didn't mind my quotations on the walls and he never said a word about all the roses I painted through the years. There were so many things he could have resented, but he never did. He loved our home, and he loved you kids, and most of all . . . he loved me."

"Did you love him, Mom? Really love Dad?"

"Of course I did. Beth, there are all sorts of love in this world. Your daddy didn't sweep me off my feet like a knight in shining armor. He wasn't the hero in some epic romance. But I didn't need that. I needed a man who would take care of me and my child. I needed someone who could accept me for who I was. A husband who would protect me. John did all that and more. True love goes far beyond the silly, dizzy feeling that makes you act without thinking. It's a real commitment to another person. Love is a promise to stick together through thick and thin."

"So, it can't just happen all at once? You don't believe in love at first sight?"

"Not real love. Attraction. Passion, maybe. Affection. Fascination. But deep, abiding love is much more than that. It can't happen until you really know someone fully. Warts and all."

Beth swirled the ice around in her lemonade glass. Then she took a sip. After she swallowed, she let out a deep breath.

"I just don't know," she said, as if pronouncing the end of a conversation that she'd been having with someone other than Jan.

"What don't you know, sweetie?"

"I don't know what to do."

"Something is bothering you. Why don't you tell me about it, Beth? I may not have answers, but I'm a good listener."

"It's this man I met."

A thrill of hope shot up Jan's spine. A man! Well, now, this was unexpected news! Beth had dated in high school and college, but she never got serious with any of her boyfriends. In fact, that's all they really were. Male friends. Jan had begun to wonder if any of her children would find mates. She worried that three years of watching their father's health decline might have erased all the good memories of their happy, busy, active family. Maybe they only saw marriage as a burden, a duty, one person taking care of another as everything went slowly right down the drain.

"Tell me about the man," Jan said, hoping she sounded relaxed and indifferent. "Did you meet in New York?"

"No, in Africa."

Oh, dear! That sounded like a recipe for problems. Where would he and Beth choose to live? Did they even speak the same language? Was the man a Christian? How could they ever agree on the right way to raise a child? And would they expect Jan to go to Africa to see her grandchildren?

She took too big a mouthful of lemonade and nearly choked getting it down. This was not a happy announcement. No matter how much Jan wanted Beth to find love and joy in a marriage, this sort of situation simply could not be good. But how could a mother ward it off? What could even be said in such a case?

"You met in Africa?" she managed to blurt out.

"He was the guy who kept putting his feet on my luggage while I was talking with you on the phone in the Nairobi airport. He's president of a tea company in London. Miles is his name. He gave me his business card, and then I went to his office, and then we went to lunch, and then he told me he was falling in love with me. Just like that. I don't think it's possible at all, for him or for me, except that I can't stop remembering the things he said to me. He asked me some questions, you know? And he told me what he'd been thinking about. Anyway, I left my Bible on the table in the pub, and he found my business address in New York, and he sent it to me. He had written me a note, and he wants to see me again. But I'm just not sure that's a good idea. What do you think?"

Jan sat stock-still, as though she'd been pegged right down the spine by a steel bar. Information overload.

A man with his feet on Beth's luggage—Jan remembered that, and she hadn't wanted such a person anywhere near her daughter. This was bad.

But he was president of a tea company. This was good.

Beth had gone to his office when they'd only just met? Bad.

He had told her he was falling in love with her on the first date. Very bad.

Beth had her Bible out on the table—now, that was good.

But they had been in a pub at the time—oh, bad, bad, bad.

Jan raked her fingers through her hair. She hadn't remembered to put in gel. Forget gentle curls. Her hair would be standing straight out from her head by morning. But who could think of hair care when a daughter came along asking strange questions and then making indecipherable announcements?

"Now, let me get this right," Jan said, laying her hands flat on the table. "This man is an African."

"No, he's British. Some kind of an aristocrat. He has a brother, and the two of them reminded me so much of . . . well, they were like Bob and Bill. Goofy. Bugging each other. I felt comfortable with them. Comfortable with Miles."

"But he had been very rude and obnoxious at the airport, hadn't he?"

"He calls himself boorish. I don't think it's necessarily bad, though. He inserts himself wherever he wants—as though he has total confidence in his ability to fit in. Except with me. He said he couldn't peg me."

"Who can?" Jan chuckled, though she didn't think it was all that funny. "Oh, Beth, this fellow has fallen for your enigmatic charms, just like all the other boys! I'm sure he was enraptured. But I don't believe he could have been serious when he said he was in love with you. He doesn't know you."

"But . . . we sort of do. We know each other." She

161

shook her head. "I can't explain it. What I'm thinking sounds too ridiculous to even put into words. It's like . . . it feels as though God put Miles into my life. Maybe the way He put Dad into your life."

"But your father came along to rescue me. You don't need rescuing, Beth."

"I don't need anything. Or anyone. I'm happy. I *was* happy. Now, I just keep thinking about him. Miles, Miles, Miles. He pops into my mind when I least expect it. It's like he stormed in and took over. But he isn't right, Mom. He's not a Christian, for one thing. I mean, that's the main issue. He doesn't even own a Bible. How could God have put Miles into my life if he's not a believer? And of course, there's the fact that he lives in London. That would make dating difficult. It's impossible to think we could work anything out."

"But you like him."

Beth's dark eyes focused on her mother. "I do. I want to see him again. I keep almost picking up the phone and calling him. But I'm so afraid it's wrong. I've tried hard to be true to my faith, and I can't bear to think that I'd do something stupid and mess up my life. Miles can't be from God, can he? This must be some kind of temptation I'm supposed to withstand. Right?"

Jan sank back in her chair, recalling with some chagrin the fact that she had no idea where her own Bible was stashed. No doubt it was inside one of the cardboard boxes she hadn't yet brought herself to open. She hadn't felt any need for it, not even the couple of times she'd been to church recently. After all, they had

Bibles in the pews if a person wanted to look something up.

As a young woman, Jan had been nothing like Beth. Worrying about being true to her faith? Rejecting a man because he wasn't a Christian? Her main focus in those days had been how tight she could wear her jeans without making her father mad. How to control her coarse red hair. How to pass math.

And Thomas. Jan definitely had been all wrapped up in Thomas Wood.

Chapter Ten

She did not like his feet, and she was thankful he never wore sandals. In fact, Jan rarely saw Thomas in anything but his leather, steel-toed work boots. Winter, spring, summer and fall, the man kept his great big clodhopper feet tucked inside a pair of bleached white socks and those well-worn boots.

But Jan knew Thomas's feet. They were like his hands to her now, so familiar she could draw a perfect picture of them from memory. During two years together, Thomas and Jan had bit by bit uncovered every private, intimate part of each other's bodies.

At first they had done nothing but hold hands. Jan adored Thomas's big, callused fingers and thick palms. They made her feel small and fragile. A man with hands like that could take care of a girl. And Thomas had.

But he wasn't satisfied with just threading his fingers through Jan's. Neither was she. Pretty soon, they were kissing. And then holding each other close. And finally came the day he took off his boots.

"Good gravy!" she exclaimed as he peeled off a sweaty white sock. "Thomas, that is the most enormous foot I've ever seen!"

He grinned, his thick brown hair hanging down over his collar and his dark eyes sparkling. "Wood feet," he said. "We've all got 'em."

Thomas wiggled his toes, cartoon toes with white nails like fish scales. He stuck his foot down into the water of the stream, where he always took Jan to be alone with her. Then he unlaced his other boot, pulled off his sock and put that foot into the stream.

"Wood feet, Wood hands, that's me." He looked at her sideways, a crooked grin on his mouth. "I'm Wood all the way. What do your feet look like?"

"Normal, thank goodness." She kicked off her sneakers and set her bare feet beside his legs. "These are what normal toes look like."

"Mmm." He picked up her foot in both his hands, bent over and kissed it.

"Thomas Wood!" Jerking away, she let out a squeal. "That is gross. My feet are sweaty!"

"I love your feet." He grabbed it again and spoke in a West Texas drawl. "Gimme them purty little feet, girl."

Before she could stop him, he was cradling both her feet, rubbing them up and down with his thumbs and kissing her toes. His lips on her soles sent a fire roaring up through her chest. She gasped and flopped back onto the green, green grass.

And that was how it went. Day after day. Night after night. They had been like two firecrackers, fuses lit up and ready to pop. Did they do a thing to prevent it? On the contrary. They just stoked the fire.

By the first semester of Thomas's senior year at the university, Jan was so mad for him that she could hardly make it through her classes. She was a sophomore, but just barely. Telling her parents she had been too young to start college at seventeen anyway, she managed to talk them into letting her take just a few courses that fall. She spent the rest of her time improving her tan, fixing her hair and working at the ice cream shop enough hours to pay for the constant stream of new clothes she felt sure she needed.

Not that she had any trouble keeping Thomas's eyes fixed squarely on her. The man made a beeline to her house after his last class every day. They hopped into his car and drove somewhere. By that time they had several favorite places to be alone, and Jan had long ago gotten past the surprise of bare feet.

"I've got to tell you something, and I'm not sure how," Thomas had said one afternoon as they sat together on a blanket by the stream. "I don't want you to get upset."

Jan had realized he wasn't himself the minute she climbed into his big blue Mercury and scooted over beside him. He was holding on to the steering wheel as

165

though the car might suddenly decide to take them off on a joyride. Eyes on the road, he had driven out to the stream, helped her spread the blanket and unloaded the picnic she'd packed for them. Instead of his usual talk about what he was learning in his college classes—Thomas loved his agriculture major and couldn't think of much else besides school and hanging out with Jan—he had been silent.

They ate sandwiches, and she told him about a dress she had her eye on in one of the department stores. It was a pink-and-orange sundress with little strings that tied at the shoulders. She didn't think her dad would let her keep it if she brought it home, even though she would pay for it with her own money that she'd worked hard to earn. Her parents were so conservative. They had no idea what the real world was all about.

Jan had chatted on and on, and the whole time, Thomas kept picking up pebbles and shooting them like marbles into the stream. Finally, she'd had enough of his preoccupation and asked him what was going on.

"Well, just go ahead and say what you have to tell me," she said, "and then you'll know whether it's going to upset me or not."

"You'll be mad. I know you will."

She stared at him, her mouth going dry. "You want to go out with someone else?"

"No!" He swung around, clamping his hands on her shoulders. "No, Jan. Never. You're the only girl I've ever loved this way. You're all I want. All I'll ever

166

want. You have to believe that."

"Okay." Her voice was hushed. "Then what is it? What can be so bad?"

He dropped his hands and looked away. "I got my internship assignment."

"Well . . . we knew that was coming. You'll be out of town for a semester. But we can call and write. And you can come home on weekends. It won't be fun, but we can make it, Thomas."

"Jan, I wasn't placed near Tyler."

"Where, then? You told me you thought you might get the internship in Shreveport. That was the one you wanted, wasn't it?"

"They didn't give me Shreveport." He flipped another pebble. "I decided not to tell you this, because I figured it would never happen . . . but there were two openings overseas. I went ahead and applied for them, because you know how I've always wanted to travel. And I got one. It's in Sri Lanka. A tea estate up in the highlands. The tea company will pay for my flight and my room and board and everything. This afternoon, I went over to the Ag building and talked to Dr. Heffert about whether I should do it. He thinks it's a great opportunity, and he says I should go. So I accepted."

He reached for a pebble, and Jan grabbed his hand. "Wait a minute—you're leaving America? You're going overseas?"

"Sri Lanka. It's an island near India. It used to be called Ceylon, and they grow amazing tea there."

"I don't care what it's called or what they grow!

167

Thomas, how can you abandon me for an entire semester? We won't see each other that whole time!"

"Jan, listen, it's not that bad." He turned and cupped the side of her face with his hand. "Please don't worry. We can write letters every day. I'll be back in time for my graduation in May."

"May! But that's forever!"

"Five months from the day I leave Tyler. It'll go fast, I promise. I'll be working hard to learn everything I can. And you'll be busy with your classes and your friends. Look at it this way—you'll be free to do whatever you want. You can go to girl movies and the mall and stuff. And Jan, you can spend more time on your paintings. I really want you to go somewhere with your art. This way, you won't have me around bugging you all the time."

"You don't bug me! I love you, Thomas. I want to be with you. I don't care about movies or the mall. And my paintings are stupid. I wish I'd never even shown them to you."

Tears began to well, and she battled to keep them back. The few times she had cried, Thomas fell apart. He couldn't stand to see a single tear, and he just went all to pieces. She had to speak firmly and make him understand that this simply was not possible! Five months on some foreign island growing tea? Absolutely not. He belonged in Tyler, Texas, and she was going to be strong enough to force him to see that.

"You don't want to learn how to grow tea," she informed him. Swallowing at the lump in her throat,

she squared her shoulders and continued with her argument. "You're Thomas Wood. Why would a Wood want to know about tea? Woods grow roses. Woods have grown roses for generations. You should be doing your internship with your father at his nursery like I told you."

"Jan, the college won't let me do that, and besides . . . I'm not sure I want to grow roses for a living."

"What? You never said anything to me about that."

"I know everything there is to know about roses. There's no challenge to it. I want change. I want adventure. I want to go different places and try new things."

With every sentence, Jan felt as though Thomas had punched her in the stomach. She blinked, but the tears welled up anyway. How could this be happening? It was far worse than just going overseas for five months. Thomas was telling her he was choosing a whole different life from the one she wanted.

"But you're a Wood," she managed to choke out, as if repeating it would somehow make him change his mind. "You can't grow tea."

"I can grow anything I want." He leaned back on his arms and lifted his face to the sky. "I bet I can grow tea better than they ever imagined. I bet I can streamline their production process and identify diseases and keep their trees healthier than anyone they ever hired. The whole idea of stepping into something new really appeals to me. It's change, you know. I want to change. I'm sick of being a Wood who can only grow roses.

People hear my name, and that's the first thing they think. But I want out. Out of roses, out of Tyler, even out of the States. Tea could take me all over the world. They grow it in lots of places, and there'd be no stopping me once I learned the basics."

By now, Jan could hardly see through the blur of tears streaming out of her eyes, down her cheeks and onto her blue-jean-covered knees. She couldn't believe he was saying these things. What about all her hopes of getting married and buying a white clapboard house and raising kids and dogs and growing old together on the front porch in their rockers? How could this be happening? It was a nightmare beyond her worst imaginings.

Pushing back her hair, she sniffled, and he turned his head as if surprised to find her still sitting there. "Jan?" he said. "Oh, no. Oh, baby, please don't cry. It's all right. I'm just talking, okay? Just dreaming big dreams. Don't get all upset."

"What about me?" she blubbered. "What about my dreams? What about us?"

"I see us together always, babe. I mean that. But you're young, and so am I. We don't have to settle down right away."

He tried to pull her into his arms, but she pushed him away. "How can we be together always if you're on some island and I'm in Texas? Huh? Did you think of that when you started dreaming big dreams?"

"It's not any old island, it's Sri Lanka. And it's just for five months. We'll be fine. I love you, and nothing

170

can change that. I promise. Please believe me, Jan, and stop crying. I promise I won't leave you alone. I'll be with you for the rest of our lives, okay? Okay?"

She allowed him to draw her close, and she buried her head in his shoulder. Tears of hurt and frustration surged out as though she hadn't cried in years. Was he promising marriage? Or threatening to discard her in favor of change and tea and seeing the world?

"What if you find another girlfriend?" she wept.

"I won't. Nobody on an island off the coast of India could interest me."

"You mean there might be a girl somewhere else who could interest you?"

"No, of course not!" He began kissing her wet cheeks. "Jan, please believe me. You're everything. Everything I ever wanted."

"I'm not tea!"

"But you're you. You're the woman I love."
Threading his fingers through Jan's thick hair, he pressed her against his chest. "Come on, baby, you know how much I love you. We're perfect together. We match. We fit."

She sighed and closed her eyes. Maybe things weren't so bleak. At least her reaction proved to her how much she wanted him—and proved it to Thomas, too. And they always got exactly what they wanted.

Beth opened her eyes to a shaft of sunlight streaming in through the window in the spare bedroom, and she knew immediately what she was supposed to do. Be obedient to God. Simple. She would set aside the silly rush of jangling nerves that went off every time she thought of Miles Wilson's handsome face and dry wit and suave British accent. Those things were shallow. Meaningless. What counted was his heart, and it wasn't where it needed to be.

The moment she sat up in bed and swung her legs over the side, a pang shot through her heart. But Miles was seeking! He really had wanted to know about the Bible and the Christian life and the teachings of Saint Paul. Who better than Beth to tell him? God had put Miles beside her in that airport in Kenya. Even put his feet on her luggage! How much clearer could it be? She was the one to lead Miles to Christ.

Beth stood and grabbed her bathrobe. No way. That was a complete rationalization. She wanted to see Miles again, and so she conveniently decided she was the only one to guide him onto the straight and narrow. Ha! God could use any of His servants to accomplish that task. Beth had done her part, and the Holy Spirit could do the rest.

Perhaps the Lord had put Miles into her path to spark his interest in a life of faith, but there her responsibility ended. Beth walked into the bathroom and turned on the shower. She knew all too well the perils of dating someone who didn't share her religious and moral beliefs. In fact, she thought as she stepped under the stream of warm water, dating was turning out to be a fairly bad idea all across the board. Thankfully she'd had the sense to break things off with Joe when she got back to New York after her trip to Botswana. Dumb to date your boss. Dumber to date someone with whom you could never imagine sharing a life.

Joe called himself a Christian, but he didn't give much evidence of it. He rarely spoke of his faith. Only went to church when she was in town. And certainly didn't live the most surrendered life she had ever seen. In fact, more than once, she'd heard him blatantly lie—telling his secretary to inform a caller he was out of the office when he wasn't. Little things like that taught Beth where his heart was.

When Beth had informed him she didn't intend to see him again outside the office, Joe had accused her of being rigid, morally uncompromising—as though that were a bad thing! She rinsed the shampoo out of her hair as she recalled his concluding words to her. *Your standards are too high, Beth. You'll never meet any man perfect enough to please you.*

Stepping out of the shower, she dried off and wrapped her hair in the thick pink towel her mother had provided for the guest bath. Beth peered at her reflection through the steam on the mirror. Queen rose of the rosebud garden of girls.

Right.

Were her standards really too high? Did she expect perfection in a man? And if so, wasn't that her mother's fault?

Probably so. How could any child grow up in such a happy family . . . in such a pink bedroom . . . with such zippy sayings painted on the walls . . . and not have high expectations? The Lowell family had been perfect. A model mother and father. Well-behaved children. Paintings of roses hanging in every room. Ideal.

Except not.

Nothing in this life was perfect, Beth thought as she examined her eyebrows. There were always problems like Thomas Wood and Lou Gehrig's disease and other faulty things getting in the way. That's why Christ had come, though, wasn't it? She had just read it in her Bible. "But God showed his great love for us by sending Christ to die for us while we were still sinners."

Wanting to be sure, she padded back to her room and flipped open the small book. Yes, there it was. The fifth chapter of Romans. Saint Paul had spelled out the whole thing in his explanation of the two roles of Adam and Christ. Because one person disobeyed God, many people became sinners. But because one other person obeyed God, many people will be made right in God's sight.

Right in God's sight—even though we're flawed and sinful and diseased and . . . and not even the real daughter of our daddy. Beth bent over the Bible on her lap and pressed her hands against her eyes, trying to push the tears back inside. She—who tried so hard to follow Christ, whose standards were deemed "too high," who did everything she could to be perfect— was born because of sin.

Not her own sin. The wrongdoing belonged to her mother and the man Jan Calhoun chose to have sex with before marriage. Thomas Wood.

Beth let out a growl of frustration and anger at the very thought of the man. She hated him! Why did he even have to exist? Why had he walked into her mother's young life, tempting Jan away from the truth? He was disgusting! They both were filthy. And Beth was the product of their selfish, thoughtless passion.

She felt like she needed another shower! She was illegitimate! She was a mistake! She was a blunder, an error, a lapse in judgment. She was nothing but a biological product of two stupid people who didn't even love each other and couldn't be bothered to get married and try to behave decently!

Disappointment, irritation, annoyance and resentment built into another snarl as Beth yanked off her robe and threw it on the bed. While she dressed for the day, her rage built. Nobody should be allowed to have mistake babies. Mistake babies didn't belong. They could never be part of a real, true, honest family. Mistake babies were better off never to have been born than forced to try to fit with people who didn't even really want them in the first place.

"Knock, knock, sweetheart!" Jan's voice sang out as the door swung open. "Rise and shine!"

Beth glared at the perky redhead who fairly skipped into the guest bedroom. Stepping into a pair of flip-flops, Beth watched as her mother pulled open the lacy curtains and began to sing. It was a song from *Mary Poppins*, a movie they had watched together a hundred times. Jan loved to adapt the words to fit her own children.

As she sang her own version of "Jolly Holiday" about the beautiful weather and feeling good, Jan took the bedsheet and pulled it up to the pillow as if she were the magical British nanny herself.

Gritting her teeth, Beth shoved her hands deep into the pockets of her shorts. Her mom was giving the down comforter a shake to fluff it before setting it into its place. And now the pillows. One, two, three. Largest to smallest. A tiny embroidered one for the last, set at a jaunty angle just to be cute.

Now Jan was replacing Mary's name with her daughter's in the song that she sang out as she touched up the ruffles on the pillows. "Bethy makes your heart so light!"

"Shut up, Mother!" Beth shouted. "Just shut up!" Clenching her fists as her face went hot and throbbing, she ran out of the bedroom, through the living room and onto the porch. She pushed open the screen door and sprinted down the road. Her flip-flops slapped the warm pavement, and a sheen of perspiration broke out on her forehead.

What a sham! Her whole life was just pretend, Beth thought as she raced toward the lake. All these years, her parents had been acting like people they weren't. Perfect and happy and honest! It had all been a big lie. Beth was a lie. She was nothing and nobody. An accidental union of sperm and egg, unexpected, unwanted, unloved.

Reaching the edge of the water, Beth sank down into the grass and buried her face in her hands. Her daddy had only pretended to love the baby girl, because he wanted to be married and escape his alcoholic family. Her mother had been so afraid to face the consequences of her failures that she had accepted the first good offer that came along. And there was Beth, sitting in the middle, a little illegitimate child around whom they had built their Mary Poppins life.

Something cold and wet pressed against her leg, causing Beth to gasp and look up in surprise. Beside her, a plump white poodle-looking dog lifted its head and gazed at her with soft brown eyes. The dog wagged its tail. Beth reached out and patted the fluffy head.

"Hey, there!" a voice from behind called out. "Trixie, don't bother the nice lady. Come here, girl. Get over here right now!"

Beth turned to find a stocky man with a fishing pole heading toward her and the dog. He lifted a hand. "Sorry about that. Trixie never met a stranger. We've been fishing since dawn and haven't had a nibble."

"It's okay." Beth managed to force a pleasant expression. "She's not bothering me."

"I'm Jim Blevins," he said, hunkering down into the long, green grass with some effort. "Are you new to the neighborhood?"

"My name is Beth Lowell. I'm just here for the weekend."

"Beth Lowell? Why, you must be Jan's daughter!

177

The young lady who lives in New York and travels all over the world! Your mother has told me all about you. She's proud as punch over you. Talks about all three of you kids like you were royalty. I was hoping I'd get to meet you one of these days. I helped Jan put in her new rose garden. Me and Trixie. We live just up the street, you know, and we pass the house on our walks. Your mother has been coming to our church now and then. I'm hoping she might join us one of these days."

Beth pictured the large man and his fluffy dog beside "their" church, and a genuine smile softened her face. "The roses look lovely."

"Thank you. She's got a nice variety that should bloom all summer. I did a lot of research for my late wife's garden, and so I did what I could to help your mother, too. Do you know she makes the best chicken salad I believe I have ever eaten? And lemonade. The woman can whip up a pitcher of fresh lemonade that rivals anything I've ever tasted."

"Mom has always had her specialties in the kitchen."

"I do believe that. This neighborhood sure has improved since she moved in. She's fixed up her house so nice, and she painted those sayings on the walls—and have you seen the children she draws with her pastel chalks? Usually we sit out on the screened porch when Trixie and I happen to drop by around lunchtime, but once or twice I've gone inside. She got her kitchen sink plugged one day, and we ended up calling the plumber. I can fix those things most of the time, but this job needed a pro. Anyhow, I saw the portraits she had done, and I'd like to have fallen over in a dead faint. Those children look as though they could jump off the page and run out to play in the yard."

"I got in late last night," Beth told him. "I haven't really had time to look around."

"She's shy about them, but don't let her get away with hiding them from you. They're good. Real good."

Beth studied the lake. "She used to paint roses."

"That's what she told me. When her husband was living, she had to work at her teaching job and take care of you kids. And then she took care of him, of course. She said painting bouquets of roses helped her relax. But now she doesn't have so many pressures, and these children just come tumbling out of her imagination. That's what she told me. They just tumble right out."

"Really?" Beth turned to Jim Blevins and took in his pleasant blue eyes and warm grin. This man knew more about Jan Lowell than her own daughter did. Beth had been so consumed with her own emotions that she hadn't taken time to find out what her mom was thinking and doing these days.

"Jan told me she figures the children she paints are all the ones she never had. She would have liked more of her own, but her husband said three kids was the perfect number for the perfect family." Jim winked and nodded. "I have three myself. 'Course they're all older than you. I've got so many grandchildren now I can hardly keep track of them. I know your mother

179

can't wait to have grandbabies, too."

"I'm sure that's true."

"Well, Trixie and I had better head back to the dock and put away our gear. Time to go home, put my feet up and have a cup of coffee and a cinnamon roll. I shouldn't eat a single one, but your mother brought some over the other morning, and they just sit there on that plate and call out to me, you know?"

Beth did know. She had eaten her mother's homemade cinnamon rolls nearly every morning of her childhood. Jan Lowell's chicken salad and fresh squeezed lemonade had been famous in their neighborhood in Tyler.

"It was nice to meet you, Mr. Blevins."

"Call me Jim." He shook Beth's hand. "I know you must be proud to have such a wonderful mother. And she sure is proud of you, young lady. I don't believe there's a mother anywhere who could love her daughter as much as she loves you. And those boys? Well, just take a look at the framed photographs she's got all over the living room. If there was ever a woman who got more happiness out of her family, I don't know who. You kids have got a real jewel there. Take care, now."

Jim whistled to his dog and ambled off with his fishing pole balanced on one shoulder.

Chapter Eleven

"I met your friend," Beth said. She had come back into the house about an hour after shouting at her mother and running down to the lake. "The man with the white dog? Jim Blevins."

"Oh, yes, he's over here bothering me all the time."

Jan tried to sound lighthearted, hoping her daughter couldn't tell how hurt she felt. When Beth had returned to the house that morning, she apologized for her explosion, went into the guest bedroom and shut the door. Jan could hear her making phone calls. Now they were out on the screened porch eating lunch. She had made chicken salad sandwiches, even though she secretly felt her daughter didn't merit the effort it took to create good chicken salad.

Still, a mother's love never ended, did it? While Beth was at the lakeshore pouting or fuming, or whatever it was this time, Jan had hopped in her car for a run to the grocery store. She bought everything she would need for the chicken salad, as well as some lemons, lots of fresh vegetables and a loaf of seven-grain bread. So much for her fruit-and-cereal diet. Her hips would head east and west, the way they always did when she ate too much of the wrong things, but what could she do? It wasn't like she could serve her daughter nothing but cornflakes and strawberries.

In the Lowell family, the phrase "shut up" was never

spoken. That expression of disrespect and anger was forbidden, and for good reason. Nothing could cut a person to the quick faster than those two words. Even now, seated on the porch with roses and barbecue smoke perfuming the air, Jan still stung from the reprimand.

What had she done wrong? Nothing but sing an old family movie favorite. Nothing but try to start the day on a cheerful note. Nothing but love her daughter and do her best to make the most of their short time together.

"I think he likes you, Mom," Beth was saying.

"Who?"

"Jim Blevins. He had nothing but wonderful things to say about you. He thinks you've really brightened up the neighborhood."

"I wish he and that dog would just leave me alone. You watch . . . The pair of them will stroll by here in a few minutes. Jim will wave and holler out some kind of a question that I'm supposed to answer, like—'Did you get rid of your aphids?' or 'Have you heard the white bass are biting?' Then he'll pretend he didn't hear me answer, so he and Trixie will come walking up my driveway, and the next thing you know, they'll be right here on the porch with us."

"Why don't you like him? He seems nice."

"He's nice enough. I just wish he wouldn't hang around so much. It's because his wife died and he's lonely."

"I think he's set his cap for you, Mom."

"Oh, for pity's sake. Jim is a good twenty years older than I am."

"So what? Are you going to live here by yourself tending roses and making chicken salad until you die?"

"Now what kind of a question is that, young lady? You talk like I've got one foot in the grave already."

"Well, you act like it. Mother, you're forty-five. If Jim Blevins is too old for you, what kind of man would you be looking for?"

"I'm not looking for any man. I'll have you know I've done all I ever want to do in that department. Marriage to your father was wonderful, and I'm in no hurry to find anyone else."

"But say you changed your mind. What sort of person would you choose?"

Jan looked across the table at her daughter. What on earth was going on? What was Beth getting at? She had come back to Texas and appeared at her mother's door unannounced. She said she had something to ask. The question seemed to be: Why John Lowell? Jan thought she had answered very well, but then the very next morning, Beth lashed out at her and ran away in a huff.

Now here they were again. Back to the man question. This fellow in London certainly had caused a wrinkle in Beth's well-ordered world. Maybe that was good. It was about time she learned that things didn't always go the way a person planned.

"I would choose someone who made sense to me," Jan answered, after giving the question some thought.

She wasn't about to tell the whole honest truth. "I'd look for a man who matched me in temperament and interests, like your father did. We'd have to live in the same area and have the same values and be like-minded. I certainly wouldn't do anything rash, I can tell you that. I would proceed very, very carefully, because marriage is a lifetime commitment."

"Your dream man sounds just like Jim Blevins."

"Keep your voice down, Beth!" Jan glanced around. "He's always lurking, and he certainly is not the kind of man I'd choose to marry."

"Same location, same interests, same temperament."

"And I don't care for his dog, either."

Beth laughed, but then her expression became earnest. "You don't think you'd want a man who was different from Dad? Someone exciting—maybe a little wild and crazy?"

"No. Absolutely not."

The truth was, Jan would probably jump at the opportunity to be with such a man. But she'd done that once before, and look where it got her.

No, she had to be wary. In spite of all she'd been through, she was still vulnerable, still liable to do something terribly stupid. But she had lived long enough to know what she wanted out of life. It was this small house beside this lake. It was her roses and her pastel chalk children and her fruit-and-cereal diet.

"By the way, Thomas Wood is alive," Beth announced into the silence between them. "He lives in India now."

Jan felt as though she'd been shot through the heart. "Beth!" she snapped. "We were not discussing him!"

"I think you ought to know the truth, Mom. I don't want to keep any secrets from you."

Beth arched her eyebrows to punctuate the last remark. Jan grabbed a napkin and blotted her lips. Okay, fine. So Thomas was alive. That didn't make any difference. Alive or dead, he was nothing to her except a memory.

"I don't want to hear about him," she informed Beth. "It doesn't matter to me where Thomas is living or what he's doing."

"He's the production manager for a tea estate in Darjeeling in the foothills of the Himalayas. He's married to an Indian woman. I don't know if they have any children."

"Well." Jan swallowed. She had hardly allowed herself to consider this possibility. To her, Thomas was still the lanky young man who had driven her out to their favorite stream and kissed her tears away. In her mind, he hadn't changed. He certainly wasn't married.

"Miles found out everything about him." Beth let out a deep breath. "You see, as it turns out, Miles and his brother own Wilson Teas, Ltd. Thomas Wood still works for the company."

"That was convenient for you, wasn't it?" Jan heard herself snap. "I guess you arranged it all while you were in London."

"Actually, God arranged it. In Nairobi."

Jan shrugged. "Well, that's fine, Beth. Thomas Wood

can work anywhere he wants, as far as I'm concerned. I told him so a long time ago. I'm glad he's married, and I'm certainly happy to hear he's not dead. I sure didn't want him to have drowned in that terrible tsunami."

"Miles wants to take me to India to meet him."

Jan swung toward her daughter, her heart pounding. "Beth, you can't be thinking of doing that! Tell me you won't! Promise me!"

"Why shouldn't I?"

"Because of your father! It would be awful."

"Dad is dead, Mom. I can't hurt him by meeting my birth father."

"It would hurt *me!* John and I worked very hard to give you a happy childhood, and you can't betray us by racing off to India at the first opportunity!"

"Betray you? Who betrayed who?" Beth's eyes crackled. "I'm the one who's been deceived my whole life!"

"I am not going to start this argument again, Bethany Ann Lowell. If you can't be kind and respectful toward your mother, you'd just better head back to New York. Fly away to India with your new boyfriend, if you want, but don't think you're going to get my seal of approval. And don't expect me to welcome you home with open arms. I don't approve, and I don't want you to do it, and I think it would be an enormous mistake. But I can't stop you, can I? You've always done just what you wanted! Just like him! You go wandering off as though—"

186

Catching herself, Jan began grabbing things from the table. Enough. Enough of this! She had paid for her mistake a long time ago. She had turned a teenage nightmare into a dream family, and she wasn't about to let her daughter wreck everything.

"Excuse me please." Jan picked up a plate and set it onto her own. She stood, scooting the metal chair backward across the deck. "I'll clear the dishes, and then I need to do a little weeding in my garden. You're welcome to join me outside if you want."

"Mom, please don't clam up and walk away from me again."

"Again? You're the one who shouted and ran off this morning. I was only trying to be cheerful and sing our Mary Poppins song."

"Okay, sit down and let's discuss this. I feel like you've been living a hidden, secretive life of denial all these years. It's not only that you and Dad deceived me, but you're not even being honest with yourself!"

"And just what is that supposed to mean, young lady?"

"I'm trying to *talk* to you. You're my mother. I need for you to help me figure out what to do."

"I've told you exactly what I thought. This Miles fellow lives too far away, and he's obviously an impulsive, thoughtless kind of man. If he would tell you he's falling in love with you on your first date, he'd tell that to any young woman. And now he wants to take you to India to meet Thomas? Clearly he's a playboy who sees you as a vulnerable, easy conquest. He knows you're sad because your father died, and he thinks he can zoom in and swoop you right up in his claws. Worst of all, you're just about ready to do it!"

"Mother, I came here to ask your opinion before I do anything."

"Well, I can assure you men like that are no good. How could you trust him? How could you be sure where you'd end up or what kind of life you'd have?"

"I'm sure I'd have a say in it."

"You already know what you want most, Beth. Every woman—if she's honest with herself—desires security and stability. She wants a home and children and a loving husband who can protect her. I'm warning you, if you go off to India with that stranger, there's no telling what will happen! You shouldn't do it!"

Straightening, Jan realized she'd been leaning across the table and yelling at her daughter. Mortified, she turned on her heel and practically ran for the kitchen.

Beth sat on the porch and waved as Jim Blevins and his dog shuffled past the small house. She had blown it. Totally. Her plan in returning to her mother's home had been so perfect. She wouldn't mention her discoveries in London at all. She would simply try to find out why her mother had chosen John Lowell over Thomas Wood. The heaviest concern in Beth's mind these past few weeks hadn't been her birth father. It had been Miles Wilson and what to do about her own future.

Instead, she had blurted out everything about Thomas, ordered her mother to shut up and basically acted like a naughty, spoiled child. She was never like this in her real life. In New York, Beth maneuvered through traffic and business meetings and relationships. She successfully directed the overseas unit of her department. She confidently assisted families who were settling into some of the most difficult places in the world. She negotiated red tape with immigration bureaus, housing authorities, school districts and embassies. In London, she recently had convinced a whole group of European agents who owned franchises of the moving company to sign on for her department's services. The coming months would involve hiring additional office staff, traveling to four continents and working with everyone from high-powered executives to cooks and maids. She would succeed.

But not with her own mother. Nothing Beth did with Jan Lowell worked out well. In this house beside Lake Palestine, Beth had to go and act like a bratty four-year-old. Shouting accusations. Dropping information like bombs on her unsuspecting mom. Behaving like the most self-centered, unchristian human being imaginable.

Lord, please help me, Beth silently prayed as she walked toward the kitchen. *Give me the words to say to make it right. I don't know how to begin, but I can't let this rift between us widen. I need You, Lord, I need You so much.*

Her mother was setting the last plate in the dishwasher. Carefully rinsed of every crumb, the dishes sat in gleaming white rows. Jan opened a box of detergent, filled the compartment and shut the tiny door. As she closed the dishwasher and turned it on, she spotted her daughter.

"Oh, Beth, honey, forgive me for being so bossy and talking to you in such a hateful way." She held her arms wide. Her cheeks were wet and the tip of her nose red. "Please forgive me, sweetheart."

"Mom." Beth threw herself into her mother's embrace. "I'm the one who should be apologizing. I've been so rude to you. I don't see how you can ever forgive me for what I said this morning. And I never should have mentioned Thomas Wood."

"Shh, sweetie. It's okay." Her small hand stroked her daughter's back. "This has been a stressful time for you with all that travel, and meeting your new man, and then the information you hadn't expected about your past. I understand. I'm glad you came home to me. I've missed you so much, my precious Bethy."

"I've missed you, too." Beth straightened and gazed into her mother's dear, familiar face. "Mom, I'm so confused about Miles."

"Why don't you come outside while I weed, and you can tell me more about him? Is he nice-looking?"

"This feels really stupid to admit, but . . . he's so handsome that I can't stop thinking about him."

"Well, how about that? What color is his hair?"

"Blond. Dark blond. And he has gorgeous blue eyes." Barefoot, Beth followed her mother out the front door and down the deck steps to the rose garden.

"You should hear his British accent."

"Does he sound like Burt in *Mary Poppins*?"

"Oh, Miles is nothing like a Cockney chimney sweep. He speaks more like King Arthur in *Camelot* or Henry Higgins in *My Fair Lady*."

"Now, that's romantic!"

"He told me he's an aristocrat. He could be a lord or a knight or something. I don't know any of that peerage stuff. And guess what? You just won't believe this!"

"Try me."

Beth sank cross-legged into the deep, cool grass as her mother knelt to dig out the dandelions that had begun to spring up around the rosebushes. The afternoon sun heated Beth's cheeks, and suddenly she felt like a little girl again. A good little girl. She was sitting nicely in the yard while her mommy worked in the garden. They were happy together, and it wasn't fake. And it didn't matter about Thomas Wood, either.

Beth stretched out her legs and wiggled her toes. God had an amazing way of answering prayers. Sometimes right away. Sometimes years later. Sometimes yes. Sometimes no. Today it was yes. Right now.

"Miles sits on the board of the British ALS foundation," Beth announced proudly, as though telling her mom she had just climbed to the top of the apple tree and back down again. "He knows all about Lou Gehrig's disease. In England, they call it Motor Neurone Disease or MND. Miles understood right away when I told him about Dad and what we had been through. He was so kind. So sweet."

"My goodness." Jan had stopped weeding and was sitting back on her heels. "He understands about your father and Thomas Wood, too? Maybe there's more to this Miles than I thought."

"Maybe so." Beth's focus met her mother's. "Mom, do you suppose God could have brought us together?"

Jan turned away and thrust her weeding fork deep into the soil beneath a dandelion's roots. "I don't know, Beth. I don't have a clue what God is up to these days."

Beth took a seat in the waiting area near her gate at O'Hare Airport. Why a plane from Texas had to stop in Chicago on its way to New York she would never know. She shrugged her purse strap off her shoulder and settled her bag on the floor.

Instantly she pictured Miles Wilson's boots propped on the black leather carry-on she always kept so carefully cleaned and polished. Dried mud all over those boots. Khaki slacks filthy around the hems. The man himself had been unshaven, red-eyed and rumpled. Later, he admitted to being boorish and cocky. He had forced her to go with him to that pub.

And then . . .

That's when it had happened, she realized. Right there in the smoky darkness over a couple of baked potatoes. Miles had looked into her eyes, and she had known immediately that he was honest. Genuine. Sincere. She had known . . . just known. Was this what Saint Paul meant when he wrote about a spirit of discernment? Had the Holy Spirit spoken to Beth in the confusion of that place? She needed to read the passage again to make sure.

Massaging the ache in her right temple, Beth reached into her purse for the small Bible she had previously left on the table in London. Opening it, she started to turn to the index in the back. Instead, she discovered the note Miles had written and found herself reading it again. A hundred times she had scanned the small sheet of white paper with his name and the company address printed at the top. A hundred times she had prayed about the matter of Miles Wilson. And God hadn't lessened her urge to contact the man at all.

In fact, the trip home to Texas had only made things worse. Beth reflected on her mother's perky red head bobbing as she dug in the rose garden. Jan had chosen safety. Her whole life she had managed to avoid risk and danger. Except for the brief, disastrous relationship with Thomas Wood, she had opted for security, normalcy, protection. When she recommended the same course for her daughter, Beth pictured herself living in Tyler in a three-bedroom house with three children and a professor husband. She imagined growing older and moving to a lake and tending roses. Such a routine, tranquil existence seemed like a fate worse than death.

But that wasn't the most troubling thing. During the visit, Beth had come to realize several disturbing truths about her mother.

First, there were the pictures. After the lunchtime explosion, the two had spent a peaceful afternoon puttering in the garden and then strolling by the lake. That evening, Jan had consented to show her daughter the pastel chalk artwork she had been keeping under wraps. Beth was stunned. The pictures were nothing like she had expected. True, they were children, but they weren't saccharine, trite or clichéd in any way.

Jan Lowell's children lived. Beth could almost hear them laughing and feel their warm breath and see the wind blowing in their hair. She felt as if she knew them, as though she had played with them during her own childhood, as though they were friends whose memory she had somehow misplaced over the years.

Where had the children been hiding all these years? And what had prompted them to come tumbling out onto Jan's canvases? Jim Blevins had told Beth it was the lack of pressure that had freed her mother. Jan insisted she was just missing her family.

But Beth had a sneaking suspicion it was something else altogether. Her mother was changing.

The little redhead so determined to live out her whole life in Tyler, Texas, had moved to Lake Palestine. The determined painter of a thousand bouquets of pink, red and yellow roses was suddenly bringing beautiful children to life. And maybe just as significant, the famous chicken salad, three-meals-a-day, meat-and-potatoes cook was on a fruit-and-cereal diet.

Fruit and cereal? But where's the protein? Beth had asked. Where are you going to get your vitamins? You always ordered us kids to eat our vegetables! Her mother had lifted her eyebrows and given a little smile. "Oh, well," she said simply.

Definitely, Jan was changing. But Beth felt deep concern that it wasn't all in a positive direction. At one point during their visit, Jan had casually mentioned that she rarely went to church these days. Nor could she find her Bible when they were discussing a particular passage of Scripture. She didn't pray before meals, Beth had noticed. And when Beth asked for advice, her mother never once suggested prayer or talking with a pastor or anything the least bit Christian.

When had that happened?

Had Jan wandered away from the Lord, or had she never actually been walking with Him? Beth tried to remember the details of her childhood. The whole family had gone to church every Sunday, and they'd asked a blessing at the start of each meal. Somehow, through the years of church participation, Beth had come to know Christ in a real, personal way. Much more than simply believing in Him, she had turned her whole life over to running the race she had mentioned in her phone call from Nairobi. She was striving toward the goal of obedience and surrender. Everything else took a back seat to her faith.

Beth had always believed her family was right there beside her in the long race to the finish line. Her dad had already made it to heaven ahead of the rest. Bob and Bill were living Christ-like lives. Beth felt very sure of that. All the Lowells were on the same path. Weren't they?

In that area, Beth's comfort level was ebbing. She and her mother were turning out to be polar opposites. Beth could barely speak without mentioning God. She never made a decision without prayer and consulting her Bible and her pastor or her Christian friends. She longed to be a fruitful believer, the sort of shining example of a Christian woman others looked at as a role model.

But Jan rarely mentioned God or faith or prayer. Decisions grew out of her goal of security and stability rather than the hope of perfect submission to the Lord's will. How could this have happened? And why?

Beth was far from perfect. Every day, she did selfish, sinful, stupid things. But she was consciously working to root out every wrong in her life. She wanted to be right with God. Did her mom?

The very thought that Jan might have abandoned her faith—or never had it in the first place—frightened Beth to the core. As she slipped her Bible back into her purse, her fingers grazed her phone. She lifted it out and cradled it in her palm. Then she opened it and dialed.

"There you are!"

Jan knelt beside a cardboard box and lifted out her leather-bound Bible with the gold lettering on a black cover. The visit from Beth had distressed her in so many ways, not the least of which was her daughter's constant focus on religion. Not that Jan objected, of course. She had hoped all her children would embrace

196

the faith they were brought up in.

John had found church and become a Christian fairly late in life. As a father, he insisted the whole family be present at every service their church offered—Sunday mornings and nights, Wednesday evenings and all the special events in between. They had attended countless revivals, choir cantatas, church plays and pageants. The children always participated in Vacation Bible School in the summer, and they went to Scripture-based Sunday school classes for their age group from preschool on up. A person couldn't visit that redbrick church without spotting the Lowell family, all lined up in a row in their favorite pew—five rows from the front, on the left facing the baptistery.

Jan hadn't loved every minute of those long hours of sermons and religious teachings, but she thought it was important to bring the children up right. How else would they learn good values? Ethics? Moral principles? Her own parents had felt the same way.

She set the old Bible on her lap and opened the faded cover. Funny to look at it now, after all these years. Her folks had presented the book as a high school graduation gift—so thrilled that they had discovered a modern translation of the Scripture for their bright young daughter. No longer would Jan be mired in the musty language of the old King James version, her father had told her proudly. They had no idea that the day she unwrapped their gift, Jan was poised to embark on a relationship that would almost destroy the life they had carefully structured for her.

The moment Jan met Thomas Wood—whose family members had hardly been to church a day in their lives—she let her new Bible start to collect dust. She found reasons not to go to worship services or Sunday school, and she no longer hung out with the church youth group. She began doing things she knew she shouldn't do. And those awful mistakes were the very ones she had wanted her own children to avoid.

But why had Beth become so pious? And when? She was almost like a nun or a preacher. They couldn't have a conversation without Beth saying, "I really felt God directing me toward . . ." Or "I'm trying so hard to behave the way Christ taught . . ."

Jan could hardly imagine her daughter surviving in a place like New York. The city was the epicenter of hedonism and sin, wasn't it? What did Beth's colleagues think when she went around talking about Jesus and God all the time? No wonder she didn't date much—she probably scared off all the men! Who would want to go out with a Mother Teresa clone and have to worry about saying the wrong thing or not being religious enough? It was downright intimidating to be around Beth.

Jan certainly had felt like pond scum. It was a good thing she'd found her Bible in the cardboard box at the back of her closet. She probably ought to start attending church more regularly, too. She could ride into town with Jim Blevins. That would save on gas, anyhow.

On the other hand, how could someone as holy as

Beth acted most of the time suddenly start screaming at her own mother? Telling her to shut up? Now, that wasn't right at all. Beth might think of herself as a good Christian, but she certainly hadn't behaved like one. A person could say "God this" and "God that" all she wanted, but it was how she conducted herself that really mattered.

Jan flipped through the gold-rimmed pages. They were so thin they crackled, as if the Bible had fallen into a puddle once, though it hadn't. She lifted the book and breathed in the smell of old oak church pews, a bedraggled carpet, pine-scented floor wash, even flowers on an altar. The mingled fragrances transported her back to her childhood, before the family had moved into Tyler. In their little country church, Jan had listened to her Sunday school teacher explain about salvation and righteousness and sacrifice. About Jesus dying on the cross and coming to life again to take away our sins. Crucifixion. Resurrection. Redemption. Such big words. Jan had loved the sound of them on her tongue, and she practiced saying them in her bedroom when no one was listening.

Most of what the pastor said Jan hadn't understood. But she did know she didn't want to go to hell. The whole idea scared her silly. One Sunday after their fried chicken lunch, she had burst into tears, imagining herself burning up like the biscuits her mother had left in the oven too long that morning.

"Do you believe in Jesus?" Mama had asked as she cradled her six-year-old on her lap. "Do you believe

He was the Son of God? Do you trust that He was born on this earth of the Virgin Mary and died on the cross and rose again to save you from your sins?"

Well, of course Jan believed all that. She'd been taught it from the day she took her first breath. Not that she could think of too many sins she had committed yet. Or knew what a virgin was. Or even how saving worked. All she knew was that nodding "yes" would get her into heaven with God and keep her from the fiery, smoky, sulphury-smelling furnace of the Evil One.

Not long after that, Jan and her parents had driven over to the church one day and talked to the pastor. He asked Jan the same questions her mother had, and she nodded again. A couple of Sundays later, she slipped into a white robe and waded down into the baptistery. The pastor put one arm behind her shoulders and the other over her nose and dunked her under the water. She came up gasping for air but assured that she was bound for the pearly gates.

Recalling how she had felt that day—dripping wet and so relieved she wouldn't be roasted over the coals at the end of the devil's pitchfork—Jan had to smile. She understood Christianity a lot better now, and she had tried to do a good job raising her own children in the Christian faith.

But what was all this deeply reverent yet wildly overblown rhetoric Beth kept spouting? It seemed like the young woman was on a crusade—racing at top speed down some rigidly defined path, trying so hard to root out evil and discern God's will that she turned people off, including her own mother.

Jan turned the pages of the slender volume one by one, skimming the familiar names of the different books inside it until she came to the end. Beth must be finding something terribly important in her own Bible. To Jan, the book had been little more than a collection of sayings from which preachers drew sermons and Vacation Bible School youngsters memorized verses.

Seated on the guest room floor, she lifted the Bible into focus and began to scan the words printed in red. This passage was from the third chapter of the book of Revelation, she noted. Her eyes drifted down to the fifteenth verse, which she had underlined during some long-forgotten sermon.

The ring of authority resonated through Jan as she began to silently read the words of Jesus to those in the church at Laodicea.

"I know you well—you are neither hot nor cold; I wish you were one or the other! But since you are merely lukewarm, I will spit you out of my mouth!

"You say, 'I am rich, with everything I want; I don't need a thing!' And you don't realize that spiritually you are wretched and miserable and poor and blind and naked. . . ."

Jan laid her hand on the page and lifted her head.

Chapter Twelve

Beth could hardly believe what she had done. When the wheels of her plane touched down at Heathrow Airport on the outskirts of London, she clutched her cell phone as though it were a lifeline that might drag her back toward sanity. Toward reality and common sense. She should call Miles and say she had changed her mind. Tell him not to meet her flight. Tell him to cancel their tickets to India. Tell him she never wanted to talk to him again.

Less than a week before, Beth had been sitting at the edge of a rose garden in Texas while her mother carefully explained the perils of rash behavior. Choose wisely, Jan had instructed her daughter. Your safety and security should be paramount. Don't do anything to jeopardize your future happiness.

How seriously Beth had listened as she helped pull weeds and tried to believe her mother's message. Only fools took risks. And Bethany Ann Lowell was no fool.

But the moment she was away from her mother's influence and warnings—actually while driving away from Lake Palestine in her rental car—Beth had felt a surge of desire course through her veins. When she recalled that sensation now as the jet taxied toward the terminal, she truly believed her sudden and overwhelming sense of urgency had been sent from God. She knew it so well. It was that old familiar shove as the Lord pressed her to get out there on the racetrack, run, go for the prize, take up the cross and follow Him.

Not a single true believer mentioned in the Bible ever sat around and grew roses. Back at her apartment in New York, Beth had searched the Scriptures to make sure of it. She was right—every New Testament Christian she read about had kept busy working hard on behalf of Christ, speaking out in public, making sacrifices, even putting their lives in peril.

The male disciples had taken the greatest risks. Peter and Andrew had abandoned their careers to become disciples of Jesus. Paul sailed through storms, endured shipwrecks, beatings, imprisonment and even a snakebite. Stephen had been stoned to death. There were so many others. And the women Beth found mentioned in the New Testament were no less gutsy. Many of them—including Christ's own mother—had risked their reputations and even their freedom to follow Him to the cross where He was killed. Later, a woman named Dorcas, who had been raised from the dead by Peter, went on to lead many people in the town of Joppa to a saving belief in Christ. Priscilla, the wife of Aquila, was an ardent Christian—so outspoken that she and her husband had been driven from their house in Rome and forced to move to Corinth. But even there, Priscilla risked her life by welcoming Paul into her home. She and her husband even accompanied him on his missionary journey to Ephesus.

People who really followed Christ simply couldn't sit still. That was all there was to it. Beth turned her cell phone over and over in her damp palm as the plane came to a stop, and people began unbuckling their seat belts. Christ had charged Christians with setting down their TV remote controls, getting up out of their recliners and telling the world about Him. A true believer had to go places. Speak out. Face danger.

Beth stood and tugged her black leather carry-on bag from the overhead compartment. It had been a long flight, and instead of napping, she had stewed most of the way across the Atlantic. Yes, she definitely believed that Christians were to stride out of their comfortable nests and speak boldly about Jesus whenever and wherever they could. But was that why she had phoned Miles Wilson and arranged to go to India with him to meet her birth father? Could she honestly verify that without the least qualm?

Setting down her carry-on bag, Beth released the handle and rolled the bag behind her as she followed the other passengers through the plane's door. In a few minutes, she would see him again. Had she come all this way just to lead Miles to Christ? Or was it his blue eyes and charming accent and fascinating past that had beckoned her?

Could it be both? Did God allow that sort of thing?

And what about Thomas Wood? Did Beth ache to meet the man because she needed to make sure that her birth father had heard about Christ? Or did she just want to find out if she looked like him? Was she a little missionary, trotting here and there around the globe with the aim of spreading the good news of salvation?

Or was she—as her mother had always insisted—a nosy, pushy girl who had ants in her pants and couldn't sit still and had to pry into everything that interested her?

The line through British customs seemed to take forever, and Beth finally decided to use the time to do the dreaded chore she had put off way too long. As she inched her bag forward, she dialed her mother's phone number. It would be late Saturday evening in Texas. Probably her mom would be dyeing her hair again.

But instead of the familiar "Hi, Jan Lowell speaking," Beth heard the answering machine kick on.

"Hello, this is the Lowell residence," Jan's recorded voice said. "No one's available right now, so leave a message. And remember—as Victor Hugo wrote in *Les Misérables*, 'The supreme happiness of life is the conviction that we are loved.' Have a happy day!"

Beth swallowed as the message from her mother ended. Always some infuriating quote! The joy of her teenage years had been threatened daily by her mother's ever-changing answering machine passage from some noted writer. Beth's friends had ridiculed her mercilessly, mocking Jan Lowell's perky Texas accent as she reminded them of a famous phrase that Shakespeare, Milton, Thoreau, Emily Dickinson or Larry McMurtry had written. Of course, Miz Lowell, as the kids called her, had taught high school English for so many years that most of them had been her students, and they all adored her. Still, those awful messages . . .

As the machine finally beeped, Beth's heart was hammering so hard that she half expected airport security to accost her for harboring an explosive device. *The supreme happiness of life?* Who had the luxury these days to even think about things like that? She swallowed at the nervous lump in her throat.

"Hey, Mom, it's Beth," she began after the signal. Her voice sounded way too high and trembly. "I don't know where you could be at this hour. I hope you're okay. I had planned to talk to you, but anyway, I'll just leave this message to let you know I'm in London. I, uh . . . I decided to look up Miles, after all. And I also need to tell you that . . . well, he and I are going to India. Not as a couple or anything like that, okay? It's not how you might think. Miles is just helping me get there, because, you know, he owns the tea estate and it makes sense that he could cut through the red tape and all that. So anyway . . . I wanted to tell you that I will be meeting him . . . my birth father . . . Thomas Wood . . . and I hope you're not upset about that, because I definitely don't want to hurt—"

Another beep cut Beth off as the machine in Texas hung up. She considered redialing, but she was nearly at the front of the line now. And she suddenly realized how terrible it had been to tell her mother this way. They'd had such a good time together. Seemingly in perfect harmony. Now Beth had made this decision and had just gone and done it. She hadn't asked permission—not that she needed to. Still, she could have had the courtesy to tell her mom what she was up to before actually leaving New York. This way, the cowardly way, Beth had blurted it all out to an answering machine. It felt like one of those e-mails she realized she shouldn't have written just after clicking the "send" button. Oh, she did that far too often.

"Next, please." The customs official beckoned Beth forward to his glassed-in booth.

Feeling like she might topple over from exhaustion and stress, she made it past customs and through the security gates into the terminal. She walked out onto the tiled floor. And there he was. Just like that. Miles Wilson was waiting for her as he had promised.

"Beth!" His face broke into a smile, and his blue eyes lit up. He strode toward her like a battering ram bearing down on a castle door.

She swung her purse around to blunt the first assault as Miles wrapped her in his arms and drew her close. "I'm so pleased you decided to come after all," he whispered.

The purse had done no good at all. As it turned out, the attack came from another direction entirely. Beth shivered at the warmth of his breath on her ear.

"Hello, Miles," she managed.

He leaned in to kiss her cheek, but she pulled back and stepped to one side.

"Wow, that's a long flight," she said breathlessly. "I've done it so many times, but I always forget."

"You look beautiful."

She tried not to meet his eyes. "It's nice to be here, but I am definitely going to need a nap."

"Good, then," he turned and slipped his arm under hers. "I'm putting you up at Wilson House, where morning naps are required by law. Wilson House is in Belgravia, but the traffic shouldn't disturb you. We're right on the square, and most of the homes there have been converted to embassies. Nothing but the occasional protest march or holiday ball to break the silence. Every country has its own holidays, you know, and some of the customs can be shockingly—"

"Wait!" Beth stopped walking and held up her hand. "I have a hotel reservation. I told you that in my last e-mail."

"I canceled it for you. No point in spending the money when you can stay with us."

"Us who?"

"Malcolm and me, of course." He grinned, lopsided and charming and way too handsome, as he started her moving forward again. "We've got the old family place now that Mum and Dad are sadly gone. Several nice guest rooms, a top-notch domestic staff and a French chef. You and I are leaving for India tomorrow anyway, so why not?"

"Well, but I—"

"Ah, there's Charles." He lifted a hand to wave as a shiny black limousine pulled up to the curb outside the terminal. A moment later, a liveried chauffeur had stepped out of the car and was opening the door for Beth. Miles nodded to him. "Thank you, Charles. Very good of you, my man."

"Of course, sir."

Feeling as though she had stepped back in time to a London where footmen drove carriages while lords and ladies chatted mindlessly, Beth slid onto the black leather seat and settled her purse beside her. This was not going according to plan, but she couldn't summon the resources to fend Miles off. Too handsome, too quick-witted, too well-heeled. The parapets had toppled, and the lady of the house was in grave danger of total invasion.

"I really would rather go to a hotel." She mustered one last counter move as Miles joined her in the rear seat. "Staying in a house with two bachelors doesn't make me comfortable."

"Bachelors, are we? Malcolm will like that." He chuckled. "I'm afraid we tend to think of ourselves as a pair of crotchety jossers—geezers, I think you Americans would call us—growing older and mustier by the day. Malcolm is far worse off than I. At least I have the good fortune to travel the globe. My brother ferries back and forth between the house and the office with nary a pause for breath. We should take him out, you and I. Dinner tonight, perhaps. Malcolm is fond of fish and chips, I'm sorry to say. Somewhat plebian dish for a man of his rank, but he can hardly be swayed from it. What is your opinion of fish and chips, Beth?"

The sum total of the long hours of flying, the tension of worrying that she was making a serious mistake, the lack of sleep . . . all had suddenly converged the moment Beth leaned back against the cool leather and stretched out her legs. She experienced the sensation that a one-ton weight had dropped onto her body. It sank her more deeply into the cushioned interior of the limousine as it pressed every last bit of energy from her muscles. She felt she had turned into butter somehow. She was oozing onto the seat as she swiveled her head and tried to make sense of what the man beside her was saying.

"Fish and chips?" she repeated. "Good."

"Excellent. You'll get some rest while I pop back to the office and check on Kenya. The pluckers there have asked for a raise, as they regularly do, and I'm in the midst of sorting things out. One can hardly raise the pluckers and ignore the factory labor, can one?"

Beth fought her way through dark clouds that had begun to gather around her vision. "Uh . . . pluckers?"

"Tea, of course. One never *picks* tea leaves. The bud and the top two leaves must be carefully *plucked* by hand and tossed into a basket. Incredibly laborious process, but no one has thought of a faster or more efficient way to do it. And it does provide employment. Very important in the Third World where Wilson Teas does most of our business. We considered planting tea in America once. An experiment. There are some environmentally suitable places where it might grow, you know. I'm the one who thought of it, actually. Malcolm has no imagination whatsoever. But sadly, the costs are prohibitive."

"I'm sorry," Beth mumbled, wondering what he was talking about.

"At any rate, I shall tackle the Kenya matter while

you sleep. Then, this evening at six straight up, Malcolm and I shall transport you to the finest fish and chips purveyor in Belgravia, of which there are not many. It is a rather foppish neighborhood, though not so much now as it was when Victoria reigned. Belgrave Square used to be *the* place to live. But now one can never be sure what one might find when opening the door in the morning. Incredibly diverse lot living near us these days. We have the embassies of Spain, Norway, Saudi Arabia, Ivory Coast, Turkey, Mexico and one other . . . oh, yes, Portugal, all within sight of Wilson House. Did you know that Mexicans shut down business for an entire month at Christmastime simply to celebrate? *Feria,* they call it. Dancing in the street all night long. Dreadful din. And the Norwegians . . ."

Jan tried to get through her front door without Jim following, but no such luck. He was right on her heels, asking if she still had any of that blueberry cobbler she'd served him the other day. She did, and she considered fibbing. But lately, ever since Beth went away and the old Bible came out from its cardboard box, Jan had been feeling the prick of conscience. You could hardly tell a lie when you'd just read about God giving Moses the Ten Commandments.

"Mmm-mmm, fresh blueberries," Jim mused aloud, shaking his head as he toddled after her toward the kitchen. "Frozen blueberries. I can take 'em or leave 'em. But those fresh ones just can't be beat."

Jan had no choice but to feed the man. How could she refuse? Earlier that evening, he had picked her up in his nice clean car and driven them down countless curving, dark roads to the home of a member of their Sunday school class. She would never have found her way to the fellowship dinner if Jim hadn't offered to take her.

"I'll give you the recipe," she told him. Kicking off her shoes, she stepped to the refrigerator in her stocking feet. "It's not hard to make at all. You start with biscuit mix."

"Not me." He held up a beefy hand. "I can barely boil an egg. I am getting better at cooking as time passes, I'll grant you that. But cobbler? No, I'd prefer just to drop in here and mooch a slice of yours every now and then."

"We did have dessert at the social, Jim," she reminded him. "I think you ate three of those peanut-butter cookies and a piece of pie."

"Chocolate silk pie. Now, that was good." He cocked his head at her. "Say, were you watching me? Trying to keep me honest?"

"Well, you've got diabetes, Jim, and you need to take off a few pounds. Those aren't my words, they're yours. So, I'm just telling you what you already know."

"All right, all right."

"But here. Take this cobbler and don't tell the doctor who gave it to you."

He laughed as he settled onto a chair at her kitchen

dinette. Jan cut herself a small square of the dessert and sat down across from him. As much as Jim Blevins could annoy her, she had to admit this evening had been fun. She'd been trying to read the directions with a flashlight while they negotiated the narrow, winding lanes and tried not to hit another car, a deer, a possum, an armadillo, or anything else that might think it had a right to the road. By the time they finally arrived at their host's house, they were both giggling.

People probably suspected something was going on between them, Jan surmised, but they were wrong. It just felt good to be silly occasionally. To have companionship. To share an enjoyable event with another person.

"You know, you're a killer at that trivia game," Jim observed. "I never met anyone who knew where Borneo was."

"Oh, it's just useless information. I remember some things, and other facts go straight out of my head. A few weeks ago, my daughter called me from Nairobi, and for the life of me, I couldn't figure out where she was."

"Well, where was she?"

"In Africa. Nairobi is the capital of Kenya. It's over on the east coast."

"Why would anybody ever want to go to Africa, is what I'd like to know."

"That's exactly what I thought. But Beth was helping an American family to move there. She'd found them a house and a school and all that. Beth said she loved

Botswana so much, she'd move there herself in a heartbeat."

"Botswana?"

"It's another country in Africa. Farther south and toward the middle."

"You couldn't pay me enough money to live in Africa. And it's not what you might think. I don't care whether people are black, white, yellow or purple polka dots. But all those wild animals? Snakes? Do you know they've got the fastest snake in the world in Africa? I saw a TV show about it. The mamba—mean, aggressive thing. No, just give me good ol' Texas. I'd take on a rattler before a mamba any day. At least with a rattler, you've got some warning before it strikes."

Jan carved a bite of cobbler with her spoon. She had always said she would never leave Texas, and that still made sense. But she wasn't so sure a rattlesnake was any kinder than a mamba. If Beth liked Botswana so well, maybe Jan would, too. Not that she would ever consider leaving the United States. Not in this day and age. But still. It was something to think about.

"Have you ever heard of Darjeeling?" she asked Jim suddenly.

"I've got a box of it up in my kitchen cupboard with the Earl Grey and the chamomile. Never drink the stuff, but my wife used to love it, and I haven't gotten around to throwing it out. She told me Darjeeling was flowery tasting, and I said, who wants to drink flower-flavored tea anyhow?"

"I'm not talking about the tea, Jim. Darjeeling is a place. It's in India."

"Is Beth going to India now? Pretty soon they'll have her flying off to Timbuktu."

"Timbuktu is a real city, you know. It's in Mali, which is in West Africa."

"No kidding? Timbuktu is real?" Jim wiped his mouth with a paper napkin. "Did your daughter tell you that, too?"

"It's just one of those things I know. Like Borneo."

"Well, Timbuktu, Borneo and Darjeeling can carry on without me. My wife and I went to Canada one time. That was foreign enough for me, and we weren't even in the French part. We drove to Saskatchewan. It's all a big prairie up there, as far as you can see. You'd think it wouldn't be so different from Texas, them speaking English and all. But it was. They have strange customs, and food and things like that. You're supposed to take your shoes off when you go into a house. The people eat an odd kind of dumplings. But at night . . . that's when you can see the Northern Lights. Strangest, most beautiful thing in the world. Colored lights just coming and going, streaking across the sky in waves, flashing in and out like nothing you ever saw. You ought to go up there sometime. You'd like it."

Jan set down her spoon and studied the man across the table from her. They were just alike, weren't they? Beth had noticed it first, and now even Jan could see it. Each had lost a spouse. Each had children they loved who rarely came to visit. Each had chosen Lake Palestine for retirement at the end of their lives. Only Jan wasn't anywhere close to the end of her life. At least, she didn't think so.

"If you liked things about Canada," she said, "what makes you think you wouldn't like Botswana?"

"I told you. Mambas."

"Isn't there anything dangerous in Canada? Grizzly bears, maybe?"

"I reckon there's something dangerous no matter where you go."

"Then maybe you'd like Botswana."

He focused on her, his eyes narrowing. "Are you thinking of going to Africa?"

For a moment, Jan hesitated. And that slight pause scared her silly. Of course she wasn't thinking about going to Africa. But why couldn't she just up and say it? Why did the denial hang on her tongue like one of those old-fashioned stamps when you licked it too long?

"I'm not thinking of going anywhere," she told him. "But I am thinking."

He leaned back in his chair. "What about?"

"My daughter says Christians are supposed to keep busy—like we're in a race. Heading for the finish line."

"Well, I can set your mind at ease, honey—the finish line is not in Botswana."

Honey. He had called her honey. Jan stiffened. Did she want to be Jim Blevins's honey? Did she want *any*

216

man to address her with endearments ever again? Surely not. And yet, the comfort and ease with which he had said the word made her feel strangely peaceful. It was almost as though she and John were sitting together in their little kitchen in Tyler.

"The Apostle Paul talked about running the race," Jim was saying. He had his eye on the refrigerator, and Jan knew he was wondering whether it would be rude to ask for more cobbler. "The Christian life is a race, but that doesn't mean you have to leave Lake Palestine to run it."

"Are you sure?"

"Absolutely. Jesus commanded His followers to make disciples in Jerusalem, and Judea and the uttermost parts of the earth. He didn't mean we *all* have to go to the ends of the earth. That's what missionaries are for. Some of us need to stay here and proclaim the Gospel at home."

"Do you do that?"

"Me?" He glanced up with a sheepish look on his face. "Sometimes. I used to leave Christian pamphlets in gas station bathrooms."

"Well, that's something."

"I was a seed salesman, and I traveled all over Texas for the better part of my adult life. That's a lot of gas station restrooms, let me tell you."

"I never even did that much."

"I bet you did. Didn't you teach Sunday school or Vacation Bible School?"

"Sure."

"There you go. See, we're missionaries here in America. Nothing wrong with that."

Jan let out a breath. "Oh, I don't know what's wrong with me, Jim. The more I think about my daughter, the worse I feel. Not about her. About me. She's so driven, and I've always been content to be a homebody."

"Nothing wrong with that in my book."

"But what about God's book? I stopped being a daily Bible reader a long time ago. Now that I've started up again, it feels like I'm seeing the words with new eyes. Did you know that on one of Saint Paul's journeys, he was bitten by a snake? The ship he'd been sailing in had wrecked, and he swam to shore with the other survivors. He was building a fire on the beach when a snake slithered out of the woodpile and sank its fangs into him. What I'm saying is . . . Saint Paul wasn't afraid of mambas."

"Well, I'm no saint, and I never said I was. I'm just a man doing the best he can. I had a family to feed and provide for, and I did that. I raised my kids up right, took them to church, stayed faithful to my wife—"

"And put pamphlets in gas station restrooms."

Jim heaved a deep sigh. "A man's got to make a living, Jan. We can't all be missionaries and head off to Timbuktu to preach to the natives. Some of us have to stay home and take care of our families right here in Texas."

She hung her head. "I know. It's just been bothering me . . . how I've spent my life . . . how I was so focused on myself and my own family's needs . . . how I never even bothered to try to find out what God wanted from me."

"God wanted a good mother, a loving wife, a hard-working schoolteacher and a baker of the best blue-berry cobbler in the world." Jim reached over and laid a hand on her arm. "And that's exactly what He got."

Jan lifted her head and smiled. "Thanks. That's so sweet of you."

He swallowed. "Listen, Jan, I—"

"Oh, my goodness!" she cut in, glancing at the kitchen clock and slipping her arm out from under his hand as she got to her feet. "Look how late it is. It's nearly midnight! You'd better go, Jim. I hate to be so blunt, but it's really not a good idea for you to come over here at night. I don't want the neighbors to get the wrong idea about us when we're just good friends."

Without waiting to see the reaction on Jim's face, Jan hurried into the living room. She pulled the front door open and was reaching for the porch light switch when she spotted the flashing red dot on her answering machine. Without thinking, she reached over and pressed the button.

Beth's voice filled the living room. She sounded strangely childlike and frightened. Alarm coursed down Jan's spine as her daughter spoke. ". . . I don't know where you could be at this hour. I hope you're okay. I had planned to talk to you, but anyway, I'll just leave this message to let you know I'm in London."

"London!" Jan exclaimed.

". . . I decided to look up Miles, after all," Beth went

219

on. "And I also need to tell you that . . . well, he and I are going to India."

"Oh, no!" Jan gasped and covered her mouth with her hands. "Not India!"

But Beth went on speaking, delivering the awful message. ". . . I wanted to tell you that I will be meeting him . . . my birth father . . . Thomas Wood . . . and I hope you're not upset about that, because I definitely don't want to hurt—"

The beep silenced Beth's voice, but Jan continued staring at the machine as if she could make her daughter keep talking and somehow deny the words just spoken. It couldn't be true. This must be some kind of prank. Hadn't she and Beth discussed this very thing? Hadn't Jan explained in detail the importance of stability and reason and choosing wisely? They had chatted right outside in the rose garden, and Beth had nodded at every sage word that came from her mother's mouth. Then she ran off and did this!

"Are you all right?" Jim asked hesitantly. "Maybe you should sit down."

"Go away," Jan sobbed out, fighting tears. "Please, Jim, just go home."

He knew. Jim Blevins now knew about Thomas Wood and everything! He knew Jan's most intimate secret, and she could never look him in the face again. He would probably tell the whole neighborhood.

"Sounds like your daughter is hatching some more of her far-flung schemes." Jim spoke gently as he took Jan's shoulders, turned her around and pressed her down onto the sofa. "Listen here, honey. I don't know anything about London or India or Darjeeling or any of that. But I think I understand what's got you upset. Beth isn't John's daughter?"

Jan shook her head. "He knew, though. He wanted her."

"I'm sure he did. We've all done things. Wrong things. Stupid things. And good things, too. To me, you're one of the best. You always will be."

Jan pressed her fingertips against her eyes in a vain attempt to prevent the flood. "I'm sorry, Jim."

"You didn't do anything to me. I'm glad I was here." He stood. "But I guess Trixie will be wanting out. She's always got to have that last walk of the day. I'll head for home now."

As he stepped outside, Jan bent over and wept into her hands.

Chapter Thirteen

"I warned you." Malcolm Wilson shook a finger at Beth, who sat across the table from him. Then he turned to his brother. "Miles, did I not warn Miss Lowell about you? I distinctly recall urging her to be extremely cautious."

"You did, Malcolm, but as you can see, she succumbed to my charms at last."

As hard as she might try, Beth could not take offense at the bantering between the two men. Wilson House was grander and much more opulent than she had imagined, and she was put up for the night in a magnificent guest bedroom with an attached bath. After a luxuriating soak, she had fallen deeply asleep for several hours. A shy maid woke her with a tray of tea at four that afternoon, and at six the limo arrived with Miles and Malcolm. Now sharing a booth in a rather seedy-looking restaurant, the three were digging into plates of greasy batter-fried fish and equally greasy wedges of fried potatoes. Delicious, but definitely not on Jan Lowell's fruit-and-cereal diet.

Beth couldn't help thinking of her mother as she sat across from Miles Wilson—the man Beth would like to blame for everything but couldn't. No doubt the phone message she had left at the lake house had been a shock and a huge disappointment to her mom. Beth would give anything to take it back, but it was too late. After dreading the call for days, she had impulsively made it, and now she couldn't undo anything.

"She is regretting it," Malcolm said. "I can see the truth clearly written on her face. She knows she was wrong ever to see you again, but the deed is done."

"I contacted Miles because I need to see my birth father," Beth told Malcolm, "but you're right. I am regretting it."

"What gives you pause?" Miles protested, a look of innocent dismay on his face. "Did I not collect you at the airport? Ensconce you at my ancestral family residence? Arrange for you to have a truly British meal?"

"You have been kind," Beth conceded. "But I shouldn't have accepted your invitation to travel to India. First of all, I hardly know you."

"Too true," Malcolm pointed out. "Miles is a rogue."

"Nonsense. I'm a gentleman in every sense of the word. Shut up, Malcolm, before I pinch your ear." He focused his attention on Beth. "You and I know each other well enough to fly to India in one another's company. After all, we've traveled half the continent of Africa together, haven't we? When we're back in England again, we shall declare to my doubting brother that we are great friends, and all his warnings were in vain."

"Friends," Malcolm scoffed.

"Yes, friends. Beth does not yoke herself with just anyone."

"You make the poor lady sound as if she were an ox!"

Beth spoke up. "Miles is referring to a passage from the Bible."

"Beth is very religious." Miles bent over and reached into his briefcase. "As am I. Or nearly so, anyway. Look, Malcolm, this is my new Bible, and I must tell you that if you bothered to read it, you would find it enlightening."

"Religious? You?" Malcolm snickered as his brother set a leather-bound volume on the table. Beth noticed that the Bible was nearly identical to her own. Malcolm ignored it. "Now I know you'll do anything to steal a lady's heart, Miles. Pay this man no heed, Beth.

He's wicked. You'd do better to turn your attentions to a steadier, more honorable sort of man."

Miles barked out a derisive laugh. "Like you, I suppose?"

"And why not?"

"Because you're boring."

"I like Malcolm," Beth declared. "You're exactly the kind of man my mother would choose for me."

"I'm not certain that should be taken as a compliment," he returned.

"But it is. She chose a wonderful husband. My father was as steady and honorable as they come. She was wise to marry him."

For a moment, both men fell silent, and Beth knew they were thinking of the man she was traveling to meet. Her birth father. So far, no one had broached the topic, and she hoped it would stay off-limits. Miles summoned the waitress for a refill of their soft drinks, while Malcolm suddenly busied himself flipping through his brother's new Bible.

"Our parents were lovely people, too," the older man said. "Well matched. Sadly, Mum wasn't quite as certain of this fact as Miles and I, and she took herself off to live in Australia with the captain of our father's polo team."

Beth's mouth dropped open. "Miles didn't tell me that."

"It's not the sort of thing that makes for charming conversation. Our father was heartbroken, of course."

"Yes," Miles concurred. "The dissolution of his polo

team was the saddest thing that ever happened to him. He never recovered from it."

"Oh . . ." Beth was puzzling over this information when both brothers began chuckling.

"You can't take such things too seriously," Malcolm told her. "Their divorce wasn't amusing to us at the time, but we've accepted it."

"Nothing we could do about it anyway," Miles said. "But, Malcolm, you've made it sound as if Dad died of a broken heart. It was leukemia, actually. He fought it as hard as he could, but he couldn't win. Dreadful disease."

"I'm very sorry." Beth thought of her own father's battle with ALS, and she wondered why Miles hadn't mentioned the leukemia to her earlier. It was another experience they had in common, though not a topic as cheerful as their shared interest in globetrotting. Maybe, as Malcolm implied, Miles cared only about impressing and charming her. She was another fly for his spider web.

"If I'm the sort of man your mother would choose for you," Malcolm asked Beth, "why are you winging off to India with my ne'er-do-well brother?"

"He offered."

"There you have it," Miles said. "I offered. On the other hand, I think there's more to this. I believe Beth is sitting here this evening because schemes greater than either of ours have been at work. You see, I've been reading in my Bible—give me that, Mal, you tiresome devil."

Wresting the book from his brother's hands, Miles

leafed through the pages. "Incredible amount of material to digest here," he mumbled as he searched through it. "Too much, really. Shocking things. Murders, stonings, adulteries—even a lady who hammered a tent peg through a bloke's head."

"No. Can you mean it?" Malcolm said.

"Absolutely. One can hardly think where to begin and end in reading this book. The teachings of Christ are magnificent, and at the same time difficult to comprehend. The scope is vast. It would take a great mind to truly fathom it."

"That lets you out," Malcolm muttered.

"Now then, here we are," Miles continued. "The back part of the book appears to be about Jesus and the beginnings of Christianity. The front part is all Jewish history. Quite confusing—kings and prophets and all that. I can't make much of it."

"You never will. You barely passed your A-Levels."

"Pay him no mind," Miles advised Beth. "He's jealous because I was better in football."

"Well, get on with it," Malcolm prodded. "If you're determined to preach at us, go to it."

"I found this interesting bit in the chapter titled Romans, which I decided to read because it sounded as if Saint Paul were writing a letter to me."

"Romans is a book, not a chapter," Beth clarified. She realized she had been clutching the corner of the tablecloth ever since Miles had opened his Bible. He really had bought it—and not just to impress her. He was actually reading it.

"A book within a book," Malcolm said. "I've seen that sort of thing before. I believe Tolkien's *Lord of the Rings* is set up that way."

"No, that's three separate books," Miles stated. "Honestly, Malcolm, how did *you* pass A-Levels? At any rate, here in this letter to the Romans, Saint Paul tells the Christians to think of God as a loving father, even when they suffer. He speaks of the Holy Spirit, who assists Christians in various ways, particularly by praying for them when they're too miserable to pray for themselves."

"Not a happy lot, I take it," Malcolm observed.

"They do appear very content, oddly enough. Now listen to this. I found it underlined in Beth's Bible, and I've underlined it in my own, as well. It's remarkable." He cleared his throat and began reading. " 'And we know that God causes everything to work together for the good of those who love God and are called according to His purpose for their lives.' There, what do you think of that?"

"Contradictory. First, Saint Paul writes that there will be misery. Then he says that everything will be good."

"Wrong. Everything will *work together* for good," Miles clarified. "You see the difference? Suffering will come to each of us. But in a Christian's life, all events—whether positive or negative—will work for good in the end."

"That is quite a promise. But I can't see how it applies to your pursuit of the pure and pious Miss Lowell."

Miles leaned back and contemplated the question. "It is true that I'm not the ideal gentleman," he admitted. "Perhaps I did have devious motives in asking Beth to go to India with me. And one might even argue that I purchased this Bible for all the wrong reasons . . ."

"You've utterly condemned yourself, Miles," his brother said. "Carry on."

"But that's it, you see. *We* are condemned, all of us. And yet, those who call themselves Christians are actually free of the fate they deserve. Not only that, but according to Saint Paul, they've got God Himself working to put their lives into good order. Even through the struggles. It all comes out right in the end."

"Lucky us." Malcolm took the Bible from his brother's hands and began to reread the underlined words.

"I believe," Miles said, "that God intended for Beth to meet me in the Nairobi airport. Or if we can't go quite that far, at least we can predict that God is going to use this trip to India to her benefit. And all because she's such a religious person."

Beth relaxed her grip on the tablecloth. "Oh, for pity's sake, I'm not all that religious. Religion is the outer trappings that go along with a person's faith—the church or temple or mosque, style of worship, prayer rituals, stuff like that. I have trouble with the religious aspect on a regular basis, and my faith often feels pretty weak."

"Come on," Miles said. "You're better at it than most people. You read your Bible, carry it with you everywhere, run your race."

"And you never yoke," Malcolm put in.

"I try to follow Christ," Beth said. "But look what I've done in the past few months. I've hurt my mother by flying off to meet my birth father—a man whose name she wants never mentioned again. I've argued with her, yelled at her and totally disregarded her wishes. I'm unwisely sitting here with two people I hardly know, and I'm recklessly heading off on a weeklong trip with one of them. Does that sound like a prudent thing to do? My brothers think I'm nuts. When I told them what was going on, they both advised me to drop the issue and accept the family I grew up in as my own. Oh, sure, I've prayed about this and read my Bible and talked to Christian friends, but the bottom line is that I'm doing what I want to do. I'm being selfish, and that's not Christ-like in the least."

Both brothers stared at her as though she'd been speaking a foreign language.

"Well, that does it then," Miles said. "I must cancel the trip at once."

"Absolutely," Malcolm agreed. "I won't let my brother go off to India with such a careless, self-centered creature."

"Indeed, I can't imagine spending even another minute with someone so egotistical and proud."

"She's cruel, she is. Ignoring her brothers' advice. Disobeying her mother."

"We've never done anything like that, have we, Malcolm?"

"Certainly not. We've always been good boys."

"Personally," Miles said, "I never make a move without consulting you, Mum, the board of governors, the Queen and God."

Beth's shoulders loosened. "All right, that's enough."

"I'd never go looking for my missing relations in the face of such familial disapproval," Malcolm said.

"Nor sit in a restaurant with someone I'd only known for a month."

"It's her yelling at her mother that bothers me. We never yell, do we, Miles?"

"Well, there was that awkward time when Mum ran off to Australia with the polo captain. I believe you and I might have done some yelling. A jolt in the family structure does tend to bring out the worst in a person. Do you know what I mean, Beth?"

"Yes," she said. "Okay, maybe I've behaved normally under the circumstances. I just wish I could be sure I was doing the right thing."

"But you are," Miles reminded her. "Everything works together for the good of Christians."

"That doesn't mean you can blindly go around doing anything you want. Christians are those who 'love God and are called according to His purpose for their lives,' remember? But I don't know what God's purpose is in all this. I really can't figure it out."

"Neither can I," Miles said. "And I think that's the beauty in it. In the end, all you've got is faith."

Rain spattered the windshield, droplets flying left and

right with the motion of the wipers, as the small black car labored up the steep foothills of the Himalayas. Beth sat in the back, gazing out at emerald-green ridges and distant, mist-shrouded blue mountains. Occasionally, the car passed a person climbing the winding road. A Buddhist monk in a bright orange robe. A woman bent beneath the heavy basket on her back. An old man with a cane, nudging the roadway for rocks that might make him stumble.

Beth and Miles had taken a jet from London to Calcutta. A propeller-driven plane flew them to Bagdogra airport, where a Wilson Teas car was waiting to take them the three-hour drive up to Darjeeling. At the wheel was the company's Indian liaison rather than a chauffeur, which gave Miles the perfect opportunity to discuss business while Beth tried to collect her thoughts. The two men chatted about tea production, labor issues, the coming monsoon rains and the state of the world tea market. Beth listened for a while from the backseat until eventually she tuned them out and concentrated on the scenery.

But the view didn't take her mind off her worries. She hadn't heard from her mother since leaving the awful phone message. Though Beth knew she should have called again while still in London, she couldn't bring herself to do it. The thought of Jan's tearful, accusing voice on the other end of the line was just too much.

This was all a mistake. Even the discovery of the tea set and the note inside it had been in error. From that moment, nothing had gone right. Beth and her mother had shouted at each other and wept and apologized and tried to make everything just fine. But it wasn't. Beth walked through each day feeling disoriented, as though she had inadvertently put on someone else's skin one morning instead of her own. She had been so confident, so sure of herself. Now she wasn't even positive who she was. Did genes and DNA even matter, after all? Was a person's upbringing all that really counted?

Again, she felt sick at the thought of how her father would feel if he were alive. The betrayal. The disloyalty. And after all he had done for Beth.

"You're looking a bit pale," Miles said over his shoulder. "Feeling ill? Darjeeling sits at over 7,000 feet. Thinner air, you know. And the road is tortuous."

"I'm all right." She studied his eyes, filled with concern. How attractive he'd seemed to her when they were apart. And even now, just a casual glance from him sent a tingle up her spine. But how dumb. How immature. There were thousands of nice-looking men in New York. She shouldn't have let one Brit with blue eyes send her spiraling.

"We're almost there," he told her. "Too bad we've got clouds today. We're just at the start of the monsoon season, but if we're lucky, we'll have break in the mists and get a look at Kanchenjunga."

Almost there. Beth laced her fingers together and squeezed. She had no idea what to say when she met him. Thomas Wood. Why had that name taken hold of her and possessed her? She wasn't a Wood. She was a Lowell, a proud Lowell.

"Is the Wilson Teas estate near town?" she was asking just as her cell phone warbled. "Oh, excuse me a moment . . . Hello? Beth Lowell speaking."

"Beth, it's your mother. I hope I didn't wake you up. I'm not sure about the time difference."

"Mom?" She looked at Miles. His eyes softened. He reached across the seat back and laid his hand over hers.

"Are you in India?" Jan asked.

"Yes. We're on our way up the mountains toward Darjeeling."

"Oh . . . so you haven't . . . ."

"Not yet."

"Well, then." There was a moment of silence. "I guess you're safely back on the ground anyway. I hope your flight was good. Are the roads there fairly decent?"

Before her mother could babble on further, Beth blurted out what was on her heart. "Mom, listen, I'm sorry about that message I left on your machine. I should have told you in person what I was planning to do."

"It's all right. I guess nothing you do can surprise me now."

Beth bristled, but she tried to keep her voice calm. "I realize this wasn't how we left things when I visited there the last time. You told me how you felt, and I really did listen."

"Yes, well, perhaps your mother's opinion doesn't matter anymore."

"Of course it matters. Very much." The car took a hairpin curve, and Beth thought for a moment she might be sick.

"You're cutting in and out, honey, so I guess I'll say goodbye. I hope everything goes all right for you there."

"Mom, please don't hang up yet. Just listen to me for a minute, okay? I didn't want to disappoint you. That's why I couldn't bring myself to call earlier. I knew you'd be hurt, but I felt I had to make this journey. I needed to know."

"Know what? You already know what Thomas looks like. You know where he lives and what he does. You know he's married. What else is there?"

Could Beth actually say what had been hammering in her brain when she made her travel arrangements? *I need to know that my father is a Christian. I need to make sure he shares my faith. I have to be certain of his eternal destiny.* It sounded lame. Like a weak excuse for thoughtless behavior.

"You want to know what he's like, don't you?" her mother asked. "Well, I could have told you that. Thomas Wood is a selfish, egotistical man. He has his own goals, and he doesn't care about anything else. Or anyone but himself."

Beth suddenly gripped Miles's hand more tightly. She could almost hear the words her mother hadn't spoken. *Thomas Wood is like you, Beth. The two of you are just the same.*

"Oh, dear. Wait," Jan said, a tremor in her words. "Just a second. I didn't mean that. I didn't intend to say that to you. I wanted to tell you . . . something else. Let me start over."

Closing her eyes, Beth could almost see her mother's face before her. But Jan wasn't perkily spouting pithy quotations or snapping off retorts to put her daughter back in line. What did the woman look like now—this mother whose voice had traveled halfway around the globe to reach her daughter's ear?

"Thomas was a good man," Jan began, repeating the words she had written on the note her daughter found inside the teapot. "And he was . . . he was very dear to me. I felt terribly wounded when he left for Sri Lanka the second time. It seemed like he was choosing his career and his love of adventure over me . . . and you. But he didn't know about you. So that's not fair. I can't hold him responsible for it. Oh, Beth, what can I say that will help you feel better? He was talented. He was brave. He was funny. He was passionate. He was very smart, too. One time he told me he thought he could learn to grow tea better than anyone else, and see? I bet he has."

Beth tried to respond, but she found no words.

Her mother continued. "The thing I need to remind you, Beth, is that . . . you have to remember that Thomas didn't know anything about your existence. I didn't tell him I was pregnant before he left. I didn't send him a letter when you were born, or contact him during the years while you were growing up. Thomas came back to Texas a couple of times to visit his family, but I never saw him, and I never let him know about you. His mother didn't tell him, either. Nanny agreed to go along with my wishes, because I offered to let her see you as much as she wanted if she would keep the secret. And so she did, even though it hurt her not to be able to tell her son that he was a father. I know it did. But I didn't care, you see, because I was selfish, too."

"Now, Mom, please don't—"

"No, let me finish, Beth. That's what I'm trying to tell you. *I'm* the selfish one. And it's all right that you're in India. Truly, it is. I hope you have a good experience there . . . a good meeting . . . and I hope you like him. But he won't be prepared, so I've been worrying that you might get hurt. Oh, Beth, sweetie, I don't want you to be wounded over this. I've caused you enough pain, honey. I'm so sorry. I hope you can forgive me."

Beth held her breath for a moment, hardly able to absorb the gush of words that had flowed from her mother's mouth. She was holding Miles's hand as though she were perched at the lip of a cliff, and one slight puff of breeze would send her off the edge.

"I'm sorry, too, Mom," she said. "I'm sorry for hurting you."

A sniffle echoed across the miles. "Well, I guess that's how it is sometimes when people love each other."

"I suppose so."

"Just stay safe. And be good. And call me if you want to talk. And how is . . . how is Miles?"

Beth lifted her focus to the blue eyes that gazed back at her. "Miles is fine. He's nice."

Miles held out his free hand and gave Beth a little nod. "Let me have a word with dear ol' Mum, will you please?" he murmured.

Without telling her mother, Beth handed him the cell phone. He put it to his ear. "Am I speaking to the mother of the charming Beth Lowell?" he asked. His mouth widened into a smile. "Excellent. Miles Wilson, here. Mrs. Lowell, do permit me to assure you that your daughter is in very good hands. I mean to keep her under lock and key and only let her out when I'm certain she is prepared to behave herself properly."

At the sound of Miles's mischievous tone and cocksure British accent, Beth felt her tension begin to melt. She sank into the seat.

"That is absolutely correct," he said. "She'll be staying in a company guesthouse with room for no more than one occupant. She'll be fed a wholesome diet, and I shall see that she is taken out to tour the estate, receive her daily exercise and breathe the fresh air of the Himalayas. I promise you that I shall introduce her to our staff members—particularly our production manager—in the most discreet manner, and I shall ensure her welfare and contentment at every possible moment. You have my word that nothing dreadful will happen to your lovely daughter, and she will be returned to you as whole and happy as she ever was . . . perhaps even more so."

A long breath deflated Beth's lungs as Miles went on chatting with her mother. She rested her head on the seat back and gazed out the window again. As he spoke, a pearl-gray cloud suddenly dissolved, and a slice of golden sunlight lit the car, the road, the valley below and far, far up in the distance, the peak of a snow-covered mountain.

"Perfect," Miles said. "I shall make certain that she telephones you at least twice daily. Your daughter is willful, Mrs. Lowell, but what else can one expect from such an exquisite and unique creature? . . . right, then. Signing off."

He gave the phone back to Beth and followed her eyes to the window. "Aha. Just as I'd planned. Here we are in Darjeeling—and Kanchenjunga has come out to greet us."

Chapter Fourteen

Jan spread the letters across the table on her screened porch. Four blue envelopes, onionskin paper, strangely colorful stamps, her address in squared black-ink words. He had written only four times, and she had never replied. Why had she even bothered to keep them? Hidden at the bottom of her cedar jewelry box, they had lain untouched and almost forgotten.

Almost.

Today, she would start at the beginning. A bright red

cardinal in the dogwood tree near the porch whistled as she reached for the first of the letters. Thomas had written it not long after arriving in Sri Lanka to begin his full-time job. Jan, who had been vomiting every morning, yelling at her family every afternoon, sobbing her eyes out most of each night, had barely been able to focus when her older brother brought the letter into her bedroom.

"It's from Thomas," he had announced, thrusting out the pale blue envelope with its red and navy stripes around the edges. "Pull yourself together, Jan. Everybody's getting really sick of you."

"Get out of my room!" she had screamed at him. "Just leave me alone. I hate you! I hate everything about this stupid family!"

As the door shut behind her brother, Jan had blinked through her tears at the letter in her hand. Now, all these years later, she again studied Thomas's odd penmanship. Blunt and hard-edged and earthy, like him. She slid the letter from the envelope. The photograph fell out, just as it had the first time. Thomas stared into the camera, his long, wild, brown hair trimmed into a neat, grown man's style. He wore a khaki-green uniform shirt with an embroidered logo on the breast pocket. Two tea leaves and a bud. Verdant fields of green plants stretched out behind him. He was smiling.

"Dear Jan," he had written. She read the words again, imagining him writing them and remembering herself reading them.

I'm here on the estate and settling into my job. I live in an apartment with three other guys. One is an intern from Tanzania, and the other two are Sri Lankans. We can't understand each other, so we don't talk much.

It's boring at night. The manager put me out in the field again, like I was last spring, but I am hoping to get to work in the factory pretty soon. I want to see how it runs and figure out if I can make some improvements.

I know you were really upset with me for deciding to take the job, but I wish you could get over it. You would like Sri Lanka. I still want you to come out here for a visit. I'll pay for as much of your ticket as I can afford. My relatives gave me quite a bit of money for graduation, and it's in a savings account in Tyler. My dad can get into the account and help you buy the ticket. I told him to do whatever you asked.

Jan, I realize you didn't want me to leave, but I had to. I need to figure out who I am and make my own way in life. I can't grow roses anymore. I'm sorry, but I just can't. I want to be different. I have to change. The only thing I wanted to stay the same in my life was you. I still love you, Jan. You're the only girl I've ever loved this way. Please write back to me.

Love,
Thomas

Even now, after all this time, the words brought a lump to Jan's throat. She had loved him, too. So much! So desperately! It had taken all her willpower not to pick up the phone and call Mr. Wood to ask him for Thomas's money from the bank account. She would buy a ticket and fly off to Sri Lanka for the rest of the summer.

But she couldn't do that, could she?

Laying her hand now on her softly rounded midriff that had borne three babies, Jan recalled so well that first insistent flutter—a reminder that her life was no longer her own. She shared it with the tiny heartbeat and miniature fishlike, alien creature that had appeared on the sonogram in her doctor's office the week before Thomas's letter arrived. A baby. His child.

"I wish you could get over it." A girl didn't just get over a baby growing inside her. Not unless she was willing to let some stranger tear that little beating heart out of her body. As much as Jan had hated her situation and regretted her carelessness, she wouldn't do that.

"I need to figure out who I am and make my own way in life," Thomas had written. "I want to be different. I have to change."

Different? Well, Jan was already different. She would have to make her own way in life and figure out who she was. But she wasn't selfish, like Thomas. Though the baby had made her sick, her whole family treated her like the black sheep sinner of the century and her friends never called to ask her to hang out with them anymore, Jan had remained stubbornly determined to have her baby. She was growing a life inside her. Somehow . . . somehow . . . she and the child both would survive.

Now, at forty-five, sitting out on her screened porch and listening to a cardinal sing for its mate, Jan let the tears fall. It had been hard, all of it. But she could sincerely thank God she hadn't destroyed that unwanted, inopportune, little alien fish-baby who had made her heave over the toilet every morning. After all, that unrecognizable tadpole had been Beth. Her Beth! John's Bethy-boo. Bobby and Billy's big sister. "Beff," the boys had called her. "Beff, tie my shoes . . . Beff, get me a cookie . . . I need a Band-Aid for my boo-boo, Beff."

Jan folded the letter and slipped the photograph back inside it. She would give them to Beth when her daughter returned from India. Jan would read Thomas's message out loud and explain how she had felt at the time. She would tell Beth everything she could remember about that awful year of losing a true love and welcoming a new life and becoming someone different.

She reached for the second letter. Inside this one, Thomas had enclosed a tea leaf. No doubt mailing a foreign country's vegetation to the United States had been highly illegal. It was crisp and fragile now and had turned brown. But Jan recalled how she had held the green leaf up to the sunlight and marveled at the network of veins that transported life and flavor and nourishment. Her own body was functioning in much

242

the same way, nurturing the baby who by that time had taken to performing somersaults in the middle of the night.

Dear Jan,
Did you get my letter? Why didn't you write back? You can't be that mad. Think of all the time we spent together. Think of how much we love each other. I still love you, Jan. I think about you every day, and I wish you would come and see me. I've added to my bank account in Tyler, and my dad will help you get whatever you need to buy a ticket.

I'm working in the tea factory now. It's amazing. I enjoy the machinery more than I thought I would—me being an ag major and all. I have learned how to make some repairs, because things are always breaking down. Replacement parts are hard to get over here. It's not like in Tyler.

My mom says she hasn't seen you or talked to you. How are you? Please write to me. I miss you. I love you.
  Love,
  Thomas

She had loved him, too. But summer was passing, and she had stopped vomiting every morning. She still yelled at her family, but now that the baby was showing, they treated her better. Her mother cooked whatever Jan wanted. Her father kept asking if she was

243

all right, did she need to sit down, was she feeling any funny twinges, could he help her with anything? Her brother stared at her every time he walked by the den where she was watching TV with her long bare legs stretched out on the ottoman and her stomach pooching up like a small hill under her T-shirt. That summer seemed to last forever.

And then the third letter came.

The cardinal flew past the screened porch as Jan now lifted the blue envelope and drew out the letter. The brilliant red bird had called and called, and finally his mate answered. They sang out, first one and then the other, fluttering closer and closer until they spotted each other.

Dear Jan,

Why don't you ever write to me? I know you got my last two letters. My parents get every letter I send them. I would call you, but it's too expensive and the time is backward. I would rather spend the money on your plane ticket. If you came over here, we could talk about everything. We could work things out. I know we could.

I got a promotion. I'm making more money now, and they're talking about letting me move into one of the houses they provide for midlevel employees. The houses are small but nice. We could get married while you're here. There's a missionary in Nuwara Eliya, and I already talked to him about it. He said he would do the ceremony. I was planning to marry you all along anyway, but I wanted to wait until I was settled into my job.

Jan, don't you love me anymore? I know you're upset about what I did, but I also know you can't turn off true feelings just like that. I will never stop loving you as long as I live. Please write to me.

Love,
Thomas

Jan had gotten out paper and a pen a hundred times. She had started countless letters. But she always threw them away. How could she live in a place where time was backward? How could she marry Thomas without her father to walk her down the aisle and her mother to sit crying on the front pew of their church in Tyler? What would she ever do with herself in a small, mid-level employee's house on a tea plantation in Sri Lanka? No matter how much she loved Thomas—and she still loved him to the very core of her being—she could never change that much. More important, she couldn't bring a baby into the world and expect the child to live that kind of nomadic, inse-cure existence.

Jan had to smile now as she put the letter away, and she leaned back in her chair to gaze through the screen at the lake. How hard she had worked to protect her baby from the life Thomas Wood offered. And look what had happened! Beth grew up to be a globe-trotting nomad herself!

Not only did Thomas's daughter love to travel, but

even at this moment, she was headed straight toward a tea plantation in some foreign country where people spoke strange languages and ate strange foods and had strange customs. Beth had no qualms. No hesitation. Her only worry had been her mother's reaction.

"Oh, what a tangled web we weave,
When first we practice to deceive!"

Jan shook her head at the truth in Sir Walter Scott's verse as she opened the fourth and final letter. She had worked so hard to keep her big secret. She had spun her web and laid out each thread in perfect order. But what a tangled mess she had created.

"Jan," the black ink stated matter-of-factly.

My mother told me that you got married two weeks ago. She said he's a history teacher at the college. How could you do that? Didn't you love me? Was I nothing to you? I thought you really cared about me, but I can see now I was wrong. You just wanted to stay in Tyler and have everything your way. Well, you got your wish, and now I know exactly what kind of a person you are. I'm glad I found out before it was too late. I was planning to buy a ticket and come home for Thanksgiving to see you and try to work things out, but forget it. Have a nice life.

Thomas

Her heart slamming against her ribs, Jan put the letter aside quickly and stacked the other three on top of it.

Oh, the hurt and accusations! But Thomas was right in many ways. She *had* just wanted to stay in Tyler and have everything her way. While accusing Thomas of caring only for himself, she had managed to behave in the most self-centered manner imaginable.

How could she never have written the man even a single letter? Why hadn't she given him at least one kernel of truth? Instead, she had allowed him to feel betrayed, cut off, abandoned, as she wove her web of deceit. She could argue that she had done everything in order to protect her baby. But that wasn't completely true.

Jan thought about Beth, how much she loved her daughter and how poorly they communicated. But Beth's life was turning out all right despite the conflicts with her mother. In fact, Jan had to acknowledge that somehow the little pigtailed girl who hated pink had become an amazing woman. Beth had chosen a job her mother would never have considered, a city her mother dreaded to set foot in and a young man who wasn't even from America, much less Texas. Beth's was a strange, unexpected life, but for the first time, Jan felt truly proud of her daughter. And the main reason had little to do with her choice of job or city or boyfriend. Jan was proud of Beth for herself. For her straight, square shoulders. For her determination. For her spirit.

Miles had called Beth willful. But whose will was she doing? Certainly not her mother's. Probably not her boyfriend's. And really . . . not even her own. The best thing about Beth Lowell had turned out to be her faith in God. She was trying to do God's will, and somehow the truth of that simply astonished and humbled her mother.

"Satisfactory?" Miles asked as Beth walked around the guest bungalow situated in the central compound of Wilson Teas, Ltd.'s vast Darjeeling estate. The small house's concrete floor coated in red wax supported nothing more substantial than a single bed and an unadorned wooden wardrobe. A woven brown rug covered part of the floor, a painting of a yellow orchid hung on the whitewashed wall and a door led to a small bathroom with a white ceramic toilet, sink and shower stall.

"It's perfect," she replied. She set her black leather travel bag on the red-and-brown batik coverlet that draped the bed. "Exactly what I need."

"Not quite as opulent as Wilson House, but one has to think of the intangibles."

"Oh?"

"While London has its charms, Darjeeling has the Himalayas just outside the window." He pulled open the curtain, and a wide vista of towering, snow-covered peaks filled the glass pane.

"Darjeeling wins by a mile."

He smiled. "I think so, myself, actually, but it's not the popular opinion. I'm glad you're pleased with your quarters." His eyebrows lifted. "Well, then. Shall we go and meet your father?"

Beth sucked down a gasp. "Wait, now. I just got here."

"Not going to change your mind, are you?"

She stepped past Miles onto the veranda and sank into a bamboo chair upholstered with utilitarian tan canvas. "My mother's phone call in the car ride up here . . . She reminded me that he doesn't know. No one ever told Thomas Wood about me."

"He'll be delighted." Miles took the chair beside her. "Look at what he produced. A beautiful daughter—intelligent, resourceful, successful. It will be like finding a brilliant jewel that he had no idea he possessed."

"That's the problem. How will he react to the realization that he has been kept in the dark about me for twenty-five years? He could feel cheated."

"Perhaps. But I predict he'll mostly be glad you turned out so well."

"Or extremely upset that a total stranger claiming to be his child has stepped into his otherwise comfortable life."

"You have no idea what his life is like. Perhaps it's deadly dull, and he's just hoping something will come along to liven it up. What better than you?"

Beth threaded her fingers back through her long hair, pushing it off her forehead and encountering tangles on the way down. She should take a shower, wash and brush out her hair, put on fresh makeup, dress in something that hadn't traveled half the globe on her. Anything to avoid the inevitable.

"He may not like me, Miles," she told him. "Just

because you're so quick with compliments doesn't mean Thomas Wood is going to think I'm God's gift to Darjeeling."

"We'll never know until we meet him." He stood and held out his hand. "Shall we?"

"Do you know anything about his personality? Is he quiet? Or gregarious? Or what?"

"I've only met the bloke once or twice, and I hardly remember him. I'm sure he's amiable enough. One can't succeed in the job he has without an even temperament and a confident disposition. In dealing with the labor and the factory, he's bound to face surprises all day long."

"Well, he's going to face a big one today."

"He will love you. Now get up so we can go and have a chat with Mr. Wood."

Beth set her hands on the chair's bamboo arms and pushed herself to her feet. "Don't say a word about me being his daughter, Miles. I'll tell him when the time is right. Do you promise?"

"Absolutely. This is entirely your affair. I'm merely here to facilitate."

As they walked down the path toward a row of small trucks the estate used to haul workers and tea, Beth glanced at Miles. "Why are you doing this, really? You've come all this way, and—"

"For you, my dear lady."

"Don't be sarcastic."

"Sarcastic? I'm astonished that you would say such a thing."

"You hardly know me, and you certainly don't owe me anything."

"Wrong on both counts. I know you very well. I read your Bible, remember? You underlined so many passages and wrote such personal information in its margins that I feel as if I know everything about you. You struggle to keep your tongue under good regulation. You're not fond of proud people. You have very little patience—you've begged God urgently to give you more of it."

"Okay, stop."

"You're passionate about caring for the poor, widows, orphans, the hungry, the thirsty, the sick. Enough exclamation marks alongside those verses to populate two or three complete novels."

He opened the passenger side of one of the trucks, and Beth climbed in. She couldn't believe she was actually going to do this. They would drive out onto the estate, and she would see him. It was a mistake. She should have listened to her mother and chosen safety and sense and stability.

"And as for my not owing you anything," Miles went on as he turned the key and the truck jumped to life, "the fact is I owe you everything."

"I haven't done a thing for you."

"Wrong again." The truck pulled out of the parking lot onto a narrow road, dry now but rutted by years of tire tracks through the rain and mud of the monsoon season. "It was your mention of the race, you see. And then the Bible you left on the table at The Running

Footman. And your phone call telling me you were coming back to London. I never expected any of those things. Nor did I deserve them. I am, in reality, quite unworthy of you."

"Don't be silly, Miles. I'm not going to fall for that kind of flattery, so you can just give it a rest. I know who I am and who you are, and neither one of us is perfect. Don't try to sweet-talk me, especially right now when I'm so tense." She eyed him. "I might be unable to keep my tongue under good regulation."

He laughed. "Say whatever you like. I require a good tongue-lashing now and again."

"Hang around with me very long, and you'll get one."

"I'm terrified." He rolled down a window and pointed at a long, low building in the distance. "That's the factory where we process the tea leaves for shipping. Mr. Wood might be inside, but as it's a clear afternoon and the sun's out, I imagine we'll find him in one of the fields."

Beth tried without success to think of ways to still her heartbeat and calmly draw air into her lungs. But the altitude, the curving road and the prospect of actually meeting Thomas Wood defied all her efforts. Unlike photographs she had seen of tea fields spread across flat expanses, the Wilson estate covered a series of steep rolling hills. Pluckers with baskets on their backs labored up and down the tidy rows. Mist rose from the damp ground as the sun beat down. Somewhere a bird cried out with a squawk that jangled Beth's nerves.

"There." Miles slowed the truck. "Near that tree. I believe we've found our man. He's too tall for an Indian or a Nepali, though he's certainly brown enough. Looks like he's spotted us, as well."

Beth focused on the angular, broad-shouldered man in the distance. Halfway down a precipitous slope, he was speaking to a group of women. He wore a green shirt with some kind of logo, and his dark brown hair hung in shaggy, uneven lengths down the back of his neck.

"It's him," Beth whispered. She grabbed Miles's hand and squeezed it hard. "Let's go back. Take me to the bungalow."

"I'm afraid he's seen us."

"We'll talk to him later. Now I know what he looks like, and that's enough. Let's go."

"Look, he's coming up the hill." He pulled her hand to his lips and kissed it gently. "I'm stopping the truck, and we're going to get out. I promise he'll be much more intent on me than on you. I'm his boss, remember?"

Swallowing at nothing, Beth pressed her dry lips together. She wouldn't be able to talk. Her mouth was parched, and her knees felt like noodles. She couldn't even think how to pray.

And now Thomas had climbed up to the road. She could see him better, and he looked like the boy in the senior photograph from the high school yearbook . . . only the hair at his temples was gray and deep lines fanned out from the corner of each eye. But he was tall enough. Square enough. The high cheekbones and long, straight nose, the Adam's apple . . .

"Mr. Wood?" Miles had stepped out of the truck and was walking to meet him, hand thrust out in greeting. "Miles Wilson. London office. Pleased to see you."

Beth sat rigid, small breaths hopping in and out of her scorched mouth, her nostrils dilated as though she were choking. Thomas Wood shook Miles's hand and reminded him they'd met before.

"A few years back," Thomas said. "The big Christmas party at the main house. You were here with someone . . . a girlfriend, I think. The whole event was fairly crazy. A lot of alcohol. I'm not surprised you don't remember me."

"Ah." Miles gave Beth a guilty glance. "And I should very much like you to meet another . . . friend. Beth?"

Feeling like the Tin Man without his oil can, she managed to open the truck door and step out onto the road. She willed her mouth into a smile and forced her feet to move forward one after the other.

"Beth Lowell," Miles was saying. "This is Thomas Wood. He's in charge of production here in Darjeeling. The fields as well as the factory, I believe?"

"That's right." Her father thrust out his hand. "Thomas Wood. Pleased to meet you, Ms. Lowell."

She stared at it too long. His hand, the fingers that had caressed Beth's mother. The palm that had pressed her against him. The knuckles a deep brown from years of exposure to the tropical sun. The hand that

254

was somehow connected to Beth even without a touch.

"Hello," she murmured. She set her hand in his, and he wrapped those large, brown fingers around it and gave a firm shake.

"You're an American," he said. "Where are you from?"

"Texas."

Too late!

He perked up. "I was raised in Texas. Tyler. Ever been there?"

"Yes," she breathed.

"As have I," Miles spoke up. "Dallas, at any rate. Fascinating city. The businessmen wear cowboy hats and boots with their Armani suits. A bit humid in the summer months. Beth is a travel consultant of sorts. We met in an airport in Kenya. Do tell him about your work, Beth."

"I handle global transitions for a New York moving company." To her surprise, the words came out perfectly. "Basically, I help our customers settle comfortably into a foreign country."

"She finds houses for them," Miles explained. "Hires household staff. Locates schools and country clubs. Immensely helpful. Wilson Teas would do well to make use of her services, don't you think, Mr. Wood? I'm certain you didn't have such assistance when you first came to Darjeeling."

Thomas lowered his head and chuckled. "I was sent over from the Sri Lanka estate years ago when the former production manager suddenly quit. Lawford

255

put me into one of the guest bungalows for a while. When I got married, I moved into one of the bigger houses. To tell the truth, I was too busy to realize it was a transition. But I'm sure most people could benefit from your services, Ms. Lowell."

"Lucky for us to have such an adaptable employee as you, sir," Miles observed. "My brother, Malcolm, told me you constructed a home here for yourself and your wife."

Thomas's expression sobered. "I built the new place three years ago. After she died."

"Dreadfully sorry, Mr. Wood. I had no idea you'd lost your wife. Please accept my condolences."

"Thank you."

"Well, I'm pleased to know you've got a place where you can feel comfortable, and I do wish to convey my thanks and congratulations for the excellent work you do here. I've been remiss. As president of the international division, I should have spoken with you long before now, Mr. Wood. Malcolm tells me that our Darjeeling tea continues to bring some of the highest prices on the market. And equally important, we've operated at a substantial profit from your second year as production manager to this day. Well done, sir."

"I can't claim the credit, Mr. Wilson. Lawford handles the office work—the books, the payroll, the markets, all that." Thomas Wood had turned his head and hooked his hands into his back pockets, Beth noticed. He was studying the women who had gone back to their plucking, as though he didn't trust himself to look

Miles in the eye. She wondered if the mention of his wife's death had caused the reaction.

"We can't have success without good tea," Miles pointed out. "I'm told you're actually involved in the propagation and breeding of tea here at Darjeeling. I can't think how you have time for it while overseeing the labor and the factory."

"Hybridization is a hobby of mine from way back. My family owned a big rose nursery in Tyler, and I studied agriculture at school. Once I had things running a bit more smoothly here, I thought I'd see if we couldn't breed out some of our problems and make our stock more healthy. *Camellia sinensis* is a fascinating shrub. You'd think we couldn't discover anything new about it, but I'm still learning."

"Excellent, Mr. Wood."

"Please call me Thomas." He turned to Beth, his voice lighter and his expression more cheerful. "If you'll excuse me, Ms. Lowell, I need to head over to another field and talk to the women. There's some kind of rivalry going on between that group and this one here. They tell me it's all about how I'm assigning the fields—who has to walk the steepest hills. But I've got an informer who says they're feuding over a man." He laughed, chest-deep. "It's always something."

"Women," Miles echoed.

Beth knew she should rise to the challenge, but she had hardly been able to keep breathing the whole time Miles was talking to Thomas Wood. He was real. This man. Her father by birth. She drank him in like a thirsty child, trying to absorb and know everything about him. He had endowed her with those dark brown eyes, that long face, the olive skin. He was smart. Inventive. Good with people. Adaptable. Had he given her those things, too? She ached to throw her arms around him and feel his embrace. At the same time, she wanted to run away as fast as her legs would carry her.

Who was he? Who was she? What was she supposed to do now?

"Right, then," Miles spoke up, taking her arm. "Listen, Thomas, might I entice you to dinner with us this evening? We won't be in Darjeeling long, and I should like to make it up to you for focusing so much attention on Lawford's end of things. I'd enjoy hearing more about your hybridization program. And I certainly want to hear how you sort out these pesky troubles with your labor."

"Thanks for the offer, but I'm busy tonight," Thomas said. "It's Wednesday. Church."

"Church?" Beth blurted out.

His dark eyes turned on her. "There's a prayer service in the factory dining hall on Wednesday evenings. You're welcome to come."

"Thanks," she managed.

He faced Miles again. "How about tomorrow for dinner? I'm free then."

"Tomorrow will be perfect." Miles attempted to turn Beth toward the truck. "Seven, then. We'll meet at the main building and drive into Darjeeling. Perhaps you can show us some of the local color."

"Be glad to." He smiled. "Thanks for dropping by, Mr. Wilson. And nice to meet you, Ms. Lowell."

"Beth," she said.

"Beth." He repeated the word. Then he turned and walked back down the road.

Chapter Fifteen

"On the floor?" Beth whispered the question as she slipped into the darkened room. Miles held her hand and led her to an unoccupied straw mat.

"We're in India," he reminded her.

They sat down together, cross-legged, and she was thankful she'd chosen to put on a full skirt that afternoon following her shower. In every window of the factory employees' dining hall sat a shallow clay bowl filled with oil. A white cotton wick transferred oil to the flame that cast a soft, glowing light about the room. A stick of fragrant sandalwood incense on a low table near the front of the room sent gray smoke upward to waft around the fan that rotated slowly at the center of the ceiling. Close by, a young woman with black hair and a pale, creamy yellow sari sang a hymn that Beth recognized. The tune was one she had heard in her home church in Tyler as well as at the services she attended in New York. But the words must have been in an Indian tongue.

For a moment, Beth glanced around the room in

search of Thomas. Unable to locate him in the dim light, she bowed her head and listened to the hymn, saying the words to herself in English. Miles had released her hand, but she could feel his knee pressing into hers. She was thankful for his presence.

Miles had finally discovered the door—Christ—that led onto the straight and narrow path of faith. Though he hadn't yet stepped through, Beth realized he was changing already. His warmth and sincerity had taken on a deeper dimension. He had gone out of his way to make the trip to India a good experience for her. During their encounter with her father, he had stepped in to ease Beth's awkwardness and cover her stumbles. After an early supper that evening, he had suggested they attend the prayer service. The man both Miles and his brother had termed a boorish cad had disappeared. In his place stood a witty, kind, charming gentleman who might sweep Beth right off her feet if she weren't careful.

Having upset her mother, met her birth father and acknowledged her attraction to Miles, Beth felt herself approaching overload. She silently prayed for clarity, discernment and, above all, peace. When the hymn ended, she lifted her head to find Thomas settling behind the low table where the incense burned. He opened a Bible and began sorting through a sheaf of notes.

She turned to Miles in surprise. "*He's* the minister?" she whispered.

"Apparently so."

When Thomas began to speak, a shiver ran down Beth's spine. He was leading the service. Her father! She tried to listen as he spoke first in English, then in Hindi, then mingling the two languages in a way that both she and his audience seemed to understand. He directed the small group of men and women gathered in the room to a passage in I Corinthians. While Miles fumbled around with his Bible, Beth quickly flipped through hers and located the first chapter and the eighteenth verse of the epistle. She shared her book with the man beside her as Thomas read aloud the words of Saint Paul.

" 'I know very well how foolish the message of the cross sounds to those who are on the road to destruction. But we who are being saved recognize this message as the very power of God.' "

In a low but strong voice, Thomas explained that God's way of thinking is different from the way the rest of the world thinks. "In fact," he told the group in the room, "the truth that God sent His only Son to die on a cross sounds silly to many. Why would God care enough about man to come to Earth in human form? If He really was God, why did He allow people to nail Him to a cross and kill Him? How could it be possible to die and then come back to life? Why would Christians risk everything to tell others that God has done this thing for them?"

As he spoke, Beth reflected on the familiar message of Christianity and tried to imagine what she would have thought on hearing it for the first time. She had always known about Jesus on the cross, she realized. A God who died and came alive again sounded perfectly natural to her. It hadn't required much faith for her to believe in something that all her life she'd been told was the truth.

Nor did it take much effort to practice her faith in this Christian God. Beth hadn't ever faced any danger for being a Christian in Tyler, Texas. And if a few New Yorkers lifted their eyebrows at her strict devotion to her beliefs, they certainly didn't persecute or torment her for them. In fact, saying you were a Christian in the United States required practically nothing from people—not even the guts to actually follow through and live by Christ's teachings.

Beth leaned forward with her elbows on her knees just as Thomas lifted his head and focused his gaze directly on her. "My wife," he said evenly, "suffered and died for her faith in Jesus. Her family killed her because she dared to speak aloud the message of the cross. Many of you knew Nirmala and loved her as I did. Many of us are here tonight because she was willing to give us a message we once thought was foolish. When we listened and understood, the message completely changed us, didn't it? It transformed us into men and women who are entirely different from the way we were before."

He looked down at his Bible again. "Saint Paul goes on to write that the people in the country where he lived were offended by the message or thought it was nonsense. In verses 25-29 Saint Paul explains that

262

God's so-called 'foolish' plan is much wiser than the wisest of human plans.

"'Remember, dear brothers and sisters, that few of you were wise in the world's eyes, or powerful, or wealthy when God called you. Instead, God deliberately chose things the world considers foolish in order to shame those who think they are wise. And He chose those who are powerless to shame those who are powerful. God chose things despised by the world, things counted as nothing at all, and used them to bring to nothing what the world considers important, so that no one can ever boast in the presence of God.'

"I am one of those foolish, weak people," Thomas went on. "I have no power. Some might believe I am powerful because I have the job of production manager for Wilson Teas—but please understand this work was given to me by God. I, myself, am nothing. The Lord brought me here to Darjeeling and allowed me to meet the staff doctor, Nirmala Shah. Nirmala is the one who explained to me that I could never be good enough to win God's love. I could never be smart enough or powerful enough to get into Heaven by my own efforts. Nirmala showed me that I deserved death for the wrong things I had done in my life. And believe me, I had done a lot of wrong things."

As Thomas spoke of his past sins, Beth flinched inside. She was the direct, living result of this man's wrongdoing. How would he feel if she mustered the courage to tell him who she really was? Might he view her as his sin come to life? Standing there in front of him, Beth would be the evidence that the consequences of his transgressions lived on.

No human—not even the most faithful and pure—could escape the fact that there were penalties to sin. By sacrificing Himself on the cross, Christ had taken away the ultimate punishment of damnation and eternal separation from God after death. But smaller, earthly results of human wrongdoing lived on. Disease. Pain. Estrangement. And unexpected grown-up daughters.

"When I finally understood the meaning of the 'foolish' message Nirmala had told me," Thomas was saying, "everything became clear. I saw that nothing I could do would ever erase my past. Only Jesus could do that. Like Nirmala, I became His servant and began to worship Him as the Lord of my life."

He paused and looked around the room before continuing. "In the ninth verse of chapter two, Saint Paul tells believers that 'No eye has seen, no ear has heard, and no mind has imagined what God has prepared for those who love him.' That is true. Here on Earth, God blessed me by allowing me to marry Nirmala. Even though she was killed, I know I'll see her again in Heaven. That's where Jesus waits for us with all the wonderful things He has prepared for those of us who love Him. I wonder if we could spend our last minutes here tonight thanking God for letting us understand the truth that so many others believe to be foolish. Could we tell our Lord Jesus Christ how grateful we are for the things He has done for us here on Earth? Could we praise Him for all that He has prepared for us in the future?"

As she bowed her head again, Beth felt Miles rise beside her. She glanced up to see him slipping out the dining room door into the darkness. Her heart ached as she listened to the voices in the room, one by one speaking in a language she couldn't understand. But God understood. He knew.

Jan had chosen the little girl with hair the color of rich molasses and eyes like glistening black pebbles in a stream. A plain wood frame from a hobby shop in Tyler fit the drawing perfectly, and a pale green mat accented the color in the grass where the child crouched to examine a black-and-yellow caterpillar. Jan laid the sheet of heavy sketch paper facedown on the framed glass and began to press the clips that would hold it in place.

"She reminds me of your daughter." Jim Blevins spoke up. Having dropped by for a glass of lemonade, he had settled on a kitchen chair while Trixie sniffed for crumbs under the table. "Was that on purpose?"

Jan picked up the frame and turned it over to study the pastel chalk picture. To her surprise, the child did look like Beth.

"You know, I never thought of that while I was drawing her," she said. "It was the caterpillar. I found it on a leaf out in my garden, and suddenly right there in my mind was a skinny, dark-haired girl poking at it with her finger. But now that I think of it, Beth loved caterpillars and worms. She brought them to me all the time. I was mortified, but John thought it was wonderful. He would put the worms in the rose bed, and he'd kill the caterpillars."

"Killed 'em? I hope Beth didn't see that."

"Oh, no. She never knew. Most of the caterpillars she brought in were the destructive kind. Beth thought they were so pretty with all their bright colors, but they were eating our tomatoes and cabbages and corn. John said our daughter's hobby was a lot safer for the environment than insect sprays, and we ought to hire her out to the neighbors."

Jim chuckled as Jan gazed at the picture. "Maybe this *is* Beth," she said. "I've been trying to paint my daughter for months, but—"

When the phone rang, Jan jumped. She had spent hours preparing herself for the call, but it did no good. The past three times, someone other than Beth had been on the line. A plumbing company, checking to make sure her pipes were still working. A woman from church, wondering if Jan would be willing to help teach Vacation Bible School. And Billy, asking if she would mind doing his laundry just one last time, because he had gotten really busy at work, and he would never ask again.

"Here," Jim said, hauling himself to his feet. "I'll hang the picture while you get the phone. It's bound to be her this time."

How had he known whom she was expecting? Jan fretted at having let Jim so far into her life when she

266

hadn't intended to at all. Now they were going to church together every Sunday, eating supper out at least once a week and taking Trixie for her last walk most evenings. This wasn't supposed to happen! Jan didn't want a man in her life. She had been freed of all that responsibility, all the tangles of a relationship, all the expectations and worries.

"Hello?"

"Hi, Mom. It's me."

"Beth! This is a nice surprise." Jan glanced at Jim, who was studiously straightening the picture and pretending not to listen. She slipped out onto the screened porch. "Are you still in India?"

"Yes, and everything's fine." Beth hesitated a moment. "Almost everything. For some reason, Miles went back to London. I don't know what happened. We had a good day yesterday, I thought, but this morning he was gone. He left a message saying he needed to attend to some things at the home office, and he hoped I wouldn't mind."

"You're all by yourself?" Jan didn't know whether to be happy or sad that Miles was gone, but she was certainly worried about her daughter in that strange place.

"Well . . . I'm not exactly alone." Beth's anxious breathing sounded across the vast empty space between them. "I've met Thomas Wood. But it's all right, Mom. He doesn't know I'm his daughter. I just wanted to tell you that I feel all right about it. About him."

"I see." Jan couldn't make anything else come out.

Questions buzzed through her mind like bees around a hive, but she couldn't capture a single one.

"He's nice, Mom. Do you mind if I say that?"

"No, of course not, honey. I'm glad you like him. I knew you would—unless he's changed drastically."

"He has, though. You'd be so surprised if you saw him now. I mean, he's different compared to what you told me he was like before. Guess what—he's a Christian!" Her daughter's voice sounded happier than Jan had heard it in weeks.

And suddenly Beth was babbling. "Thomas ministers with a group of converts who work on the estate or live nearby. He's not a preacher, but he teaches from the Bible and conducts prayer meetings and worship services. Oh, Mom, you wouldn't believe how dedicated he is. Everything he says is tinged with his faith. Today he showed me around the factory, and then we drove out into the fields to greet the pluckers, and when he talks, you can just tell he's totally committed to Christ. He has dramatically increased production on the estate, plus he's working with propagation and breeding. He showed me the place where he keeps the tea bushes he hybridizes. They have to be separate from the fields. You wouldn't believe how smart he is. Everyone admires and respects him—from the pluckers to the factory workers to the tea tasters. The general manager, Mr. Lawford, couldn't say enough good things about him at lunch today, and it was all I could do to keep from blurting out that I was his daughter."

"My goodness," Jan mumbled.

"We're having dinner this evening in town," Beth hurried on. "You see, Miles had invited Thomas to join us, but then Miles took off, so I said I thought we should go out to eat anyway. The town is so quaint. I've only seen it passing through, but I can't wait to walk around and explore. You would just love Darjeeling, Mom. They've got all kinds of craftwork. Brass, fabric, leather. The women wear amazing glass beads and embroidered shirts. You can see prayer flags flying on the hills. Most of the people are Buddhist, but there are Hindus here, too. Only a few Christians are brave enough to stand up publicly for their faith, and you can see why. Did I tell you about Thomas's wife? She was a Hindu convert to Christianity, and her family killed her! She went back to her home village for a visit. When she didn't return to the estate, Thomas went looking for her, and there was an investigation, and it turned out they had murdered her! Just because she had become a Christian. Isn't that awful?"

Jan had managed to seat herself in one of the chairs on the porch. She pushed her hand down on the table edge, impressing the metal pattern into her palm. It was too much. The information kept coming and coming, and she couldn't process it.

"His wife is dead?"

"Nirmala was her name. She was the doctor for the estate. They never had any children. She's the one who led him to Christ."

"I'm so sorry. That she died, I mean."

"Mom, I'm going to tell him tonight. Do you think that's a good idea? I don't want to ruin it. He seems to like me. He thinks I'm Miles's girlfriend. He's assuming we had a spat. I can't just leave tomorrow without setting Thomas straight. But what if he reacts badly? What if he . . . rejects me?"

The hurt in her daughter's voice drew out Jan's mother instinct. "Oh, Beth, honey, he won't do that. I told you in that note in the teapot that Thomas was a good man. I can't imagine what he's like now—not from all these things you're saying—but I'm sure he's still kind. He'll be surprised, maybe even shocked, but he'll be nice to you."

"You weren't sure before. In our last phone conversation, you were worried that I might get hurt. Do you think he'll be angry?"

Jan rubbed her hand across the rough tabletop. "If he is, it won't be directed at you."

"I won't let him blame you, Mom. I promise."

"*You* blamed me, Beth. You've been very angry with me for keeping your birth father a secret. Why wouldn't Thomas blame me? Why *shouldn't* he?"

"Because I can explain everything to him. I understand it better now. I do."

"Are you sure?"

"I wouldn't have chosen to do what you did, but I see why you acted that way. I know you were afraid, and I realize that Thomas hurt you by leaving."

"I should have told him."

"I wish you had."

"But then everything might have turned out so differently. Maybe he would have felt compelled to give up his dreams, marry me and work in the Wood family rose business. He would have been miserable, and he'd have blamed me, and maybe we would have ended up divorced. He might never have met his Indian wife and become a Christian. And John wouldn't have been your father—such a wonderful father—and we would never have had Bobby and Billy . . ."

"Mom, don't cry. Please."

Jan sniffled. "It might not have been the right decision, but it's the one I made. And if Thomas is angry about it, let him blame me. You tell him it's my fault, not yours, Beth. Do you hear me, honey?"

"Okay."

She felt herself grow stronger. "You remind Thomas he made choices, too. We bear equal responsibility for what happened. And you tell him that what happened was *you*—Bethany Ann Lowell—and you're not a mistake. You're wonderful and beautiful and just about perfect. You tell that man I loved him, and I would have done almost anything for him. But not that. Not leave my home and my family and fly off to some island when I was pregnant with his child. We both played our parts, and now we can both be adult about this and face the consequences of our actions. All right?"

Beth didn't speak for a moment. "All right, Mom. I'll tell him."

"Don't let him turn his anger on you."

"I won't."

"If he wants to fuss and pout, let him be mad at me."

"Okay."

"And you just remind him that I was only nineteen when he was begging me to go off to Sri Lanka. Nineteen!"

"Mom?"

"And tell him that I would have answered his letters—which I *did* get, and I *do* have—but I happened to be sick as a dog and terribly confused and everyone was treating me like dirt for getting pregnant. So that's why I didn't write. Tell him that. And you can also remind him that I had always wanted to be a teacher, and he knew it, so why did he think I would just—"

"Mom?" Beth cut in.

Jan pinched her lips together, breathing hard.

"Mom, maybe you should talk to him."

"No! Oh, Beth, I couldn't possibly do that."

"It sounds like there are a lot of things the two of you need to say to each other."

"I don't need to say a thing. Just don't let him get angry at you. That's all. That's what I was trying to tell you."

"Well, I'd better hop in the shower and then get ready for dinner. I wish you were here."

Jan shivered. "Beth, honey, you know I could never go all the way over there."

"Pray for me, Mom. Pray that I tell him the right way. Pray about how he might feel toward Nanny and everyone who kept the secret."

"I will, sweetheart. Everything's going to be fine. You'll see. He's a good man."

As they said their goodbyes and hung up, Jan turned to find Jim Blevins standing behind her. He had a hammer in his hand and a couple of nails sticking out from one corner of his mouth.

Chapter Sixteen

"Heard anything from him yet?"

"He hasn't called." Beth reached across the dinner table for her bottled cola. Her lips burned, and she blinked back tears generated by the fiery hot curry dinner she'd just eaten. A swig of her soft drink didn't help at all.

"I'm not worried about Miles," she said. "He's a busy man."

Thomas nodded. His fingers were stained yellow with turmeric as he took another piece of round, flat bread. Chapatis, they were called, and he had shown Beth how to use one to scoop up a mouthful of rice and curry with her fingers. Sitting inside a restaurant on a bustling street in Darjeeling, she wondered how eating with chopsticks came to her easily, yet she couldn't quite get the knack of hand-feeding herself curry.

"Men get cold feet sometimes," Thomas observed. He tore a chapati in half and went to work on the last of his dinner. "Especially when they're in danger of falling in love. I nearly lost Nirmala that way. I was crazy about her, but I'd been hurt in the past. So I kept taking one step forward and two steps back, you know? She finally got fed up with me and went to Bombay for a few months to enroll in a course and update her medical license. By the time she got back, I had wised up."

Beth held the glass soda bottle tightly between both hands. "Who had hurt you before?"

He looked out the window. "College girl in Texas. Beautiful. Red hair. Bright blue eyes. Gangly little thing with long legs and pretty feet. Oh, I loved that gal. But some things just don't work out."

"Well, why not?" Beth demanded. When he glanced at her in surprise at her tone, she swallowed. "I mean . . . if you loved her so much, why didn't you make it work?"

"Are you asking because Miles claims to love you, and you don't understand why he left?"

"Probably," she breathed. "That's part of it."

"In my case, I had dreams that were just too big for Miss Jan. She was a homegrown Texas rose who wanted to stay put. I couldn't wait to get away from my family's business. Try out my wings. See if I could fly on my own. As it turned out, I flew off without the love of my life and never laid eyes on her again."

"Surely you wrote."

"Yes, but she didn't answer. I guess I had scared her away for good." He sighed and leaned back in his chair. "Well, no point in getting off track here. I think if Miles Wilson knows what's good for him, he'll be calling you before long. To be honest, the man has earned himself a reputation as a bit of a playboy, and I can tell you're not that kind of girl. He's probably figured out that you're the best thing ever to come along in his life, and he'd better straighten up and fly right if he wants to keep you."

"Like you did with Nirmala?"

"Oh, no. That's different. I had changed my ways before I ever fell in love with her. Not long after I started at the estate, I began hearing rumors that someone was stirring up problems among the laborers. People told me the staff doctor was a troublemaker—holding meetings and trying to ruffle the waters. I envisioned some kind of political activist—maybe a union organizer or a socialist radical. When I slipped into the back of one of Dr. Shah's meetings, I couldn't have been more shocked. There on the floor in a soft pink sari sat this exotic Indian creature—and she was teaching from the Bible."

"Who had come to listen?"

"Some of the women. The pluckers. They'd been to the clinic for various things, and Dr. Shah had invited them to a Bible study. She didn't want me in the room—said she didn't believe women ought to teach men Scripture, but once I'd heard her speak, I couldn't stop going. Not long after that, one plucker's husband became a Christian, and he started a Bible study for men. Then things really got going. Talk about trouble. The Buddhists were angry. The Hindus were angry. The Muslims were angry. Lawford was angry. I managed to calm things down enough to let the groups keep going."

"What about you?"

"It's strange. I had left Texas in search of change, but nothing I did made a difference. By that time, I knew change had to come from another source. I repented of my past sins, and I pledged to follow Christ. I had no idea exactly what that meant, but I was put to the test right away. It was a struggle. Every day."

"I know what you mean."

He smiled almost sadly. "Too bad we Christians get attacked so often, but that's part of carrying your cross. Nirmala never soft-pedaled the consequences of becoming a Christian. Anyway, I was attending the men's group, and I hardly ever saw her. Then, after a vacation in Calcutta, I came down with malaria. While the good doctor was treating me, I fell head over heels in love with her. Nirmala wasn't so quick to give her heart to an ugly ol' cowboy, especially one with cold feet, but eventually she came around. We got married, and everything seemed to be going well. Then she decided to go home and visit her family. I never saw her alive again."

Beth reached across the table and laid her hand on his. "I'm so sorry."

He nodded. "Me, too. Nirmala always used to tell me that suffering was a good thing. She said it was a way that we humans could identify with the price Christ paid for our sins. I never really understood what she meant until I lost her."

"You've suffered a lot." Beth knotted her fingers together in her lap and wondered what effect her news would have on Thomas. Would she be adding to his pain? Or could knowing he had a daughter bring him joy? Would he feel his past sins hadn't really been forgiven by God? Or might he see Beth as a blessing?

Thomas shook his head. "Enough of this. Tell me about Texas. I haven't been back in years. How are things in the Lone Star state?"

An open door. Beth decided to walk through it.

"I doubt it's too different since you were there," she said. "I'm from Tyler, too."

His dark eyes flashed. "You're kidding! Why didn't you say something before now? Do you know any Woods?"

"My babysitter was a Wood. My two brothers and I called her Nanny, but her real name was Nancy."

"Nancy? My mother's name was Nancy. What street did your babysitter live on?"

It was going too fast, but Beth couldn't figure out how to slow it down.

"Aldrich Lane," she said.

"That's where I grew up!" He was beaming from ear to ear. "Your babysitter must have been my mother, Beth! If that doesn't beat all."

"Nancy Wood was my grandmother." She spoke the words softly, then she watched as the animation in Thomas's face went from surprised delight to confusion.

"Your grandmother? But that would mean my sister

is your . . . ? Mom never told me. . . ."

"I'm not your niece. My mother's name is Jan. Jan Calhoun Lowell."

He stared at her.

Beth found she couldn't meet his eyes. Fighting unanticipated tears, she looked out the window. "My mother was pregnant with me when you left Tyler for your job in Sri Lanka. She married John Lowell, and they raised me as his daughter. I have two brothers, Bob and Bill Lowell. My dad died two years ago of Lou Gehrig's disease. This past spring, I opened a box in my mother's house and found the antique tea set you had given her. The one you bought in London. That's when she told me."

"She told you that I . . . that we . . . that I'm your . . ." He blew out a breath, pushed back from the table and stood. "Whoa. Uh, excuse me just a minute. I need to . . . uh . . ."

Before Beth could react, he had fled the restaurant. She grabbed her purse and tried to summon a waiter. What if Thomas vanished? What if he ran away, like her mother said he had done before? What if he abandoned her the way Miles had? She needed to pay the bill.

"Hey!" She waved at a waiter taking an order near the back of the restaurant. People in the room scowled at her. "I'm sorry, but . . ."

And then Thomas was back inside, pulling money from his wallet and tossing it on the table, taking her arm and lifting her from the chair, leading her out the

278

door and walking her down the sidewalk so fast she could barely keep up.

"Janice Calhoun," he said. "She's your mother?"

"Janice Amelia Calhoun Lowell. Yes."

"Nancy Wood is your grandmother?"

"Yes."

"And Jan told you that I . . . that she and I . . ."

"You're my father, Thomas." Beth pulled her arm from his hand and stopped walking. "You're my birth father. John Lowell is my dad. He's the one who raised me, and if you don't want . . . if it bothers you to . . . It's okay if you'd rather not talk about it anymore. I came here, because after I found out, I needed to see you. I had to know. . . . Mainly, I wanted to make sure you were a Christian, and now that I know you are, I didn't have to tell you about the rest. But I did. So . . . I'm sorry."

"Sorry?" He set his hands on her shoulders. "Beth Lowell? You're my daughter?"

"It's Bethany Ann Lowell on my birth certificate."

"Jan was pregnant?"

"Yes. Barely."

"Why didn't she tell me?" he exploded, his hands flying up into the air, then clamping down on his head, his fingers threading through his hair. "That's . . . that's unbelievable! She was pregnant, and she didn't tell me? And my mother! Are you telling me my own mother knew all this? She was your *babysitter?* Why didn't she say something to me? All that time? All those years?"

"It was a secret," Beth told him. "They agreed not to talk about it to anyone. Mom said Nanny could babysit me as long as she didn't tell you."

"What?" he barked. "Why wasn't I told? I had a right to know! I was the father. I went off to Sri Lanka and no one said anything! I wrote to Jan and she never even answered!"

"She didn't write because she was too sick and confused. And everyone was upset with her for getting pregnant."

"But I could have . . . I could have helped. I would have married her. I wanted to marry her." He shook his head. "This is not right. They should have told me. My mother took this secret to her grave. Why did Jan do this? What did she think I was, some kind of loser? Did she think I couldn't take care of her? Did she think—"

"I don't know what she thought!" Beth cried out. "I don't know anything. You should talk to her yourself, because you're both blaming each other, and it's not fair to me. I'm the daughter. I wasn't there."

He studied her. "You're my daughter?"

Beth's shoulders sagged. "I told you that."

"But you came here with Miles Wilson. He told me he met you in the Nairobi airport. You're his girl-friend."

"No, I'm not. Not really. Well . . . one time he did say he was falling in love with me, but now he's gone, so I have no idea how he feels. Miles helped me find you. He offered to bring me here. Are you upset with me?"

"With *you?*" Thomas shoved his hands into his back

pockets and looked up at the night sky over Darjeeling. "Bethany Ann," he said. His voice was deep, husky. "Bethany Ann. A daughter. I always wanted children, and I thought . . . Nirmala and I . . . it didn't happen for us, and we . . ."

Beth frantically wiped at the tears streaming down her cheeks. "I'm sorry. Sorry about you and Nirmala. But I'm here. Is that okay?"

He focused on her again. "It's more than okay, Beth. You're precious . . . and sweet and . . . But this is just a lot to absorb, you know. I need to go back to my house and take some time to think it through."

"Of course." She recalled fleeing the lake house the first time she heard the news. And later she had yelled at her mother and run down to the water's edge. Beth couldn't blame Thomas for being in shock. But her secret hope—the small dream that he would throw his arms around her and welcome her into his life—was fading fast.

He was striding ahead of her now, toward the staff car he'd driven to town. Fewer people walked the winding streets at this late hour. A night breeze fanned down from the high peaks, sweeping away the smells of curry, tanned leather and animal waste. It was cold. Beth shivered as she slid onto the car seat beside Thomas.

"I can give you my mother's address and phone number," she said. He drove in silence out of Darjeeling toward the tea estate. She tried again. "She lives beside Lake Palestine now. After my father died, she taught school in Tyler until she could retire early. Then she sold the house that my brothers and I grew up in and moved to the lake. She paints and grows roses."

Thomas shifted gears, maneuvering the narrow, rutted roadway. Beth could see his Adam's apple moving up and down, as if he were trying to swallow something but couldn't. She wondered if it was anger. Or sorrow. It certainly wasn't joy.

"Mom kept the teapot in the bottom of a cardboard box." Beth decided to keep talking. It was better than riding in the still emptiness between them. "I wasn't supposed to find it until after her death. But one time when I was visiting, I noticed the box and I opened it. She had put a note inside the teapot. It had your name on it. Mom had written that you were my birth father, and she said you were a good man."

"I see." He fell silent again.

"We've had a rough time since I found out. Mom didn't want to face her past. She had thought she could hide everything and pretend that we Lowells had been this perfect American family. But we weren't perfect. No family is."

"That's true," he mumbled.

"She's starting to soften about it now. I think she might even regret having kept you a secret from me. At first she didn't want to talk about you at all. But now she tells me things."

"Like what?"

"She told me she had loved you, but she was only nineteen and very afraid. You chose to go overseas even though she asked you not to, and she believed you were choosing that life above her. She wanted to protect herself . . . and me. So she chose security. My dad was a history professor. They loved each other a lot. He knew everything, yet he treated me like his own daughter."

He nodded. "That's good."

"So I didn't . . . I didn't really need to find you. It was something I wanted to do. Mom told me you were dead. She thought you had died in the tsunami that hit Sri Lanka in 2004. She had looked for your name in the list of the dead, and she found a Wood."

Glancing at Beth with a frown, he said, "No, I wasn't living there then."

"I know. After I met Miles Wilson in the airport, he ran a search on his company's employee list and found you in Darjeeling. Mom begged me to abandon the idea of meeting you, and I thought I could. But then I called Miles and came to India anyway."

Thomas had pulled the car up to the front of the guesthouse. With the engine still running, he set the brake and leaned back in the seat. He rubbed a hand over his eyes, massaging his temples with his thumb and forefinger.

"Beth," he said, exhaling the word in a deep breath. "I'm a quiet man with an insulated life here. I guess I'm like your mother in that I tried to put my past away. Part of becoming a Christian was repenting . . . of Jan . . . of the way I had been with her . . . the things we had done . . . the fact that I left her . . . my selfishness,

283

immaturity, immorality. All of it. I wanted it behind me, and God helped me put things into place."

He dropped his hand into his lap and looked at her. "Now you're here," he said. "A shock. A miracle."

Shaking his head, he battled an obvious struggle against a tide of emotion as he continued speaking. "I'm sorry, Beth. I wish I knew the right things to say to you. A daughter. *My* daughter. But I don't have a plan in place for this. I don't . . . I don't know what to do."

Beth set her hand on the door release. "It's okay. I didn't know what to do when I found out, either. I'll let you go home now. I'm leaving in the morning, so . . . it was nice to meet you, Thomas. Thank you for the dinner. I'm glad we talked."

He nodded, his lips trembling as Beth left the car and shut the door behind her. By the time she had unlocked the guesthouse door and stepped inside, he was gone.

Beth walked into her New York apartment, kicked off her high heels and glanced at the blinking light on the answering machine. Not again. Her mother must have called her five times a day since she got back from India. Finally Beth had to ask her to stop using the cell phone and just leave messages at the home number.

Things weren't going the way they ought to. Applicants for the new positions at work didn't have the right qualifications. Beth had hoped to hire employees who had traveled extensively or lived overseas. She needed intelligent, adaptable, eager young souls who could be shaped into copies of herself. But they were turning out to be shy or undereducated or just plain flaky. Most agreed to travel to certain countries, but not just anywhere. The Middle East was off-limits. Most of Africa seemed too chancy. And certainly they wouldn't go to places where political unrest, economic instability or climate extremes might cause a problem. No one wanted to get caught in a riot, an earthquake or, heaven forbid, a dirty hotel room.

Beth dropped her bag on the floor and headed for the phone. No doubt her mother's voice would pipe up about something inconsequential. Did Beth remember the words to the poem that had always hung in the guest bathroom? Was she still suffering from that little bout of intestinal discomfort after her India trip? Did she think Jan ought to find a way to limit Jim Blevins's visits to the house? On and on.

The real reason for all the calls was, of course, Thomas Wood.

No matter how many times Beth repeated every detail of their few conversations, her mom wanted further clarification. How had Thomas looked when he said such and such? What was the exact wording when she told him this or that? Did he happen to mention so-and-so? Beth had decided this was the inevitable result of failing to end a relationship properly.

Which was why Miles Wilson was driving her crazy. Or rather, the absence of the man. Though it nearly killed her not to see him, she had decided against phoning Miles when she passed through London on her way home. He hadn't called her, and she felt it was his responsibility to remedy the situation. The fact was, she had to admit, he had turned out to be a boor, after all. A cad. A rogue. Awful! How could he have run off like that? Abandoning her in India, alone with her birth father for the first time. Unconscionable! She regretted ever calling him the first time. Why had she let the man into her life at all?

And Thomas Wood was no better. All that expense and effort to find a man who couldn't bother to show up and say goodbye to his own daughter. Beth had left Darjeeling without getting even a last glimpse of the man. And just as well. He clearly had gone into some kind of shell—hiding himself from pain and reality, trying to protect his "insulated life" just the way Jan had so many years before. They were two of a kind.

Fuming, Beth plopped down onto the sofa and reached for the phone. It rang just as her fingertips touched the receiver. She dropped her hand in her lap and stared at it. Did she really have the energy to talk to her mother? Did she really want to hear more questions about a man who obviously had no interest in the woman he had put out of his mind and the daughter who was too much trouble to deal with?

But what choice did Beth have? She couldn't very well cut off her mom and tell Jan to shut up, the way she had once before. With a sigh, she started to pick up the phone, but she had waited so long that the answering machine kicked on.

"Yeah, uh, this is Thomas Wood." The voice sounded

like it was in the next room. "From India. Darjeeling. Well, I just wanted to speak to Beth and say—"

She jammed the receiver to her ear. "Hello?"

"Oh, you're there." Silence. "Well, this is Thomas Wood, your . . . um . . . father. Birth father."

"Yes. Hi."

"Listen, Beth . . . I don't want to take up your time, but I did want to say I'm sorry I didn't make it over to the guesthouse before you left. That was wrong of me. I was . . . uh, still kind of reeling, I guess."

She picked up the pillow beside her and held it tight. "It's all right."

"I've done a lot of thinking and praying . . . I should have called you sooner."

"Really, it's okay."

"I want to tell you that I'm . . ." He went quiet for a moment. When he came on again, his voice was choked. "I'm thankful. I'm so thankful for you."

"Really?" She sounded squeaky and fragile, like a shy little girl.

"You're a gift I never expected. I don't deserve you. Not after what I did to your mother. How I behaved. The way I lived my life. And yet God brought you to me. It's . . . it's grace, you know? Unearned favor. God granted me grace, and I'm overwhelmed by it."

"I figured you might be thinking of me as the unfortunate consequence of sin, or something like that."

"Unfortunate?" He gave a low laugh. "Bethany Ann Lowell, you are the prettiest, sweetest, smartest, best daughter a man could hope for. I'm just having trouble believing that a man like me could have played any part in creating you."

By now, Beth was a puddle on the sofa, and she couldn't make herself say a single word. This was what she had ached to hear. This was what she had craved—this blessing, this affirmation. He didn't stop.

"I've been trying to think how I can make it up," Thomas said. "How can I get back the lost years? What can I do for you? I need some way to show you how grateful I am that you came to India to find me. Such a long distance. And the way you told me. It was just right, Beth. It was fine. The best possible situation to convey information like that. We already respected each other as fellow Christians. And we had enjoyed our dinner together. I just . . . well, that's all I've done for you. . . . All I did was pay for the meal. One meal. I wish I could do more. I guess you've already been to college."

"Yes. I got some scholarships. My parents helped with the rest, and I worked." Trying to sniffle down tears, she sounded like a drain unclogging. "Don't think about that, okay. Please? That's not why I wanted to meet you. I don't need anything like money or gifts. Just . . . a phone call now and then. Or a letter. Maybe when you have vacation time, we could meet some-where. And talk."

"I'd like that. I'll plan on it." He hesitated. "Do you think you might send me a photo or two? Maybe from when you were younger, and also one from now? I'd really like to show you off. I know Lawford met you and so did some of the Christians in the prayer group, but no one realized you were my daughter. People were focused on Miles, him being the owner and all. He's a wreck, by the way."

"Miles Wilson?"

"That's how I got your number. It was just what I told you. He got cold feet. Says he figured out during the prayer service that he wasn't worthy of you. Thinks he's a loser. *Boorish,* I think, is the word he used. He's struggling, but he's crazy in love with you. Can't say as I blame him. He'd be more than boorish to let you go—he'd be a fool. I told him that. He said he knew."

Beth kept wiping tears, and they kept flowing. "It's good to know why he left. But neither of you should put me on a pedestal. I'm not that great. Really. Just ask my mom. I've acted awful toward her, especially since all this came out. I've yelled at her, accused her, blamed her. I keep trying to figure out the Christ-like way to handle this, and I run into a wall. There's just no excuse for the secret she kept."

"Yeah, there is. You think about your mom, Beth. What kind of a girl is she? Jan is a homebody. She used to make me fresh lemonade. She could bake cobbler like nobody's business. And when she drew or painted, it was always the same thing. Roses. She loved Tyler and her family. She loved that old house where she grew up. She was created to be a wife and mother in a little house with a white picket fence and laundry drying on the line. I was a tornado that tore through her world and blew everything to pieces. I was just so different—wild and ornery. Each of us had a little bit of what the other was missing, and we fell in love. But it was a disaster waiting to happen."

"Me. I was what happened."

"Not you!" His voice grew harsh. "You'd better hear me say this, Beth. Your mother and I did a lot of wrong and foolish things in our relationship. But you—the child God allowed to be born—you are not a mistake. You are not a sin."

"I'm a sinner."

"But not because of Jan and me. Not because of how you came into existence. God permitted your existence. And you are a blessed gift."

Beth nodded, trying to stem the tears. "Mom says that, too."

"Good. Mom is wise. So . . . uh, how is she? Your mother."

"She's fine."

"Jan left Tyler? She moved to Lake Palestine?"

"Yes. She bought a little house and fixed it up. She planted roses."

He chuckled. "I could have guessed that. I . . . uh, I was wondering if she was happy. Did she have a good life? So far, I mean?"

"I think so. I don't know if she married my dad out of fear, or what, but they loved each other. They had a happy relationship."

"And you have two brothers?"

"Bob and Bill."

"Your mom . . . what did she say . . . what does she

think of me? Did you tell her you met me in Dar-jeeling? Did she say anything?"

Now this. Beth suddenly had to restrain herself to keep from laughing. She felt exactly like she had in the sixth grade while acting as a go-between for a timid girl and a bashful boy. *Does she like me? What did he say?* It was crazy!

Beth unfolded her legs from the sofa and stepped to the window. "I'll tell you the same thing I've been telling my mom," she said. "If you want to know about each other, why don't you talk? Call her. Here's her number."

After reading it to him, Beth glanced at the framed family portrait on the table beside the sofa. Jan and John Lowell sat surrounded by their three children: Beth, Bob and Bill. Did Beth really want her mother to talk to Thomas Wood again? What about her dad? John Lowell was dead, but would this reconnection violate his honor and his memory? He had been such a great father. And how would Bob and Bill feel if their sister let this stranger into their mother's life?

"Thanks," Thomas told Beth, "but I'll probably just call you now and then. Not that I'm upset with Jan for keeping her pregnancy from me. I think I'm past that. I understand the choice she made, and I've made peace with it. I'd just prefer to visit with you, and you can let me know how your mom is doing."

Beth rolled her eyes. More phone calls filled with questions about each other, no doubt. "All right. That's fine with me."

"Well, then, I guess I'll let you go," he said. "But Beth, I just wanted to . . . I learned a lot from Nirmala, you see. From her life and also from her death. I know not to take anything for granted. So, I want to say . . . right now before I hang up . . . I want to tell you that I love you."

Biting her lower lip, Beth let the words soak in. They filled her chest, ran like rivers down her arms and legs and lit her up with a glow of happiness that radiated warmth.

He loved her. Her father loved her!

"I'm glad," she said. Then she nodded. "I love you, too. And I'm proud to be your daughter."

Chapter Seventeen

Jan didn't know when she'd ever been so scared in all her life. Or so excited. She held Beth's hand as the taxi inched through traffic, regularly zipping forward and then coming to a screeching halt when another car pulled out in front or a pedestrian took a step into the street. New York City was a crazy place. Horns honking, sirens wailing, and people. Everywhere . . . people.

"Don't they get tired of each other?" she asked. Without meaning to, Jan had scooted across the taxi's back seat and was now sitting shoulder to shoulder with her daughter. "You'd think they would want to see more grass and trees. They're like ducklings, all headed in one direction, but there's no mama duck in sight."

Beth laughed. "How can you get tired of people when you never see the same one twice? And there's more grass in New York than tourists think. I'll take you to Central Park. It's enormous."

"I can't imagine a park in the middle of all these buildings. There must be so much shade. How can anything grow?"

"Mom! Now you're being silly."

"No, I'm not! Everything is choking here. And shadowy. Dirty, too, in a way. So crowded. It's really frightening, don't you think?"

"I think it's wonderful. People from all over the world live in the city. If you wanted, you could eat at a different restaurant every night for a year. I can't wait to take you to my church and let everyone meet you. You'll love our pastor. He's Nigerian."

"Nigerian?"

"New York is exciting all the time. There are plays, art exhibitions, musical events—"

"Don't even mention art exhibitions. Oh, Beth, I have no idea why I let you talk me into bringing my pictures here. Compared to what artists in New York must create, my little drawings will look primitive—as though a third grader did them."

Beth lifted her mother's hand and kissed the soft, pale skin. "We already know Harry Kellner likes the pictures well enough to ask for a closer look. He might have a manuscript in mind to go with them. And he wants to talk to you about some other concepts, too. So, you're not bringing your art in cold."

"But it's just children! Everyone can draw children, Beth!"

"No, Mom. Not everyone. Yours are different. Special."

"Oh, dear." Jan's stomach twisted into an even tighter knot. She couldn't see how her pictures were different or special or anything else! "Maybe it's not too late to cancel the meetings. We could go to the park instead. And I do want to see a Broadway play."

"You're here for a week. We'll have time for everything, including our appointments with Harry Kellner and the others."

The taxi swerved toward the curb and came to a sudden stop. The driver, who was clearly Middle Eastern in origin, turned around and hooked his arm over the back of the seat. Jan shivered. She'd been worrying about terrorists for two weeks, ever since Beth had coerced her into this harebrained idea of bringing the pastel chalk artwork to children's book publishers and greeting card companies in New York. Now here they were, two helpless women, in the very palm of an extremist who would probably try to rob them or kidnap them or something even more horrible.

Why had Jan ever permitted her daughter to show the pictures to a friend from church—a man who just happened to head the art department of a publishing company? Beth insisted God's hand was at work, but Jan knew it was just her nosy, assertive, interfering first-

294

born. The pastel chalk portraits of children were meant to hang in a frame in Jan's kitchen or by the front door, as had all the rose bouquets she had painted through the years. Not like this! Not packed into a leather portfolio and stashed inside a taxi driven by a man who was clearly the leader of a terrorist cell!

"Forgive me, I heard you speaking," he said as he hung over the seat, smiling at them from under his thick black mustache. "You are Christians?"

Before Jan could warn her daughter not to answer, Beth nodded cheerfully. "Yes," she said. "Are you?"

"I am. I was born in Argentina—Buenos Aires—and I have come to New York as a missionary. Of course, my job is to drive a taxi, but I do God's work during my free time."

A *missionary*. Jan would have dropped her teeth if they hadn't been attached.

Beth smiled as though this were the most ordinary announcement in the world. "Great!" she said. She handed the man a small card. "Here's where I go to church. We support a lot of missionary work through prayer."

"Prayer is what we need most. I am Pedro. *Peter,* you may call me. If your pastor agrees, I shall visit your church and ask for prayer. My ministry is with youth. My wife and I, along with some others, we have started an after-school recreation center. Thank you, *señorita.*"

He reached across the seat and shook Beth's hand.

"*Señora,*" he said.

Jan held her hand out tentatively. The man grabbed it

and gave a powerful shake. Then he stepped from the taxi and helped them unload the bags and the art portfolio. After Beth had paid their taxi-driving Argentine missionary, she steered Jan toward the front door of an apartment building. In moments, they were inside.

"Your pastor is a Nigerian?" Jan asked. "You never told me that. And how can that driver claim to be a missionary to people here in America? *We're* the ones who send missionaries to foreign lands."

"Missionaries and ministers are coming to the States from all over the world. We're one of the last major unchurched people groups in the world. Ironic, isn't it?"

"Beth, how can you call Americans unchurched? Our founding fathers—"

"Forget the founding fathers, Mom." Beth carried the portfolio and an overnight bag into an elevator that looked dangerously old. "I'm talking *now.* Think about the way Americans live. Most of our TV shows, movies, lifestyles are so ungodly. Even the behavior of some church leaders. People here are far from Christ and the teachings of the Bible, and they're moving farther away every day. Nowadays, some of the greatest Christian movements are in Asia, Africa, South America. And they're coming our way. Christ expects His followers to evangelize the world, and we need to get busy in the U.S. and Europe."

Jan hurried after Beth, shocked at the grime in the hallway and worried about the rickety elevator. How could her daughter live in a place like this? And what was her problem with the founding fathers? After a groaning, lurching ride up sixteen floors, the elevator doors opened, and the two women lugged the baggage down a narrow corridor.

Jan wanted to dispute her daughter's point of view, but she wasn't even sure what to say. How could Beth forget the way the United States had begun—founded by Christian men to become a Christian nation with a Christian constitution? It was all just too much. So confusing. Missionary taxi drivers and Nigerian pastors. What next?

"Oh!" Beth's gasp knocked her mother's heart clean out of whack.

"What on earth?" Jan cried. "Honey, what's wrong?"

"He's here."

A vision of Thomas Wood filled Jan's imagination, and she thought she was going to faint.

"He *is?*" she breathed out. "Where?"

"Here. In New York." Beth bent over a note that had been stuck to her door. "He sent this up with the doorman. Listen to this. 'I flew in last night. Had to see you. Must talk.'"

Jan dropped her purse to the floor and leaned back against the wall. This was unbelievable. She had barely found the courage to fly to New York, and now she was going to have to face Thomas Wood. What would she do? And say? And wear? How would it feel to see him again?

Her heartbeat steadied but began to pump heavily. Did she look all right? She had tried a new shade of hair color, Autumn Blaze, from an entirely different company—and to her surprise, it had turned out even more natural looking than Desert Sunset. Hard to imagine that something new could look better, but it did.

At least . . . she thought it did. Would Thomas think so? She'd had long hair the last time he saw her, and she was thin and young and oh, she'd been pregnant and such a mess!

"I can't believe this," Beth said, pushing open her door and scooting her mother's bags inside with her foot. "Why now? And without even telling me!"

"I can't imagine." Jan followed Beth into the small apartment and tried to absorb her surroundings along with the shocking news. "What could he want?"

"I have no idea. That's all he says. 'Had to see you. Must talk.'"

"Did you tell him I was coming? Maybe he wants to talk to me."

"To you?" Beth tossed the note onto a narrow counter that divided the kitchenette from the rest of the room. "Why would he want to talk to you, Mom? Oh, this is just absurd. We haven't been in contact for weeks."

Jan glanced at the note. "But you told me Thomas had called you several times. You said he asked about me."

At that moment, her eye fell on the signature. "Miles Wilson." She turned her head quickly, hoping her daughter couldn't see her startled expression or the

298

flush that was now spreading across her cheeks.

"The message is from Miles, Mom," Beth said.

"Oh, sure. I was thinking you meant . . . well, never mind." She took a step toward the seating area. "This is a cute apartment, honey. You've fixed it up so nice. And look at that window! I bet you get a lot of sunshine. I'm really surprised."

"Mother." Beth's voice held that familiar note. "You thought the note was from Thomas."

"Well, you didn't say who wrote it. We had a mix-up, that's all. But it's interesting that Miles has flown here to see you. I wonder what he wants . . . Is that a philodendron in the corner?"

"You were hoping it was him, weren't you?"

"Who? Thomas? I was having heart failure over the very idea of it. Imagine him seeing me after all these years, when I've changed so much. Perish the thought. But Miles . . . now, I must say that's a different story. You two have had quite a tumultuous long-distance relationship."

"You're not getting out of this so easily, Mom." Beth shook her finger at her mother. "You wanted to see Thomas. You were hoping he had come to New York!"

"Honestly, Beth, I—" A loud buzz filled the room, cutting her off. Thank goodness.

"Oh, no, what if that's him?" Beth's brown eyes darted from her mother to the door and back again. "Mom, I don't want to talk to Miles Wilson. He drives me crazy. I can't see him."

"Answer that buzzer, Bethany Ann," Jan commanded. "The poor man has come all the way from London, and you owe him the courtesy of a conversation."

Beth pressed the button by her door. "Yes?"

"Beth. It's Miles. May I . . . no, better, will you come down? Please. I must speak with you."

Jan waved encouragement at her daughter. "Invite him in. I want to meet this suitor of yours."

Beth's worried expression transformed into a sly smile. "Sure, Miles. But you come up. There's someone I'd like you to meet."

"That should put the fear of God into him, honey." Beth's mother settled onto the sofa by the window. "Miles will probably think you have a boyfriend up here."

"I hope he does. Serve him right for coming to New York without even a warning."

Beth couldn't stop herself from pacing back and forth as she waited for Miles to make the elevator journey to the sixteenth floor. Why had he come? He ought to have called first! She shouldn't be feeling this nervous. They had nothing in common, no relationship, not even regular communication. Maybe he was here for some other reason and thought he'd look her up. She could appear casual and unaffected, even though her palms were sweating and her mouth had dried out.

And look at her mother! Sitting over there like the Queen of Sheba! Jan was ready to inspect Miles as though he were an unusual beetle that had stopped to visit her prize rosebush—perhaps threatening to take a nibble of the queen rose in the rosebud garden of girls. . . .

Yet five minutes ago, Jan had been the one about to collapse. She had believed Thomas Wood was in New York. And Beth had no doubt about the meaning of that pink flush on her mother's cheeks. She had hoped to see him.

So Jan Lowell wanted to meet Thomas Wood again. And it was more than just curiosity that drew the two of them together. They had never really ended their love, had they? Beth recalled how Saint Paul had taught the Corinthians that if a man joined himself to a woman, they became one body. A single flesh. He had reminded believers of the teaching in Genesis that when a man leaves his father and is joined to his wife, the two are united into one.

Jan and Thomas were still joined, attached to each other by a thin cord, a filament so slender it was almost invisible. They'd hidden this thread from others and denied it to themselves. But it was there, and it was pulling them closer every minute. Beth could hardly believe this was all happening, but she couldn't deny it, either.

A knock at the door nailed her feet to the floor. Miles. Oh, why now? Why on this day of days, when she had finally managed to lure her mother to New York? When they needed to talk about Thomas and remember John Lowell and try to understand everything.

Beth didn't want to see Miles. She would tell him that. "Sorry, but I'm busy with my mom," she would say. "Get lost."

"Are you planning to answer the door?" Jan had cocked her head to one side like a parakeet. That's what she was, too, a bouncy little bird just waiting to produce some sort of pithy quotation or some pert observation about Miles.

"Beth, sweetie? Miles is knocking."

Deep breath. Shoulders back. Chin up. She would take care of this so she and her mother could get back to the real matter at hand.

Beth walked to the door and peered through the peephole. And there he was. Looking just like he always did. Too good. Too British. Too handsome.

She turned the knob and willed her mouth into a smile. "Miles. What a surprise."

He stepped inside the room, turned to her and took her shoulders in his hands. "Beth, please listen to me." His voice was raspy, forcing out the words. "I'm sorry to come to you like this without warning. Very improper. Highly irregular, I know. Malcolm urged me not to come, but I had to. Beth, I love you. I do. I've tried not to, but I simply cannot change what is true and right. I beg you not to think me mad.

"Since Darjeeling, I have been in absolute and utter agony. Let me say, before you throw me out, that I do realize I'm perfectly wrong for you. I don't deserve you, I could never deserve you and moreover, I am quite convinced I shall never have you. But nothing can be done about the fact that I must try to convince you to love me in return.

"Now, if I were you, trust me, I'd run in the opposite direction as quickly as I could. Knowing myself as I do, I can honestly tell you that any woman in her right mind—as you obviously are—would be a fool to seriously care the slightest whit about me. I fancy myself dashing and charming. But I am actually nothing. Nothing but rot. A dustbin full of rot. I know this, I see it, I admit it.

"I'm determined to change myself, but at this precise moment, I've not accomplished it. I believe change has something to do with God and morality and Bible reading and several other important issues, which are unfortunately rather vague to me. But this realization of my need to change is why, dearest Beth, I left you alone in Darjeeling—a wrong and boorish thing to do. I apologize, and I mean to make amends if you'll allow it. But I must say that as desperately as I do love you and wish to transform myself into a man worthy of your affection and admiration—"

"Enough!" Beth covered his mouth with her hand. "Stop talking, Miles. You make me crazy."

"Darling, please give me one chance." He took both her hands in his. "I love you. Love can alter a man, no matter how far off the mark he may be. Thomas tells me God must do the changing, which I am fully willing to allow. In fact, I—"

"Wait." Beth held up a hand. "Thomas Wood told you to change? *My* Thomas Wood?"

"We speak regularly by phone, and he does have excellent advice—though I fear my ability to follow it is limited. But please, you must permit me to try to win you, Beth. Can you do that?"

She gave a groan of exasperation. "Miles, turn around and meet my mother." With a shove on one shoulder, she pivoted him toward the window. "Mom, this madman from England is Miles Wilson. Miles, this is my mother, Jan Lowell."

Beth watched as her mother rose from the sofa and fairly glided across the floor. "Miles." She held out her hand. "So pleased to meet Beth's young man. My daughter has told me a great deal about you."

"No, I haven't. Mom!"

Jan smiled at her daughter. "You didn't mention that Miles was so passionate."

"I beg your pardon, Mrs. Lowell. The previous conversation . . . it was intended for Beth."

"I could tell." Jan gestured toward the sofa. "Won't you sit down, Miles? I believe Beth told me she had made some fresh lemonade for my visit. Maybe she'll remember her manners and pour us each a glass."

Beth watched as her mother led Miles across the room. This was not supposed to happen! Why was her mom suddenly acting like a Southern belle? Why was Miles blurting out long speeches that made no sense? Had she remembered to put sugar in the lemonade?

From behind the kitchen counter, Beth watched as her mother chatted with Miles Wilson. They might as well be on some porch in Texas the way the woman smiled and tilted her head and said interesting things in her honeyed Southern accent. In the past ten minutes, Miles had gone from impassioned to stunned to utterly beguiled. As Beth stirred ice into the pitcher, she could see the man relax, stretching out across the chair like a panther on a tree limb, gesturing as he shared some fascinating detail with her mother.

Great. The pair of them had charmed the socks off each other immediately. No doubt Jan would insist that Miles go out to dinner with them. And Miles would want to hear all about Beth's plans for her mother's artwork. He would admire the pastel chalk children and say amusing British things, which would tickle Jan pink. Before long, they would be the best of chums, and Beth would have to figure a way to pry Miles loose so she could kick him out the door and back to London.

As she set three glasses on a tray, Beth thought about his speech to her at the door. Let's see. He loved her. He wasn't worthy of her. He wanted to change. He thought God was the answer, but he hadn't figured out how. He'd been talking regularly to Thomas Wood.

Now that last part was really annoying! Beth had finally found Thomas, and he belonged to her. What right did Miles have to ask him for advice? Thomas's loyalties were supposed to lie with his daughter, not with this upstart . . . dashing . . . crazy . . . adorable . . .

"Lemonade," she announced, grabbing the tray and nearly slinging the glasses to the floor as she rounded the counter and headed for the coffee table in front of the sofa. "Freshly squeezed lemons, cold water, ice, lots of sugar. And a twist."

"What?" Jan's head shot up in surprise. "What have you done to my lemonade?"

"Made it mine." She set the tray on the low table. "Taste it."

Her mother gingerly took a glass and sipped. "Mint!" she exclaimed. "Fresh mint! I never thought the old recipe could get any better, but here you are, sweetheart . . . tinkering with it. Miles, try some. You won't believe how good it is."

Beth settled onto the sofa beside her mother as Miles drank long and deep. When he had drained the glass, he set it on the tray, let out a breath and pronounced, "Excellent."

Jan laughed. "Well, Beth, you've won him over. And me, too. I'll put mint in my next batch. Jim Blevins will wonder what's come over me."

"How is Jim?" Beth asked.

"Shocked to pieces that I would fly all the way to New York to see you. He didn't think I had it in me. But he's quite a few years older, you know. I'm only forty-five. A woman my age has a lot of life left."

"That's why you came, Mrs. Lowell?" Miles inquired. "You're ready to start living again? Phase Two, so to speak?"

Beth glanced at her mother in alarm. But Jan was still smiling. "It's my daughter's fault," she said. "I was ready to settle into my cocoon and never come out. I'd raised my children, worked long enough to retire, enjoyed a happy marriage and buried my husband. It may sound crazy, but I figured I was next, and it was just a matter of waiting around."

"Then Beth discovered the tea set," Miles stated. "And that brought you back to life."

"Oh, no. Not the tea set. It was Beth and her faith. She kept quoting the Bible to me and reminding me of this and that about the Christian life. My daughter can be very persistent. You ought to be made aware of that if you're so sure you're in love with her. Beth just kept challenging me."

"Making you feel as if you needed to get back in the race, eh?"

"Get *back* in the race? I've been watching from the sidelines most of my life. I'm a Christian, and I believe all the right things. But I never thought about actually having any responsibility to God other than raising a good family and being a moral person. I wanted to do *my* will—which was to be safely tucked away in Tyler, Texas, with my own little family and my own little life until Saint Peter called me to the pearly gates. Then my daughter started living her life in front of me. . . ."

"She did that to me, too," Miles said. "It's why I adore her."

Beth took a quick drink of lemonade. This was strange. Unnerving. She'd merely been doing what she thought all believers ought to do—and, in truth, she hadn't been particularly good at it. Yelling at her mother. Stressed out about work. Unsettled and nervous every time she so much as thought of Miles Wilson. Christians were supposed to bear the fruit of the Holy Spirit—love, patience, gentleness, long-suffering . . . Not shouting, floundering, worrying . . .

"Your daughter makes me want to change, Mrs. Lowell," Miles was saying. "I can't go on living the way I was. But I'm not quite certain what sort of man I'm to be."

"Neither am I. I haven't found the blueprint for Phase Two. And please call me Jan."

"Let's ask Beth, shall we?" Miles said. He turned his blue eyes on her. "You've told us that Christians are meant to become new creatures in Christ. We're to change. How?"

"Well, for pity's sake, don't look at me!" Beth exclaimed, rising to her feet and pacing toward the wall where the Murphy bed was hidden behind a panel. "I don't know how to change anyone. That's the job of the Holy Spirit. You're supposed to read the Bible and try to pattern your life after Christ. That's what I do, and I'm pretty horrible at it, actually, so I wish the two of you would quit using me as your example of Christian perfection. I'm just a regular person—"

"No, you're not," Jan said.

"You glow." Miles was nodding as he spoke. "I heard it in your voice in the Nairobi Airport, and then I saw it on your face."

"I'm glowing right now, because I really do wish that both of you would just . . . just . . ."

The phone rang, and Beth could have kissed it. She

308

excused herself and grabbed the receiver. "Beth Lowell," she said.

"Beth, it's Joe. Something's come up at work."

"I'm off this week, Joe. Remember? My mom is here from Texas. We're going to do the sights and try to market her artwork. I told you that. If there's a problem, talk to Sean. I've trained him, and I'm confident that he's capable of handling things there until I get back."

"It's Congo, Beth."

"What about it?"

"Haven't you seen the news? There's an uprising in the works. Maybe a full-fledged coup. It's looking like Kinshasa may go down in the next few days. The U.S. government is moving all its people out, and companies we worked with in the past have been calling us night and day for the last forty-eight hours. They want to try to transfer as much employee property out of the capital as they can, but they're even more concerned about moving personnel. Some companies are sending people to Kenya, and others are trying to put them in Europe to wait it out. That toothpaste factory we worked with wants to send their top dogs to Uganda."

"Uganda? So, what are these companies needing from us—the names of hotels?" Beth grabbed her black leather bag from its usual place by the sofa and opened the clasps. She slid her computer onto her lap and brought it to life. "How many people are we talking about moving, Joe? And why do they want us?"

"They want *you*. You moved a lot of these families safely into place in Congo, and now they want you to get them safely out."

"I can't move people out of a country in the middle of a coup. That's not even close to my job description, Joe."

"We'll take care of the transportation end. You just find clean, safe, comfortable places for us to put them."

"Kenya's best hotels are going to cost a fortune." She pressed a few keys and pulled up a screen. "In Uganda, I can't guarantee the quality. Which countries in Europe do they want to use? If the unrest runs into the start of the school year, it's going to really mess up the children. These companies can't just toss kids around from one country to another."

"Well, they certainly can't leave them in Congo to get shot at with AK47s. If they fly everyone to the States and the coup fizzles out, then the companies have to bear the cost of getting their people back in place again. And you know how these uprisings work. The deal could blow up and then be over, and things could be stable again in a month."

"All right, I'll be at the office in twenty minutes. What can I . . ." Beth lifted her head to find her mother and Miles Wilson staring at her.

Chapter Eighteen

Jan didn't know when she'd ever had so much fun. She and Miles were headed up the elevator to Beth's apartment when the realization hit. She loved New York!

"What's so amusing?" he asked as she unsuccessfully stifled a laugh.

"Me. I used to think I was old. I thought I was shy. I thought I was scared to try new things."

"You?" He grinned. "I've never met anyone quite so adventurous. You've taken the city by storm."

"I wouldn't go that far."

"The Empire State Building, the Metropolitan Museum of Art, Central Park and shopping . . . lots of shopping . . . all in one day. I'm exhausted."

A giggle welled up inside Jan as the elevator door opened and she thought of the past four days. She'd seen so many things! Done so much! Met hundreds of people! It felt like hundreds, anyway. The only downside to the visit had been the absence of her daughter.

Poor Beth had been forced back into her office to deal with the Congo crisis. She joined Miles and Jan whenever she could, and the visits to publishers and card companies had gone much better than anyone expected. In fact, Jan wouldn't be surprised if one of these days she got a phone call from someone asking her to illustrate a book. Or maybe they would even want to purchase the art she already had completed.

Who would have thought? A second career. A whole new life. Phase Two.

Newness, joy and giddy elation seemed to come bubbling up and out of Jan all the time. Miles said he felt happier than he had in years. Mainly it was because Beth hadn't yet thrown him out, he claimed. But Jan thought there was something more.

She and her daughter's young admirer had become good friends. Confidantes. Coconspirators. Jan was certain she could tell Miles almost anything. He had openly confessed his love for Beth—and his certainty that nothing could come of it. He talked of his past, the breakup of his parents' marriage, his relationship with his brother, the importance of his work in the tea company. But more than anything, he and Jan simply had fun exploring the city together.

"I'll see you safely inside," Miles said as the elevator doors opened and they stepped out into the corridor. "Then I'll pop back to my hotel, have a bath and be ready to escort Beth to dinner when she comes home. You sure you won't join us?"

"Absolutely. You're going to have a serious talk with her, remember? You're going to tell her exactly how you feel—this time without the theatrics." Jan sighed as she unlocked the apartment door. "Besides, I'm bushed. I could fall asleep on my feet."

"Now that's something I'd like to see." Miles waited as Jan went inside, then he elbowed his way through the door. Loaded down with boxes and bags, he had become her personal packhorse. Though she hated to spend so much money, it was hard to resist the art shops filled with wonderful supplies. She certainly wouldn't find such a large selection of pastel chalks anywhere in Tyler. And she had bought a set of oil paints, too, just to give them a try. Maybe she was the next Mary Cassatt. Why not?

"Have a look at this," Miles said from the kitchenette counter. "Beth must have come home for lunch. She's left us a note."

"Read it to me." Jan sagged into the overstuffed chair by the sofa, shook off her shoes and propped her feet on the coffee table.

" 'Dear Mom and Miles,' " he read. " 'Thomas called from India this morning. He has decided to take some time off next week, and he wants me to meet him. Since I've lost most of this vacation to the Congo problem, Joe is giving me a break. Thomas has booked us a couple of rooms at a bed-and-breakfast in London. He said he'd like to see Miles. Thought I'd let Twee-dledum and Tweedledee put their heads together and think on this before I get home. Love, Beth.' "

Miles set the note back on the countertop and looked at Jan. "Tweedledum and Tweedledee? Is that you and me?"

She shrugged. "I guess so."

"Not sure I fancy being Tweedledum."

"Just exactly why are they meeting *now?*" Jan demanded, surging up from the chair in a burst of energy. "So soon after Darjeeling. It sounds like

313

Thomas is pushing her. He wants Beth to spend her free time with him instead of with me. We've hardly seen her this week, and off she goes to London!"

"My dear Jan, Beth isn't choosing Thomas over you," Miles assured her. "He has some holiday time, and he wants to see his daughter. That's reasonable."

"Why London? Why doesn't he come to New York, if he wants to see Beth so badly? He's never done a thing for the child, and now he's making her fly all the way across the Atlantic again. It's not fair. That man is so self-centered! Look at me—I came to New York, didn't I? I saw Beth's apartment and her office. I wanted to be part of my daughter's life and experience her world. But Thomas—he expects Beth to bend to his wishes, and you know what? That's how he always was. He didn't care . . . he was so . . . oh, I don't know, I wish he would just leave us alone, stop interfering—"

She covered her eyes with her hands and turned to the window. No, she would not cry. Not on this day, after so much fun, and with sacks full of pastels and oil paints, and visions of Van Gogh, Picasso and Renoir floating in her head. . . .

"Mrs. Lowell—Jan," Miles said. "Beth adores you. She knows you love her, and you gave her a wonderful childhood. But now you need to grant her permission to spend time with the man who helped to create her."

"The only thing Thomas Wood contributed was his DNA!" Jan snapped. Then her shoulders sagged. "No, that's wrong. I didn't let him know about the baby, so how could he do anything for her? It's all my fault. If Beth wants Thomas, how can I blame her? How can I blame him?"

"Do you feel betrayed?"

Jan rested her head on the cool glass windowpane. "I guess I do. But I'm not sure why."

"What would Beth tell us to do about these obstacles in our path? You and Thomas and your unsettled past. My impossible love for an unreachable woman." He laid a hand on Jan's shoulder. "What would that glowing light say to Tweedledum and Tweedledee?"

She wiped her damp cheeks. "Some Bible verse, no doubt."

He stepped away, sat down on the sofa and patted the chair across from it. "Beth would tell us to run the race that is set before us. She would encourage us to forgive those who've hurt us and embrace God."

"I'm pretty sure I forgave Thomas years ago, but I'm not sure he can ever forgive me for what I did to him. And I have no idea how to forgive myself."

"Nor do I," Miles said. "And the Lord knows I need forgiveness."

Jan settled back down on the chair. "So do I. Not Thomas. Certainly not Beth. I'm the offender. I gave myself to a man who wasn't my husband. I kept his child a secret. I hid the truth from everyone. I even made Thomas's own parents deceive him."

"You're a spotless lily compared to me," Miles said. "It's a wonder I'm alive, honestly. Endless women. Drunken parties. Drugs. Please don't look so shocked.

I told you about the treatment center, didn't I?"

"No," Jan sniffled, "but how are we so different? I was awful to Thomas. You were awful to yourself."

"What did Beth tell us last night at dinner? Our bodies are meant to be a temple?"

"The temple of the Holy Spirit." Jan hung her head. "Our pastor used to preach about it. If you're a Christian, then God's Holy Spirit lives inside you. Your body is like a temple or a church. It's a wonderful thought—one you wish you had realized the truth of before you defiled yourself."

"Amen." Miles dropped his head back on the sofa cushion and stared at the ceiling. "Do you suppose God can really forgive people? Do you think He can actually absolve us of our past?"

"Yes. I believe that He can, and He will."

"So do I."

"But I should apologize to Thomas first." Jan wove her fingers together and squeezed. "That's what I need to do. I can't ask God to forgive me until Thomas has."

"By that argument, I've got to locate and apologize to all the women and half the men I ever knew."

She blew out a breath. "Never mind making amends with everyone. It's humanly impossible to fix everything with each person we've hurt."

"Then we have no choice but to accept the consequences."

"On earth, yes. But not for eternity. We should go straight to God and ask His forgiveness for our wrong

316

behavior. If He pardons us, and people see that we've changed, maybe they can forgive us, too. The main thing is to repent—to turn away from sin. That's what Christians do."

Miles grimaced. "I'm not certain I'm a Christian, actually. Not in the sense that Beth means it."

"I'm a Christian, but you'd hardly know it. Either way, Miles, we have to repent. Then, you need to become a Christian, and I need to have a . . . oh, what did they always call it during church revivals? A recommitment. I need to recommit my life to Christ. I used to roll my eyes when people went down the aisle at church. Someone was always getting saved or recommitting their life. But that's it, really. It's what we ought to do."

"Then let's get on with it."

Jan looked across at him . . . such a sweet young man with such nice blue eyes. And so in love with her daughter. What did Jan know about helping Miles become a Christian? Look at her, for pity's sake. She was a mess. A scheming, selfish, lying, heartless creature who probably couldn't even find John 3:16 if she had a Bible with her, which she didn't.

Miles was staring at her. "Is it a ceremony? Do we need to go to church?"

"I think you can repent anywhere. Jesus forgave the thief who was being crucified on the cross next to His."

"We might kneel," Miles suggested.

In unison, they got down on their knees. Jan edged over until she was beside Miles at the sofa. They folded their hands, bent their heads and closed their eyes.

"I shall begin." Miles's voice was strong. "I've heard Beth pray, and I believe I can do it. This is something I've been wanting . . . and needing . . . to do for a very long time."

"All right," Jan said. "Go ahead."

"Dear God. Our Father which art in heaven." He paused. "Well, that's not off to a very good start."

"You're doing all right." Jan elbowed him. "Keep going."

"Dear God," he said, "this is Miles Wilson, president of the international division of Wilson Teas, Ltd. But I'm sure You knew that. Yes, of course You did. At any rate, I'm here this afternoon with Beth's mother, recalling my past exploits, most of which were despicable. I admit that I was . . . and am still . . . among the most vile of human beings. I have used people. Women, in particular. I have also badly mistreated my body, which You gave me. In fact, dear God, I am wholly and completely flawed. I can't think how to make up for it. There's nothing I can do to repair the damage I've done to myself and to others. I've botched my life. I most certainly don't deserve Your love or Your acceptance. I know very well that You came to earth on behalf of people like me. And You sacrificed Yourself. And I am . . . unworthy of that gift. I beg You to forgive me for everything I've done, even though I know I can't right my wrongs. I ask You to please accept me as I am and convert me . . . transform me . . .

change me completely into a new man. I want to be a Christian. I want to glow. Thank you. Amen."

Jan swallowed. "I want to glow, too, Father," she whispered. "I'm a baby Christian. I never grew up. My own daughter is older and wiser in her faith than I can ever hope to be. Thank You for Beth, Lord. Thank You for Miles. Father, I know You forgave him, and I pray that You'll forgive me, too. I was wrong to defile my body, Your church. I was wrong to deceive Thomas. And Beth. I know I hurt John, too, in so many ways. And Nanny. I'm powerless to fix any of it, dear God, and I admit that I need You so much. Please forgive me. Please take charge of my life and transform me into a new and better woman. I want to live Phase Two for You. I ask all this in the name of Jesus Christ, my Lord and Savior. Amen."

Unaware of the elapsing time, Jan knelt beside Miles and continued to pour out her heart to God in silence. Every sin she could remember, she confessed. Little white lies. Angry outbursts that had hurt her family. Deceptions. And especially the mess she had made of the situation with Thomas and Beth.

As she prayed, she could hear Miles beside her, sniffling. She put her arm around his shoulders. Then she handed him a tissue from her purse. This was a good man. Better than most. He had looked himself in the face and seen who he really was—unvarnished. Miles had built a facade with his charm and his wealth and his position, just as she had built one with her rose gardens, lemonade and perfect family. But he knew the truth about himself, as did she. God knew, too, and somehow in Beth's tiny studio apartment, He had descended and filled two repentant hearts with Himself.

"We ought to do something," Miles murmured. He lifted his head. "Something to prove it."

Jan pushed herself up onto the sofa and rubbed her knees. "What do you mean?"

"A step of faith." He stood and walked to the window. "I have to prove that I'm a Christian. You have to show that you've recommitted yourself to God. If we don't do something, no one will know."

"They'll see the difference in us. In how we act and what we say. Beth shows she's a Christian by carrying her Bible with her, by using Scripture as the filter for right and wrong, by acting so moral that . . . well, it's a wonder anyone likes her."

"I love her. It's her morality that drew me to her. She made me want to change, because I saw myself in her eyes."

"Well, I don't have any idea how to prove I've changed," Jan said. "I'll just have to do what Beth does and immerse myself in God."

"You've got to go to India and speak to Thomas."

Jan gaped at the young man who had begun pacing back and forth across the same floor Beth had paced a few days before.

"Go to India?" She shook her head. "That's not the kind of change God asks of us. Christians don't have to go traveling across the world just to prove they're new people, Miles."

"But *you* do. Beth and I shall go with you. The time together will give her the chance to see the difference in me. And God will heal your rift with Thomas. It can only be a good thing."

"No, it can only be a *bad* thing!" Jan rose and hugged her stomach. "I don't want to go to India."

"Yes, you do. You've just told God that you want to restore every broken thing in your life, and this is how you must do it. Do you suppose I really want to face the ridicule of my brother and all our friends and associates? What will they say when I tell them I've given my life to God, and I mean to behave in every way as a Christian? They'll think I'm mad. They'll do everything in their power to lure me back into my old ways. And why shouldn't they? I was the perfect companion. I won't be that anymore, and they won't like it. If I can prove to Beth that I'm a new man, I shall be ready to face my brother. If you can make amends with Thomas, you'll show your daughter that you've changed, too. We'll prove our faith not only to others and to God—but to ourselves."

Jan pursed her lips together. This was much more than she had anticipated. She had intended to go back to her little house on Lake Palestine and bake a cherry cobbler for Jim Blevins. She would read her Bible every day and pray more faithfully, and maybe even think up a ministry she could volunteer to undertake.

But a trip to India? That was extreme. She studied Miles. His blue eyes burned.

"I'm going to win Beth," he said. "I'll show her who I can be."

"Don't base your Christian faith on Beth. She's a human—believe me. She'll disappoint you. After you've known her a while, you'll see how flawed she is."

"I'm not a Christian for Beth. This is for me. But Beth is the one who showed me the path. I watched her run, and I wanted to run, too. Now I have to show her I'm in the race. Come on, Jan, let's go to India."

"But Thomas and Beth are meeting in London. Maybe we could go there."

Jan couldn't believe she had just said that. She didn't want to fly across the ocean! She surely didn't want to talk to Thomas!

"Darjeeling." Miles was adamant. "You must meet Thomas on his own ground. You have to completely rid yourself of every need for safety and throw yourself into God's arms. That way you'll prove you trust Him."

"And you? You get to trot along wooing my daughter while I have to face the worst thing that ever happened to me?"

"Has any man ever won Beth's heart, Mrs. Lowell?"

"No."

"Then I'm heading into a battle as fierce as yours. What do you say, then? Comrades in arms?"

Jan smiled reluctantly. "Tweedledum and Tweedledee."

"We talked the toothpaste people out of sending their

employees to Uganda. I consider that a major victory. Uganda's a beautiful country, and there are some good hotels, but I really wanted the children to feel safe. Botswana has turned out to be perfect."

Beth scooped up the last spoonful of chocolate mousse and popped it into her mouth. The dinner had been fabulous, and both her mother and Miles were in high spirits. They had regaled Beth with the details of their outing into the city that day. Jan actually giggled a few times during the account of the shopping expedition, so Beth knew her mom was having fun. Though it had been terribly disappointing to be called into the office because of the Congo crisis, she was grateful for Miles.

More than grateful. He and Jan got along well, and he had shown himself to be a true gentleman. Every time the three of them were together, Beth realized that she liked Miles more and more. He was not only handsome and smart and witty. He had something else. An earnest quality. A sincerity she rarely saw these days.

Miles was fascinated with her work, and he drew her out on details that others might have found boring. His international background made him a perfect fit with her own interests. When Beth remarked, "I'm concerned that one of the children we're bringing out of Congo may have contracted bilharzia," Miles replied, "The Hospital for Tropical Diseases in London is an excellent place to find treatment for schistosomiasis and other such diseases. I've been there twice for malaria." How often had something like that happened? Never.

If she could trust her emotions—which she had never done successfully—Beth might even say she was falling in love with Miles. All the signs were there. She couldn't stop thinking about him. She wanted to be with him when they were apart. He amused and intrigued and delighted her.

But when they spent time together, there always seemed to be something missing. The thought of Miles taking her into his arms and kissing her brought a warmth surging through Beth's heart. On the other hand, the idea of spending her life with him was impossible. They lived an ocean apart. Though he was coming to share her faith, she believed there were still vast differences in their values and dreams. Yet she couldn't imagine a time when this man would be absent from her life.

Jovially unaware of her mental struggles, Miles was now urging Beth to tell them how she had managed her part of the situation in Congo. "Every American we were responsible for is out of the country," she told him, "except a family who refused to leave without their dogs. With the government in a mess, I couldn't get the paperwork to transport the animals quickly and safely out of Congo and into another country. I did everything in my power to persuade the owners to leave the dogs with their household staff. They wouldn't hear of it."

"A man and his dog are not soon parted," Miles said.

Jan laughed. "Unlike a fool and his money."

"You parted with quite a bit of money today, Jan, my dear. What shall we deduce about you?"

His smirk tickled Beth and sent her mother into another round of giggles. Despite the conflict in her heart, Beth could honestly say that for this single moment she felt truly at peace. Her business crisis was now under control. The meal she had just eaten was delicious. Jan seemed happier than Beth could remember. And Miles . . . Miles was simply . . . wonderful.

"Well," he said, setting his palms firmly on the table. "It's time for an announcement, Miss Bethany Ann Lowell."

"A surprise?" She rubbed her hands together. "Did you get orchestra-level tickets for a Broadway show?"

"Oh, much better than that," he answered. "We're going to Darjeeling."

Beth clamped her mouth shut. What could he mean? Darjeeling? She glanced at her mother, who had gone completely white.

"Sweetheart, I've decided to talk to Thomas," Jan said in a low voice. "In person. In India."

For some reason, Beth still couldn't speak. She had barely managed to get her mother to visit New York. Only after Beth had made several appointments with publishing house art departments had Jan nervously agreed to make the trip. How could it be possible that the queen rose of the rosebud garden of girls would step out of her safe haven and fly away to India? It wasn't possible. This had to be a joke.

"We're all going together." Miles spoke up. "My brother has reluctantly agreed to allow me another week away from the London office as long as I go to our Kenya estate directly afterward. You already have permission from your employer to have a holiday next week. And we have told Thomas about the change in plan. He's delighted."

"Not about me," Jan put in quickly. "Miles didn't tell him that part yet. We've been trying to decide whether it's better to let him know beforehand or not. As you remember, he ran off and left you the minute you broke your news." Her mouth gave a little twist of disgust. "Typical of Thomas. Always ready to bolt. But anyway, he did call and make it up to you. So, we might tell him now to get the shock over with, but we might not tell him."

"Another secret?" Beth heard the sarcasm in her own voice. "I'm sure Thomas will appreciate that."

"Beth, do you object to going back to India?" Miles asked. "If you do, we'll meet Thomas in London. But I think your mum ought to go to Darjeeling."

Beth turned on him. "Why? Why is she going anywhere? My mother doesn't go to India. She's from Texas. What have you done to her, Miles?"

"It wasn't Miles, honey," Jan said softly, laying a hand over her daughter's clenched fist. "It was you. Your life showed me that something was missing in mine. I needed to welcome God back onto the throne. I needed to let Him be in charge. This afternoon, Miles and I . . . well, we prayed together, and now . . ." She shrugged.

Stunned, Beth studied first her mother and then the man beside her. "Now what? I don't understand what you're saying."

"I am now a Christian," Miles informed her, as if he had just joined a new country club. "You need to know that my life is going to change radically."

"And I recommitted myself to Christ," Jan said. "We did it together. After discussing our lives during all these days together, Miles and I realized we just didn't want to go on being the same people we had been before. And we also decided . . . actually, Miles suggested, and I agreed . . . that it's past time for me to talk to Thomas. And to prove I'm a new woman, I'm going to India to do just that. Miles is coming, too."

"What's he proving?" Beth asked.

Her mother and Miles glanced at each other.

"Dear Beth," he said. "I'm going to conquer your heart."

Chapter Nineteen

Jan perched on the edge of the bed in the little guest-house and tried to collect herself. Back in New York, Beth had pulled some strings and gotten her mother a passport in record time. Beth's frequent flier miles had covered costs for both of them. And so it was done.

Somehow Jan had made it from Texas to New York.

She had survived eight hours in the air to London. She had managed to endure a marathon journey to Calcutta. A bumpy flight to some small Indian town with an unpronounceable name. And a three-hour ride up a muddy road into the highest mountains in the world. But all of that was easy.

Now she had to meet Thomas.

They had decided to tell him. Miles broke the news over the phone before they left New York. Beth wept as her birth father asked to speak to her and told her it was all right. Jan had sat mute on the sofa and wondered what on earth she was doing.

Now they were here, and Beth was fussing with her hair in the bathroom. Miles had gone to the estate office to talk to Mr. Lawford, and then he would return to pick up the women for dinner. Thomas was to join them.

Jan had expected to feel nineteen again at the thought of seeing the man she once had loved so intensely. Instead, she felt every bit forty-five years old, with dyed hair and a soft tummy and crow's-feet at the corners of her eyes. Her dress was too tight. Her feet were swollen. Her nail polish had chipped. Her roots were showing.

She was not different. Recommitting her life to Christ hadn't changed a thing. Flying to India hadn't altered her in the least. She was still just Jan Lowell who painted roses and children, who had taught school and given birth to three babies and made chicken salad at least once a week. She still felt worries and fears.

She still got annoyed with her daughter. And coming to meet Thomas was a really dumb idea.

"Silver or gold, Mom?" Beth called from the bathroom. "With this blue dress, what do you think?"

She stuck her head out into the room where a pair of single beds would provide their only respite for the next four days. Beth held up a gold stud earring in one hand and a silver dangler in the other. Jan stared at them, unable to make herself see much difference.

"Silver," she said finally.

"This is exciting!" Beth's brown eyes sparkled. "I can't believe it! I'm going to see the two of you together. I know this doesn't negate Dad, okay? Dad was Dad, and nothing can change that. I'll love him forever, and he'll always be my daddy and I'll always be his Bethy-boo. But this is awesome! It'll be fun!"

Fun?

Jan's eyes felt like sandpaper. Beth said it was jet lag. Those jets hadn't lagged. They had hurtled her halfway around the globe and left her feeling like something a dog had dug up in the backyard.

Miles knocked on the door and Jan caught her breath. So, it was time. They would walk over to the estate's main dining hall, and there he would be. Thomas.

"Can you get the door, Mom?" Beth called. "I have to brush my teeth. Do you really think Miles will like this dress?"

"He'll love it."

He loves you, Jan wanted to say. *It doesn't matter what you're wearing.* She pushed herself up from the bed and forced her feet to the door. It had been strange to watch her daughter and Miles during their long trip. The two of them talked nonstop. Beth cast shy glances at Miles. He poked her ribs or twiddled with her hair or lightly kissed her cheek. When he teased her, she tee-heed like a schoolgirl. Whether she knew it or not, Beth was in love.

Jan tugged on the door handle. "She's not quite ready, Miles."

Thomas Wood stood on the veranda. He had shaggy brown hair streaked with gray. And crow's-feet. And the same brown eyes into which she had fallen so many years before.

"Hello, Jan," he said.

Her heartbeat sounded like a locomotive in a tunnel. "Oh, Thomas. Hi."

He cracked a smile. "All these years."

She looked down. "Twenty-five."

"And you're still beautiful."

"I dye my hair," she blurted out.

"Same color I remember."

"Do you think so? Autumn Blaze. It's new actually."

"You look just like you always did."

That couldn't be true. Could it? Jan tried to think of something to say to keep the dam of emotion welling up inside her from bursting wide open. "You haven't changed much."

He shrugged. "More than you might imagine."

"Beth told me about you. About your job. Your wife."

"She told me about you, too. That you stayed in Tyler."

"I thought you had drowned in the tidal wave that hit Sri Lanka."

He shook his head. "I was surprised you looked for me."

"I always cared what happened to you, Thomas." Before he could see how she felt, she stepped past him onto the veranda. The rain had stopped, and the sun was spreading wreaths of gold and pink across the blue sky.

Jan wrapped her hands around the bamboo rail that edged the veranda. Thomas had joined her, his muscular shoulder just an inch from hers. How could it be that she had let him leave? Yet how could they ever have survived the tumult of the life that would have awaited them?

Closing her eyes, Jan lifted up a prayer. She wanted God's presence. She ached for Him. More than anything, in this moment, she needed her Lord.

Might she have just a small measure of the courage and strength He had displayed going to the cross? Might He fill her with His Holy Spirit and grant her the right words to say to this one she had hurt so badly? As she prayed, Jan sensed the shadow of wings falling over her, and a peace flooded her heart.

"Thomas," she said, turning to the man beside her, "I came to India to tell you how sorry I am. Please forgive me. I let you leave and didn't say anything about the baby. I made everyone keep Beth a secret from you. It was wrong, and I'm very sorry."

He leaned forward, his face to the mountains. "Why, Jan? I can't understand why you did it. You knew I loved you."

"I was selfish. I was scared. You had said you wanted to go, and no matter how much I begged you to stay in Texas with me, you wouldn't. I didn't want to use my pregnancy to keep you. So I hid it. I was angry, and I decided to punish you by keeping our daughter's existence a secret."

"I would have married you. I would have taken care of you. And the baby."

"I know. But you would have stayed in Tyler and grown roses and been miserable. I didn't want to keep you out of obligation. I wanted you to stay because you loved me. And you wouldn't do that."

He pressed his hands down on the railing. "Jan, I'm sorry. If I'd known . . . if it had ever occurred to me that you were pregnant . . . Why was I so stupid? So blind?"

"We both were. We were kids." She sighed. "You can be a stupid adult, too. I've learned that."

"But you had a good marriage, and you raised a beautiful daughter."

"Yes. Beth is amazing."

"She reminds me of you."

Jan looked at him in surprise. "Me? I always thought she was so much like you!"

"She's the spitting image of you. She talks all the

time. She's full of ideas. She's creative and has so much energy. And she's very emotional."

"But she's got your brown eyes and hair. And she's terribly independent. Look how she flew out of my perfect little nest and made a whole new life for herself without me."

"Is that what I did?"

Jan swallowed. "It felt that way. But you know . . . now that I'm here . . . India is very pretty. I'm tired from the trip, Thomas, but I'm not afraid. I was sure I'd be scared."

"What made you come?"

"The reason I'm not afraid. God. I needed to make some changes . . . starting with you."

"Well, then," he said, "I forgive you. We'll never know how it might have turned out. But we can trust God with the rest of it."

"Thank you, Thomas." Jan reached over and covered his hand with hers. "Thank you for pardoning me."

He looked at her, his eyes dark. "You make it sound like you were a criminal, sentenced to life in prison. I don't fault you for your decision. When you let me walk away, Jan, you thought you were doing the right thing. For yourself. And for the baby. I'm the one who took your precious . . . sweet . . ." He shook his head. "You didn't belong to me, and I took you anyway. I'm sorry, Jan. I hope you can forgive me."

"I do. We loved each other, Thomas. We made mistakes. And now . . . maybe now we can let go of the past."

As she stood looking up toward the great, snow-capped Himalayan peaks, Jan felt Thomas's arm slip around her shoulders. With a shiver, she stepped closer to him and rested her head on his shoulder. It was good. It was right.

"Hey there, Mom." Beth's low voice beside her startled Jan. The young woman leaned against the rail and smiled. "Hey, Thomas."

"Hey, Beth," they said in unison.

"In Texas, do you greet people with hay?" Miles stepped to the edge of the veranda. "Here in India, we do it with tea."

He held out a green sprig. Two long, thin emerald leaves. A tiny round bud.

"From this small, fragile gift, we build our lives," he said, his own arm encircling Beth's shoulders. "The bud is the promise of a new beginning. And the leaves . . . these are the leaves of hope."